It is 1983 and Elsa is a four-year-old who is traumatized when her mother is the first victim of a serial killer later known as the Harvester. Although the horrific memory is suppressed, it has a dramatic impact on the rest of her life.

She and her father learn to move on and find happiness, but each autumn the Harvester strikes again, reviving the pain. Despite this and other heart-wrenching tragedies that befall her, Elsa develops into a strong and determined young woman, though one with a darkness lurking inside her mind.

Twenty years after her mother was ripped from her life, the Harvester is continuing to claim victims and elude the FBI. Elsa decides to take the law into her own hands. She adopts an alias and devotes her life to killing the Harvester, drawing him out by making herself a target. Training, discipline, and tapping into that darkness make her a dangerous weapon; a weapon that finds more than one target.

About the Author

Michael Selmer was born and raised in Maryland, but now calls Wyoming home. He is a writer and a runner who completed the Leadville 100 mile Race Across the Sky. He spends his spare time hiking mountain trails with his wife of thirty-five years or out on the roads running with the characters from his stories... and inventing new ones.

Harvest of the Heart

Published by Snowy Range Press

PRINTING HISTORY
Snowy Range Press edition/ December, 2011

Cover art:
Imagined by Michael Selmer
Created by Bob Vahn

For information address: Snowy Range Press
165 Wind River Road, Laramie, WY 82070

ISBN: 0984768106
ISBN-13: 9780984768103
Library of Congress Control Number: 2011919181
Snowy Range Press, Laramie, WY

PRINTED IN THE UNITED STATES OF AMERICA

Harvest of the Heart

Michael Selmer

Snowy Range Press
Laramie, Wyoming

To Mother,
Who loved her children, and reading.
You may not have gotten much else right,
But those were enough.
Your heart leapt at the thought that I might one day write.
Wherever you are,
I hope you are doing cartwheels.

PART I

First Steps

A malign figure bathes in the heavy shadows; he imagines his body absorbing their dark energy. He has become so powerful, his thoughts so brilliant, that he is concerned they might radiate through the pores of his head like some ghostly aura.

Although the still night air that surrounds him is warm, he pulls a black stocking cap from his pocket and pulls it tightly down over his head. She'll be coming through the door soon and without it he is sure he would stand out like a lighthouse on a bleak and dark shoreline.

The tall, athletic woman slips through her patio door into a darkness that seems to be winning its daily battle with the approaching dawn. Purpose and determination are visible from the first step she takes into the weak glow of the security light on her apartment building.

Walking into the grass, she clasps her fingers above her head and rises onto her toes, releasing a night-time's worth of tightness from her muscles. Then she sits and stretches, ignoring the dampness of the grass, knowing that soon she will be soaked in her own sweat.

Standing, she glances at the slender blades of green that cling to her hands and legs. A wistful look crosses her face as a long-forgotten memory of a summer many years ago becomes vibrant and clear...

CHAPTER 1

Saturday, July 18, 1981

The scruffy young man on his hands and knees shook his head and growled. Grass from the newly-mown yard stuck to his arms and decorated the legs of his worn jeans. His shoulder length brown hair dangled around his face as he bounced up and down on his hands. A giggling little girl stood in front of him. She is dressed in tattered yard sale clothes; her tangled clumps of blonde hair are sprinkled with bits of grass and frame her face. Dirt smudges accessorize her outfit as well as her cheeks, her arms, her legs… a classic ragamuffin and, to this young man, a vision of beauty.

With a Little People doll in one hand, the youngster raised her arms, squealed and ran toward her father. He lowered his shoulders and bumped his head into her tummy. While she was falling he snatched the doll from her hands. An expression of alarm lit up her face, her mouth formed a big 'O' and she dropped to the ground on her diapered bottom.

"Gotcha!" Martin Danforth laughed. As he watched his daughter's face, he was surprised to see the look of alarm turn to one of fierce determination; toddling girls don't normally look quite so dangerous. In a very mature fashion, the offended child put her hands in the grass and pushed up onto her bare feet. She looked at the blades of green on her tiny hands and brushed them on her stained shirt. Then she straightened her shoulders and glared ferociously at her challenger.

"Now honey," he said. "Daddy's just playing."

From the concrete stoop of their row house came the sound of his wife's laughter.

"Now you're in trouble! You should know better than to mess with a lioness and her cub!" Anne Danforth pulled another string bean from the basket between her feet, broke off the stem and dropped the plump green pod into the water-filled pot beside her.

Before the little girl came into this world, her parents had picked names for the expected newborn. But there would be no Emma or Brian. When the squalling, disgruntled infant made her appearance, a nurse said she sounded like a little lion cub. _Born Free_ had been Anne's favorite movie as a child... so her baby became Elsa.

The would-be lion was pawing the ground with her feet and growling. She balled her fists and charged the ogre that had taken her doll. Without slowing, she plowed into him with all of her twenty-five pounds and began to pummel his head and shoulders. No whining, no crying; only an instinctive desire to protect what was hers.

Her dad rolled onto his back in surrender and held up the doll. Elsa grabbed it and immediately jumped on top of him, knees driving into his stomach. "Gotcha!" she squealed... laughing, just like a little girl. He held her up in his hands, balanced at arm's length above him so Elsa could extend her arms as he zoomed her to and fro like an airplane.

At times, Martin Danforth wondered at the depth of love and happiness that had filled his life. Martin's family had been a mainstay of New England upper crust society since the Revolutionary War. In the Danforth clan, even the Vanderbilt's were considered nouveau-riche. To his parents, preserving the family's wealth and influence were more important than providing their only child a loving home.

Martin had felt stifled and out of place throughout his youth, often feeling that his presence in the Danforth household must have been the result of some strange circumstance, as if he had been swapped at birth. He emerged from his adolescence a confused and lonely young man who had come to question the privileged status of his family. In the end, he'd scorned his birthright and left his family behind.

Before Anne and Elsa, his life had been cold and formal. Now it was bright and warm, like the rays of sun shining through his daughter's golden hair.

The last bean plopped into the pot and Anne moved the basket from between her legs. She stretched out and leaned back against the red brick. Closing her eyes she tilted her face up into the sunshine, listened to the playful sounds of Martin and Elsa, and enjoyed the warmth on her face. The gentle rays were so different from the harsh sun of her Wyoming birthplace.

Growing up in the Petersen household had been rocky and dry like a sun-baked creek bed during the short, but blazing, Wyoming summer. Anne's father was one of those men who always felt life was dealing them a raw hand. Her mother felt trapped by an unplanned pregnancy. Love and tenderness skipped a generation.

The Peace Corp provided an escape for Anne. There she met another escapee in Martin. Along the banks of the Jamuna River in Bangladesh, they found more than enough love to replace what was missing from their estranged parents.

Married in January of 1979, Martin and Anne loved each other with a passion so complete they were sure it was all their hearts could contain. The birth of Elsa proved them wrong.

Anne watched her husband where he lay on his back in the yard with his laughing, grass-covered little girl on his chest.

She marveled at their perfect life.

CHAPTER 2

Sunday morning, September 18, 1983

Anne watched the steady rise and fall of her husband's chest beneath the thin sheet. With pursed lips and a light puff, she blew one of her long blonde hairs from his face. He stirred and kicked his legs, contributing to the night-long movement of the blanket off the bed. She laid her head on his shoulder and began to consider a replay of last night's bedtime exercises. When she kissed his chest, he snored and rolled away, taking most of the sheet with him.

Guess I'll get my run in after all. That should burn off this excess energy.

She swung out of bed, grabbed her shoes, a shirt, and shorts and headed for the bathroom.

Dressed and ready to run, she slipped into Elsa's room and looked down on the precious birthday girl. Placing a soft kiss on her daughter's forehead, Anne moved to the foot of the bed and prepared the first surprise of the day.

—◦◦◦◦◦—

"The blue, summery dress," A dreaming Elsa said, "For my birthday, I wanna wear the blue, summery dress with the yellow flowers." Hazy sunlight was streaming into her room and everything had that blurry, soft look, even her mommy.

Shifting, the dream next showed her wearing that light, cotton sundress and skipping between her parents as they cross the parking lot toward her favorite restaurant, Bob's Big Boy. They are holding her hands and on every third step they lift her up and swing her gently into a long jump. She laughed as they passed the tall statue in front of the restaurant; the chubby Big Boy in the red, checkered overalls with the funny, black hair *always* made her laugh.

Then she was back in her room. Elsa saw herself, asleep in her bed, as her mommy slipped into the room and started to write on her easel. Elsa tried to wake up; she wanted to surprise her mommy and jump on her back and tickle her and say "Mommy, that's my easel!" But the hazy edges of the dream turned dark and closed in on her mommy. The dream became scary and she wanted to wake up, but the darkness grew until her mother disappeared.

Elsa woke with a start, facing a light green wall. A wavering white line of sunshine rose out of the shadow of her rumpled head and reached toward the ceiling. She sat up and looked around her room while the sleepy, confused expression of a wakening child slowly drained from her face. Care Bear curtains rippled gently, stirred by the light breeze blowing through the small space between the powder blue frame and white sash of the window. She peered at the combination toy chest and bookshelf to the left of the window, and then her gaze moved steadily left around the room.

It passed her basket of stuffed toys and the Elsa-sized wooden rocker in the corner where she read to her floppy friends. Moving on, it paused briefly at the brightly-colored ABC poster hanging on the wall above her little table with the flowered plastic teapot and its matching cups and saucers.

Her visual tour ended when her eyes reached the foot of her bed and fell upon the large Crayola easel where her parents helped her learn to make numbers, letters, and words. It held a large spool of white paper at the top that could be fed down through a slot, so a talented artist could make dozens of masterpieces every day.

A jazzy abstract (the most popular artistic style for three-year-olds) she had drawn yesterday was gone, replaced by fresh paper with three words carefully printed across the top and spots spread across the rest of the sheet.

She remembered that today was her birthday and Elsa was pretty sure the three words read 'Happy Birthday Elsa'. For sure she knew her own name! Turning to her open door, she confirmed it.

Yep! E... L... S... A... My door. My room. My name.

She crawled down the bed to the easel and picked up a red crayon to follow the dots her mommy had quietly drawn. Tracing from dot to dot she created the words MOMMY and RUN on the paper. Mommy was doing her run.

With a thud, Elsa fell away from the easel and bumped her head on the wall. Her eyes were tightly shut, trying to squeeze out the ugly image that had burst from a dark corner of her mind.

"Oh no! Mommy!" A scary feeling that something was wrong grew quickly, pushing Elsa out of bed to make her way carefully down the stairs. She stood at the door to the kitchen where her father was preparing breakfast.

"Daddy, I'm worried," she said.

Concern was etched in her face and her bottom lip was on the edge of doing that trembling motion that always wrenches the heart of a parent.

Martin Danforth placed the spatula on the counter and knelt to hug his little girl.

"Elsa, honey, you're turning four years old today and it's an absolutely beautiful Sunday morning. You shouldn't be worried about a thing."

She buried her head on daddy's shoulder. He could hardly make out her words. "Mommy's in trouble, I think something bad happened."

Another parent would have ignored the words and sought only to comfort an imaginative child. But ever since she was a toddler, Elsa had demonstrated an unusual connection with her mother. Once, she had been taking a nap while her mother was cooking dinner. When Anne's hand touched a hot burner, a pained yelp had not yet escaped her lips when Elsa screamed from her bed on the second floor. That wasn't the first time, or the last, that Elsa had reacted to something that happened to his wife, so Martin didn't comfort or ignore his daughter.

"You know mommy is out for her run, don't you?" he said.

Elsa nodded.

"And you think maybe she got hurt?" He pictured his wife limping along the shoulder of the road with a sprained ankle and a pissed-off look on her face. She could be a challenge to live with when she was injured and couldn't run.

He watched her nod again. "Ok, then. We'd better hop in the car and go rescue her." He hoped to draw a smile from her, but her head dropped back to his shoulder.

"Come on, let's get you dressed." He stood and headed for the stairs, the home fries on the stove forgotten.

"No Daddy, please!" cried Elsa. "We need to hurry."

A sudden chill clawed its way up Martin's spine, radiating goose bumps as it rose. Instead of climbing the stairs, he grabbed the car keys and headed out the door.

—⸺⊰⊱⸺—

They had driven Anne's normal Sunday morning route twice without any sign of her. The first time around Elsa had been on her knees in the back seat looking anxiously through the windows for her mother. By the time Martin started a second circuit, Elsa was sitting quietly with her hands clutched together in her lap. Her sobs were muffled, barely audible over the engine… yet they throbbed in his ears like the first grindings of an earthquake that would shake his world apart.

"Elsa, please don't cry. We'll find Mommy soon." He tried to feel the confidence he hoped was in the words he spoke.

"We'll find Mommy soon," he repeated weakly.

—⸺⊰⊱⸺—

She arrived after lunchtime, tapping lightly on Bill Pendry's door.

"Daddy asked could you watch me for a while," a subdued Elsa said.

"Sure, honey. Come on in." The old man picked her up, sat her on his chair and placed a book in her lap. "Just sit right here. I'll be back in a minute."

Elsa's morning had been a confusing blur of brief, frightening images that appeared without warning. These were mixed with long periods of nothing but darkness pressing in on her. Her mommy was hurting and in danger, which left Elsa feeling scared and helpless. She settled listlessly into the cushions and hugged her knees.

—⸺⊰⊱⸺—

Through the screen door Bill Pendry could see his neighbor sitting slumped at the dining room table. When he entered, Martin's head lifted and his eyes followed his tall, balding neighbor into the room.

"They won't do anything, Bill." Anger, frustration, and fear dripped from each word that dragged itself passed his lips. "I called 911. For Christ's sake, she's been gone almost seven hours, of course I called 911. But seven hours isn't enough."

His shoulders tensed and each word grew louder than the one before it.

"They won't do anything!" Martin yelled. He jumped up and knocked over his chair, pounding both fists on the worn oak table and glaring at his neighbor. Their eyes met and Bill could see a jittery panic in them. Moments passed in silence before Martin's shoulders slumped and his head dropped low between them.

Bill squeezed Martin's shoulder firmly. "Keep it together. They have their procedures to follow, as asinine as they may be. What did they tell you?"

"The dispatcher told me to go to the precinct station and file a report, but they won't start an investigation until at least twelve hours have passed. They're not going to send a patrol car out here until six o'clock tonight," he answered.

"Elsa and I drove around all morning. We were going slow, checking everywhere, asking everyone we saw." He laughed bitterly. "A cop pulled me over and tried to give me a ticket for driving too slow. When I told him what we were doing all he said was 'Sorry, I can't help'. He had time to pull me over for Sunday driving, but no time to help me find my wife."

Bill shifted from one foot to another, feeling powerless, unsure of what to do or say. Anne and Martin had been neighbors for almost four years, ever since they moved in next door with a newborn Elsa in their arms. The next day he'd whipped up one of his special cherry cobblers and taken it over as a welcoming gift. Anne had invited him over for dinner that night and they'd become his closest friends; unusual, considering the fifty-year gap in their ages.

"What can I do to help?" he asked.

Martin continued talking as if he hadn't heard. "Elsa knew right away that something had happened to Anne. You know how she is." He leveled a penetrating gaze at the older man, searching for some hope. Bill quailed before those beseeching eyes. He did know how Elsa was and could only agree.

"I'm going to the station to file the report and then I'll drive around some more. I can't just sit here and watch the clock, waiting for their damn twelve hours to pass." Martin's fists pounded the table once more.

Bill waited patiently while his friend worked to control his emotion.

"Can you keep Elsa with you for a while?"

"Of course," Bill answered, "for as long as you need. I'll plan on fixing dinner for both of you."

"Thanks Bill. I feel half crazy with fear and half crazy with anger." Martin paused and then a wry smile briefly touched his lips. "Those two halves leave me wholly unstable. I don't want Elsa to see me like this."

He picked up the chair and then walked Bill to the door.

"Try to distract her when the cops finally get here. If they start in with that 'have you had any fights lately' crap, it may get loud."

———

Fists clenched and teeth grinding, he paced in a circle around the hospital stretcher. Being his first time, he had expected there might be problems, but this was ridiculous.

At the snatch, she had been much tougher to subdue than planned; for several minutes he had been dangerously exposed. If just one car had come by during that time, the driver would have had to been blind not to see that a woman was being pulled off the street against her will. Her wind-milling arms and legs and his hand over her mouth were sure giveaways.

Even after he got her in the van, the halothane took much too long to put her out. Then the clever bitch had surprised him by pretending to still be under the anesthetic when he was moving her from the van to the warehouse. The stretcher had toppled over when she started struggling violently against her restraints and, when her head hit the concrete, the resulting gash bled profusely for several minutes before he could get her patched up. Getting that overhead door fixed would be a priority.

A puddle of blood on the ground outside of the warehouse entrance was easily handled. Early on a Sunday morning this decaying industrial area was deserted. Acres of cracked asphalt sprouted weeds between the sprawling brick buildings.

The real problem was her loss of blood so early in the day. He wasn't sure how much of a problem it might be when he started the procedure later in the afternoon.

It had taken so long to get her stabilized and secured that he was behind schedule. He had to hurry to a safe phone and make the call. They would be bitchy about the timing and would have to rush things a bit. But if they didn't know what was coming, they wouldn't be ready when it got there. That would be such a waste. Next time he would do a much better job.

———

Her eyelids fluttered; with the first touch of consciousness, Anne felt the throbbing above her right ear. Occasionally she woke with a headache such as this and her initial drowsy thought was 'Aw, not on Elsa's birthday!' When she tried to lift her hand to massage her head, it didn't want to move.

In a bewildering rush, images flashed through her mind: stepping off her porch as the first blush of dawn was touching the sky; running down the sidewalk along Sligo Parkway; the tire jack leaning against a white van by the road; an injured man against the tree between the sidewalk and the car, holding a bloody hand; a red-gloved hand clapping a red rag over her mouth; fighting desperately to keep from being pulled into the van; the inside of a white van close above her head, and then blue sky changing to hard gray before pitch black came rushing in.

A wide piece of duct tape was stretched across her mouth. Legs, arms, hips, shoulders were all secured firmly, even painfully, to what felt like a stainless steel table. It was only when she noticed the cold steel touching her arms and back that she realized she was naked from the waist up.

Lifting her head, she could see her breasts backlit by red light. Beyond her feet a weakly glowing exit sign hung high on the wall. As her eyes adjusted to the dim light, it illuminated her chest and the series of black dashes drawn upon it. One started at her belly button and marched straight up her body until it disappeared from sight under her chin. Another intersected the first line just below her rib cage, falling off to either side of her body. The last started high under her right arm, crossed that center line and ended under her left.

She watched as a wave of goose bumps washed across her smooth skin and left her shivering on the frigid table. For a time Anne surrendered to the terror that pressed upon her. She screamed through the tape that covered her mouth until, lightheaded, she fell into a daze.

———

The City of Baltimore was resplendent through the high glass walls of the Johns Hopkins Heart Center. Bright afternoon sunshine had followed a passing shower and transformed pot-holed Monument Street and the tenements that lined it with a glittering crystal shroud.

Ringing interrupted the quiet musings of a bored medical technician who longed to be out enjoying the brief breath of fresh air the rain had brought. This urban atmosphere would quickly regain its gritty, acrid bouquet.

She sighed and reached for the phone. "Transplant Center, How may I help you?"

"This is Dr. Kauffman from the Washington Hospital Center," said a stern male voice on the line. "We have a twenty-four-year-old female heart donor, blood type AB+."

The technician sat up alertly, no longer bored.

"We are assembling our team and preparing to harvest the heart for transport to your center if you can have a recipient ready on such short notice."

The voice lost some its officious tone.

"Look, I know this could be a problem for you guys, being Sunday afternoon and all. We expect to start extraction around 6:00 p.m., so the heart should be viable for transplantation until at least midnight. We can have it delivered to you by eight. I'm willing to hold while you get confirmation."

The technician took a deep breath. The Heart Center had only been open for six months. There were protocols in place for exactly this circumstance, but this was the first time she had been the one to set them into motion.

"Thank you Doctor," was her efficient response. "I'll put you on hold and make the calls."

Pagers went off around the city as a result of the technician's efforts. Minutes later she was back on the line.

"Dr. Kauffman?" she said with excitement in her voice.

"I'm still here."

"We have an AB+ recipient who will be ready and waiting."

"Excellent! We'll get the ball rolling on our end."

"Thank you so much, Doctor."

"Oh, you're so very welcome."

Anne alternately clinched and relaxed her muscles, trying to generate some body heat. Each pulse of her muscles caused the ache in her head to blossom, but she fought through the pain. She started with her feet and moved up, working her way through major and minor muscle groups. It gave her something on which to concentrate. Gradually her body temperature rose and her terror level fell.

Her eyes shifted left and right as she tried to make sense of the shadowy forms around her. The arrow on the exit sign pointed to the left, but she couldn't make out a door, or even a wall in either direction. Blurry images of chairs, tables, file cabinets and various pieces of equipment dissolved into the murky distance.

Hanging only a few feet above her, centered over her chest was a large fixture almost three feet across the middle. As she peered up into the dark recesses of the circular shape, a dull red glow appeared in the center. She stared. There was a small spark, and then the entire circle exploded into a blazing white light. Her eyes closed much too late, and an amorphous white cloud drifted on a field of red behind her eyelids.

Distant steps across a hard floor trickled from the gloom. She turned her aching head toward the sound and opened her eyes, but a drifting white cloud was all she could see.

An unintelligible voice called faintly from behind the cloud. Anne's heart beat faster as hope flickered. Her muffled 'help' seemed to bring the steps closer. Though her eyes were still blind, hope flared brightly as she heard the clear and welcome words.

"Hello? Is anyone there?"

CHAPTER 3

Sunday evening, September 18, 1983

Martin leaned heavily against the frame of the screen door. His eyes followed two men as they got out of the police cruiser, walked up the sidewalk and onto the porch. The older of the two had short, fading black hair peppered generously with flecks of gray; he was dressed in a white shirt and tie and carried a jacket draped over his left arm. The colors in its herringbone weave matched his hair perfectly. He was followed by a young, uniformed officer carrying a clipboard. Martin opened the door and stepped out.

"Mr. Danforth?" the older gentleman said. When a nod was given, he continued, "I'm Detective Spence and this is Patrolman Reed."

"Thanks for coming so quickly," Martin said, the sarcasm in his voice was poorly hidden. He gestured toward the door. Following them into the house, he waved a hand toward the chairs around the dining room table. "Please, have a seat."

Spence wasted no time. "The way we work the start of this investigation may be difficult for you, but the more you cooperate and the more complete and accurate your answers are, the easier it will be to find your wife." Patrolman Reed put the clipboard in front of Spence, who clicked his pen and leaned forward. "Can we get started?"

With an obvious effort, Martin nodded.

Anne's right cheek was pressed firmly on the stainless steel table, facing the sound of the steady, powerful steps that were approaching. She blinked and the white spots in her eyes shrunk. The glaring surgical light above the table pushed against the darkness, revealing more of the cavernous warehouse. A blurry, pale mass in her vision resolved into a man dressed in white walking out of the distant shadows.

"Oh my God!" he said, and ran toward her.

Tears of relief from Anne's eyes splashed on the table as he carefully pulled the tape from her mouth. Her emotions were too strong for words. A low keening escaped from her lips.

"Shush now, you'll be all right." he said. Working quickly, he removed the restraints that held her down. Swinging her legs off the table, he helped her sit on the edge. His left hand felt warm and strong on her bicep, and he put his right arm around her to support her upper body. She shivered and leaned into the warmth of his body while he lifted her off the table and onto her feet.

White haze filled her head and her senses dimmed. Her legs buckled and only his firm grip kept her off the floor.

"Whoa, hold on there," he said, "let's get you to this chair." He sat her down and stepped away, returning with a thin hospital blanket to wrap around her shoulders.

"I'm going to get you a glass of water. Can you hold on to the arms of the chair?" he asked. "It will only take a moment."

Anne gathered her strength and forced a hollow 'yes' from her parched mouth.

"Good," he responded as he walked behind her, "you're getting your voice back."

Disembodied thoughts floated out of reach of her fuzzy awareness. Unarticulated warnings, vague fears, promising hopes bounced against her consciousness without sticking.

"You must have lost a lot of blood," he said above the sound of running water. "By the size of that bandage, you've got a nasty cut on your head."

She flinched as he stepped in front of her.

"Easy there, I've got some water and some pills to help you with that headache I'm sure you have." He held a glass in front of her. Anne willed her hand to take the glass, but it shook uncontrollably when she lifted it from the chair.

"That's ok," he said. "I'll help you." He held the glass to her lips and tilted. The cool liquid felt heavenly as it made its soothing way down her throat. The glass was almost drained when he pulled it back and placed the pills on her tongue.

"Swallow these," he instructed as he placed the glass back to her lips. She gulped them down and finished the water.

"Let's check your blood pressure," he said, and opened the cabinet next to the chair. He slipped the cuff over her arm and put on the stethoscope. Anne felt the pressure spread from her arm to her face and head as he pumped the bulb. It all felt so normal and, at the same time, so strange, under the circumstances. He turned the release valve and listened intently.

"Not great," he said as he ripped off the cuff, "but not too bad, all things considered."

He walked to the sink, talking as he went. "We really need to get more liquid into you. Between the blood loss and lying on that table all day, you're badly dehydrated."

Coherent thought was slowly becoming possible and an anxious crowd of ideas clamored for attention. Initially, the comforting notion that someone had rescued her blocked conflicting clues from her notice. One contrasting conception slowly gained strength and punched through.

Someone brought me here and he'll come back.

As Anne began to assemble an important conclusion in her mind, a sleepy, relaxed mood moved steadily throughout her body. She tried to push out of the chair, but every muscle worked in slow motion.

"We have to hurry." She slurred the words and felt his warm hand pushing her gently back down.

"You're right, Anne," he said as he came around the chair and knelt in front of her, "we do have to hurry. But first you must drink another glass of water." Once more he held the glass to her lips and tipped it up.

Drowsy confusion befuddled her. *How does he know my name? Did I tell him my name?*

"I really should have started you on an IV before I left," he mused. "I'll have to remember that next time."

Deep in the recesses of her mind that had only just awoken, panic tried to find a hold on her consciousness and shake. Adrenalin surged through her system, giving her muscles renewed strength. For a moment, her mind resisted the drugs that were attempting to send her into a deep sleep.

Anne slapped away the glass. Glittering shards and droplets danced across the gray floor when the water glass shattered on the concrete. When she pushed against the kneeling man, he stumbled backwards and fell, stunned when his head bounced off the concrete floor. Though the room was spinning as she pushed out of the chair, she fought the dizzy weakness that threatened to pull her back down.

Desperately Anne looked for a way to escape. The only source of light was above the operating table where she had been restrained. Beyond that small circle of illumination was nothing but a taunting blackness in every direction that held only an illusory promise of rescue. Anne had no choice. She raced unsteadily into the darkness.

———————

Unfocused eyes ignored the colorful book while Bill mindlessly turned the pages for the subdued child in his lap. His attention was focused on the cruiser at the curb in front of the Danforth's. The sun was beginning to set and the police had finally arrived. The wall separating the two row houses dampened the noise from the discussion going on next door, rendering it unintelligible, but it did not conceal the tone of rising anger.

Bill pulled his eyes away from the cruiser. He hoped Elsa hadn't noticed when the officers walked up the sidewalk. From the sound of it, Martin didn't like the direction the conversation was taking.

Closing the book, he laid it on the floor beside the chair and turned Elsa to face him.

"How about we put on some music?" He didn't really expect an answer. "I don't suppose you've latched on to a favorite type of music, yet." Bill reached over to the stereo and turned the knob. Soft jazz notes from Kenny G oozed through the speakers. He increased the volume enough to cloak the contentious noise from next door.

His heart ached as he watched Elsa sitting with her eyes closed, morose and lifeless on his lap. Except for the times she was absorbed in a book, he was used to seeing her active - jumping, skipping, dancing, or running after the thieving rabbits that raided his tiny garden.

He reached to brush her hair from her face, but she pushed his hand away. Her face became strained and her eyes squeezed tightly shut.

"Run Mommy... run!" Though the words were soft and mumbled, as if spoken from a dream, Bill could clearly hear the urgent desperation in the little girl's voice.

His hair stood on end as Elsa's eyes shot open. Fear radiated from them; they flashed to the right and then to the left, searching but unfocused and dilated, as if she searched in darkness.

"Elsa! What's wrong... what's happening?" Bill waved his hand in front of her face, but saw no response... to his voice or his movement.

Turning her head away from Bill, an urgent murmur escaped from her lips. When her head whipped back, a terrified child was now staring at him with unseeing eyes.

"Faster, Mommy! He's coming!" The words were tremulous and weak, fear had left her voice almost paralyzed. "Run faster!"

Elsa's legs began churning in his lap and her hands reached out in front, as if she were blindly running through a vast, dark space. Then her tiny hands balled into fists and she began swinging wildly, hitting at the air.

"Leave my Mommy alone!" Anger mixed with the terror in her voice.

Bill worried that she would fall off his lap, so he took firm hold of Elsa's hands.

Her struggling became more frantic as she yelled, "Leave my Mommy alone!"

Not knowing what to do, Bill was about to carry her next door when her fighting abruptly stopped and she took several deep, shuddering breaths. Then her head dropped to her chest.

"Elsa honey," he said, lifting her chin, "you shouldn't get so worked up. Pretty soon lots of people will be looking for your mommy. I'm sure they'll find her."

He moved his head until his gaze met hers and found himself looking into eyes that seemed older than the ones he saw every morning in the mirror.

She shook her head as if the effort was almost beyond her power. Not once through a long, frightening day had a single tear stained the soft skin of her cheeks. Now, one formed in the corner of her eye, growing bigger until it spilled over.

"Nnn... nnn... no," Elsa cried softly, "They'll never find her." Her head continued to move slowly back and forth.

"Ssh, Ssh, don't say that honey." Bill tried to comfort her, rubbing her shoulders and then pulling her to him, hugging her and rubbing her back. "Don't cry... don't cry."

After all the trouble Anne Danforth had caused him, a favorite phrase of his beloved mother came to mind. She'd usually used it while applying a belt to his backside.

"You'll be the death of me yet." The Harvester laughed and the canyon-like warehouse echoed his merry mood. His mother had been proven right in the end.

The words and laughter woke Anne.

Hazy memories floated on the edge of her consciousness; a terrifying run through the dark followed by a desperate fight. She forced her heavy eyelids to open and found that she was once again secured to the stainless steel table. The man in white was smiling down at her, a scalpel in his hand.

"Don't fight it," he said. "You really don't want to be awake for this."

Anne knew that her life was about to end, but she felt strangely numb. It was in her nature to struggle until the end and her mind attempted to formulate a few defiant last words to hurl at her captor.

"I will be…" she whispered.

"What did you say, dear?" He leaned closer and looked at her beautiful, relaxed face as the drugs slowly pulled her back to a sleep that would be permanent.

"I will be the death of you."

The Harvester felt a brief shiver and then smiled.

"I'm afraid that isn't very likely, Anne. Come now, just close your eyes."

His hands brushed down across her face and pulled her eyelids shut. A blurred scene of her husband and daughter playfully tussling on a lush field of green filled her senses. She drifted toward it on a warm comforting current and it became clearer and brighter.

He watched the rise and fall of her bare chest become slow and rhythmic. Since the moment Johns Hopkins had confirmed their ability to receive a donor heart, a synchronicity had developed, aligning his long-treasured dreams with reality. His chest puffed out with pride as he congratulated himself for the courage to follow through despite a multitude of problems.

"Too unstable to be a heart surgeon?" He pushed the button on the recorder that hung from a strap on the table. "We'll see about that."

His latex-gloved hand was rock-steady as he studied the glittering scalpel it was holding. Then he looked at the smooth, unblemished skin of the body on the table before him.

"The donor is a twenty-four-year old female in excellent health." He spoke calmly and clearly. After checking his watch, he continued. "I am beginning the procedure to harvest her heart at 6:13 p.m."

He adjusted the light, leaned over, and began to cut.

After a time, Elsa's crying had stopped and she sat quietly in his lap with her head on his shoulder. Bill was just beginning to believe that she had fallen asleep when he heard her speak seven words. Seven words that made his old bones tremble. Seven words which were all the more frightening coming from the mouth of a four-year-old.

"I will be the death of you." The elderly man felt Elsa go rigid in his arms. Then she struggled and pushed away from him.

"NO!" Elsa shook her head and wailed, "Don't cut my Mommy!"

Bill took her by the shoulders as Elsa began shaking her head faster. Her hands came up to cover her face, knocking his frail arms away. She pressed her palms hard against her eyes, as if trying to block a terrible vision.

"Don't cut my Mommy!" Elsa yelled again, louder with each word. "DON'T CUT MY MOMMY!" Tears were pouring from under her hands, spraying across his checkered shirt as her head whipped back and forth.

"Elsa don't do that, you'll hurt yourself." Bill said. Concerned for her safety, he tried to wrap his arms around her. She reacted violently, hitting him and screaming over and over...

"NO! NO! NO!"

"Your report says that you last saw your wife at approximately six o'clock this morning. Is that correct?"

Martin breathed an impatient sigh. "Yes"

"Did you speak with her at that time?"

"Not really..." Martin said. "I mean she told me she was going for a run, and I think I said 'have fun'."

"What do you mean 'you think you said'?" Spence asked.

"I was half-asleep," he responded sullenly. "I usually sleep in on Saturdays."

Spence's brow creased as he looked intently at Martin. "Are you sure that you and your wife didn't have an argument this morning?"

"No, god dammit!" Martin shouted as his head shot up. "There's no reason for her to be gone. We never fight... *never!* Neither of us is having an affair. She didn't wake up this morning with an irresistible urge to go on an all-day shopping spree, on foot, in her running shorts and t-shirt, *without any money.* None of your questions are going to help find out what's happened to wife!"

"All you are doing is demonstrating to me that you have a temper..." Spence started.

Martin's control slipped away.

"What?" he screamed and jumped to his feet. Spence and Reed followed suit.

Martin grabbed his head with both hands. "I've been tearing my hair out all day, trying to find my wife, trying to get the people who should be helping to find her, to DO THEIR JOBS!" He jabbed his finger at the officers. "You start asking idiotic questions that don't have anything to..."

Spinning away from the men, a strangled cry escaped Martin's lips and he slammed his fist through the wall. As Reed moved toward Martin, screaming could be heard from Bill Pendry's house. The officer looked at Spence who jerked his head toward the door. While Reed hurried out, Martin pulled his fist from the wall and began to follow.

"No, you wait here," Spence said. He stepped around the table and blocked the path to the door. Martin plowed through him and out of the house.

At Bill's front door, he caught up to Reed. Shouldering his way past, he stepped into the living room and saw Elsa flailing her arms as the old man tried to protect himself.

"Nooooo! Nooooo!" she wailed.

He ran to the chair and pulled the thrashing girl into his arms.

"Stop Elsa, Daddy has you, honey," he whispered in her ear, holding her tightly to his chest. "Daddy has you now."

Elsa could sense her father's love and it helped her pull away from the cold darkness. When she found her way back to the warmth that beckoned her, the uglier images that had held her so strongly retreated; they burrowed deep within her mind, out of reach of her memory.

Wrapping her arms tightly around his neck, she cried softly but clearly...

"Mommy's gone."

"Don't cry Elsa," Martin comforted, "we'll get her back."

"No, we won't..." The little girl had no words to describe the aching emptiness. "I can't feel her... Mommy's dead!"

Compiled from Harvester Task Force Archives — Official briefing documents of 1986:

Anne Danforth's body was never found. Her heart, packed in an ice-filled Styrofoam chest, was delivered to the Johns Hopkins Heart Center at 8:23 p.m. on Sunday, September 18, 1983. The doctors deemed it a viable organ. Despite desperate need and much confusion, the heart was never used. Missing donor paperwork and the strict procedures of a highly regarded institute kept a horrendous incident from becoming much worse.

Forensic psychologists put forth the theory that this murderer was a person who washed out of medical school or who had been de-certified as a surgeon; possibly one who had been rejected at an early age by his mother, or more recently by a wife or lover.

Since 1983 he has become known as 'The Harvester'. One reason is that he strikes in September or early October... harvest season; another is because the media always create a lurid moniker for serial murderers. The primary reason is a result of the medical term used when referring to the extraction of donated organs for transplantation.

CHAPTER 4

Monday, October 3, 1988

Dawn was approaching, and it painted a faint blush of deep pink on his rear view mirror. Ahead, the dark rolling hills were draped with a glittering necklace of headlights. Wispy morning fog was just beginning to rise, floating ghostly tendrils along the vales, glens and hollows that dimple the foothills of central Maryland.

The haunting beauty of the scene wasn't lost on Martin, not completely. However, it was the unbroken line of cars heading down I-270 that held much of his attention.

No matter how many roads they build, no matter how many lanes of asphalt they slap down, the congestion is only going to keep getting worse. And the people who could do something about it never listen. Listen? Hah! They have a vested interest in keeping us on the same hopeless, congested road we're following.

These thoughts weren't new to him and, under these circumstances, barely altered his blood pressure.

Sometimes it feels like I'm just beating my head against a wall.

Being a transportation engineer in the U.S. Department of Transportation was frustrating; doubly so since his specialty, his passion, was mass transportation and decentralization. Many of the drivers behind those headlights had been on the road for as much as an hour, driving from homes in places like McConnellsburg, Pennsylvania; Hancock, Maryland, or Berkeley Springs, West

Virginia. Some were probably headed for the Pentagon and still had an hour to go. The whole mess was insane! Secretaries, janitors and engineers drive from Reston, Virginia to jobs at Lockheed Martin in Bethesda, Maryland. Other secretaries, janitors and engineers drive from Bethesda to Northrup Grumman in Reston. All of them complain about the congestion, yet almost all of them cling jealously to the independence of adding their own car to the tens of thousands already on the road.

Martin shook his head, snickering quietly at himself as he glanced over his shoulder at a sleeping Elsa curled up on the back seat.

Here I am playing hooky from work and what am I doing? Thinking about work!

Unfortunately, his thoughts then turned back to those that had occupied his mind for most of the trip. He had been getting ready for bed with WTOP radio playing quietly from his alarm clock on the dresser. When the breaking news bulletin had come across, he'd sat down heavily on the bed, pajama top half on.

The newly formed Harvester Task Force has just released the name and description of a Columbia, MD woman who they believe may have been taken by the gruesome serial killer known as the Harvester. The woman is 31-year-old Cynthia Connolly. She is 5' 7" and 135 pounds. She was last seen leaving the Sears in Columbia Mall at approximately 6:00 p.m. this evening. Police are especially interested in talking with persons who may have seen any type of disturbance in the parking lot of the mall during this period. Anyone with information may...

Not again.

Every year since his wife had been murdered, it had been the same. 'Time heals all wounds' they say. Well, not if the scar is cut open again, year after year. Last September, he was in his cubicle at work, running numbers for a project, when a co-worker asked if he'd heard the news about the Harvester's latest victim, Helen Ferguson. When he returned home, a crying Elsa had come running from Bill Pendry's next door. All day, classmates had pestered her about her mom, trying to satisfy their morbid curiosity.

Her violent reaction had shocked her teacher and frightened her classmates, resulting in a series of conferences and an inconclusive session with a child psychologist.

...The Harvester has brutally reaped four previous victims, starting with Anne Danforth, a young mother from...

His fist slammed down on the radio and squelched the merciless voice that had sliced open his heart and renewed the pain that had only recently begun to recede. Right then he'd decided to keep this pain from Elsa as long as he could. He'd then break the news as gently as possible; Martin didn't want a repeat of last year.

That's why his back seat held a packed lunch, his loaded back pack and a drowsy little girl who'd been dragged out of bed in the dark of the early morning. The trails of Cunningham Falls State Park were beckoning; he vowed to banish all dark thoughts from his mind.

⸺⁂⸺

Crisp mountain air chased the sleep from her eyes and tasted clean and fresh as she breathed deeply. Her father walked close behind; the first colorful leaves of autumn swirled around them, decorating the trail as she skipped along, feeling so alive and happy. Elsa always loved hiking in the woods, but today seemed especially exciting. She was skipping school... it was Daddy's idea and he was skipping work, too!

Confidence in herself had grown, especially after her Dad signed her up for a children's karate class. What a surprise that was! After all the trouble she'd caused at school by getting into fights with the school bullies, Elsa hadn't expected her Dad to want her to become a better fighter.

But the surprise had been on her. Martial arts had taught her to discipline her mind and body; to control the darkness that seemed to jump out whenever she saw any of her friends threatened. Karate helped her to channel her anger. It had been almost a year since she'd been in a fight.

Elsa was tall for nine; most of it in her legs. This allowed her to move quickly from belt to belt, which was fun. Now, it also allowed her to set a steady pace that kept her dad working.

"Don't wear yourself out honey," said Martin. "We've got a lot of hiking to do."

"Sorry, I forgot you're too old to keep up," teased Elsa, "I'll slow down." Her dad had turned thirty in the spring, and she still kidded him every chance she got.

She squealed and jumped when he poked her in the ribs and ran past. Elsa gave chase.

Bob's Trail had risen steadily from the parking lot and now it was getting steeper as it worked its way to the overlook on Bob's Hill. Soon they were both breathing hard. Elsa grabbed on to the bouncing back pack in front of her and signaled surrender.

"Ok, ok, I give!" she said laughing.

Martin only had enough air in his lungs for a short 'Hah!' before he slowed down to a walk. After a few moments to catch his breath, he called back to Elsa...

"I know that you think you're giving your old man a break. Do I need to remind you who won the last time we raced?" He liked teasing back on occasion, especially when she knew he didn't mean it.

Against his better judgment, Martin had allowed Elsa to talk him into letting her run a 5k road race during the summer. He wasn't sure how far adolescent legs could run without risking injury to a still-developing bone structure. But, for the first time, he'd reluctantly let the 'lots of other kids do it' argument win out. And sure enough, there were dozens of kids Elsa's age, and even younger, in the crowd of almost two hundred runners. Besides, he'd been running steadily for a couple of years and was anxious for a race himself.

Elsa insisted that she didn't want her daddy babysitting her during the race. Since it was a dead flat, out and back course, he agreed to that too. Taking off with the leaders, he'd pushed hard early in the race and hit the turn-around in the top twenty. On the return route, he started looking for his daughter in the crowd of people heading out. He was surprised to see her so soon and looking so good. She was probably in the top fifty, and he hadn't seen any other kids in front of her. She'd waved merrily, floating along while the runners around her looked like they were struggling.

The sight of his daughter doing so well gave Martin a lift; he used the extra adrenaline to work even harder on the way back. He kicked by a couple of young studs in the last quarter-mile and ended up fifteenth overall. Breathing hard, he'd left the chute, grabbed a cup of water, and started back toward the course to watch his daughter finish.

He was shocked to hear "Daddy! Daddy!" as an ebullient Elsa waved to him. She hugged him across the dividing rope and continued dancing through the chute. "That was so much fun!" She'd finished 25th and won her age group by almost five minutes.

The trail became rockier and steeper as Martin tried to recover from the uphill run. Elsa was once again setting the pace. He had no doubt who'd win the next time.

With little conversation, they walked for the rest of the morning, heading north. Sometimes there was no trail and they bushwhacked through, spooking deer and squirrels as they went.

Martin enjoyed the silence and solitude of the forest and treasured these hikes with Elsa. After several years, she still seemed to enjoy them and he was thankful. He knew that someday he would hike these woods alone, but he hoped it was still many years away. Elsa, for her part, was happiest when out on an adventure with her dad.

After a steep climb, they intersected with the Cat Rock Trail, and made their way toward the main section of the park. The hiking became easier and they made good time toward the falls where they would have lunch.

———

The peanut butter and jelly sandwich was delicious and washing it down with cherry Kool-aid made it even better. Her dad even brought Jell-O chocolate pudding cups for dessert.

Elsa watched her Dad. He'd been quiet and a little tense while they ate, so she figured he had something important to say. They were sitting across from each other on the end of a picnic table, deep in the cool shade of towering oak trees, downstream from the falls. Acorns decorated the table and occasionally crashed to the ground around them.

Martin reached across the table and held his daughter's hands.

"Elsa," he said, "A hike in the woods isn't the reason I took you out of school today." Martin took a deep breath. "Do you remember last year when you had a real bad day at school?"

Elsa nodded her head and looked in her dad's eyes. She loved him so much and knew how hard he worked to protect her.

"Well, today would have been another day like that," he said.

"Because the Harvester has killed somebody else?" Elsa's head dropped as a familiar darkness began to build.

"That's right honey."

With her fists clenched in her lap, Elsa fought quietly against the fear and anger, pushing it back behind the door she had constructed in her mind. They sat in silence for a long time. The steady, low rumble of the distant falls and the burbling ripple of the stream nearby were peaceful and calming; they aided Elsa in her battle.

Martin waited patiently, surprised there had been no outburst... no tears. He'd shed plenty last night while he was alone in the bed he had shared with his wife so many years ago.

She is so strong.

Elsa lifted her head and gave him a fragile smile.

"Thanks, Daddy," she said, "you did this just right."

There were tears in his eyes as he slipped around the edge of the table and knelt next to his daughter. He leaned forward and Elsa hugged his head to her chest. After a while he wiped his eyes on Elsa's sleeve and she giggled.

"Can you stand having an old man, crybaby father?" His voice was hoarse as he moved back to his seat.

"Are you giving me a choice?" she teased, smiling broadly now, "Can I trade you in?"

"No," he said, pretending to be offended. He grabbed an acorn and threw it toward her head, missing high on purpose. At that moment the oak towering above the table dropped a big one right on the center of his own head, making a load thud.

"Owww," he cried, clapping his hand to the stinging impact point, "that really hurt!"

Elsa covered her mouth and tried to restrain her amusement.

"You," he said in mock anger as he jumped off the bench, "it was you!"

"No... it... wasn't," she forced out between laughs.

Leaping forward, he swept Elsa from her seat, swinging her around as they both laughed.

⋯⋯

Crystal water rushed with power and beauty over the rocks. Martin and Elsa were ready for the return hike and walked along the bank through the trees.

The park access road was being patched. At a picnic table along the stream bank, the rough road crew finished their lunch break and prepared for more hot, messy work. A tar-streaked laborer with a Mohawk hairdo crushed his McDonald's bag and tossed it into the stream.

"Did you see that?" Elsa scowled at the offender and then looked at her Dad. Red-faced, he was already heading for the stream. After plucking the soggy bag from the water, he stomped over to the group. The four men standing by the table looked amused.

"You dropped this," Martin said. He tried to hand the bag to the stocky guy who'd thrown it.

"Huh uh, ain't mine." The unlit cigarette danced between Mohawk's lips.

"We saw you throw it in the stream. This State Park isn't here for you to use as your personal trashcan." Martin shoved it closer and the man slapped it away.

"I said it ain't mine." He bumped Martin and joined in the laughter of his crewmates while he dug his lighter from the pocket of his frayed Levi's. After lighting up, he blew a cloud of smoke toward Martin's face. A black-eyed stare challenged Martin to continue.

While Martin was no coward, he took a moment to consider the situation. A moment was all he had. Nine-year-old Elsa flashed in front of him and delivered a kick to the groin of the man threatening her father. He doubled over to the howling laughter of his co-workers.

When Elsa grabbed a fallen branch and broke the two-inch thick club across Mohawk's face with a powerful swing; a howl of pain and angry voices replaced the short bout of laughter.

Tense seconds ticked by as the stricken man covered his face with his hands and moaned.

Then leaves crackled and the ground shook behind Martin. He watched the stormy expressions of the men change to a nervous caution. Martin looked back to see a man towering over his shoulder. Except for the black buzz cut, he looked like a kin of the massive oak trees nearby; he was dressed in the uniform of a Maryland State Trooper.

Martin felt dwarfed when the trooper stepped to his side.

"Sir, the current fire danger level is high. Carrying lighted tobacco products in the park can result in a $500 fine."

Blood was dripping from his busted nose when Mohawk dumbly lifted his hand in front of his face and stared at the cigarette that was clenched between his fingers. When he started to throw it on the ground, a growl froze him in place.

"Don't even think about it," the Trooper said. He took the McDonald's bag from Martin.

"There's also a $1000 fine for littering in a state park. But I think you may have received your punishment in lieu of a fine."

"Bu...bu..." Mohawk moaned through his swollen lips, "dis ain righ."

"What?" The Trooper pulled a ticket-pad from his back pocket. "You want me to write up some citations?"

After mumbling a final protest, Mohawk pinched off the tip of his cigarette, took the bag and retreated with the rest of his crew.

The trooper turned to Martin, who got to see a tree-trunk smile.

"We appreciate your assistance, sir. But confronting four road workers probably isn't a good idea. Even if your daughter does think she's Bruce Lee."

Martin blushed and rubbed his neck as he looked up at the trooper.

"She did get carried away a little, but I've been trying to teach my daughter that, if you see something wrong, you should try to fix it. When you see someone doing wrong, you can't ignore it."

"I won't argue with that." The trooper tipped his hat. "If everyone thought that way, there wouldn't be a need for so many people like me."

When the trooper lumbered off, Martin knelt and took Elsa's hands.

"Honey, you shouldn't have done that. It could have..."

"I'm sorry, Daddy!" Elsa pulled her hands away and wrapped her arms around his neck. "I didn't mean to do it. Everything got dark and I don't know what happened."

With her head buried on her father's shoulder, Elsa thought about the lie she was telling... and the dark anger that had exploded out of her. It had been scary when she'd opened the door and let it out.

But she did know what happened... and she wasn't sorry at all.

CHAPTER 5

Friday, June 18, 1993

Her nose pressed against the small round window while her eyes tried to take in all the sights flashing by. The plane started climbing steeply and the speed of the trees, buildings, and roads rushing beneath them began to slow and become easier to follow, until they absorbed into the misty gray of the low, wet clouds. The nebulous forms became lighter and then took on a reddish hue.

Thirteen-year-old Elsa was enchanted when they broke above the clouds to reveal a plush, rumpled carpet, painted in hues of purple, pink and red that stretched to where a burning orange ball was sinking through the horizon.

The plane turned and pointed its nose directly at the disappearing sun.

"This is the captain speaking. We've reached a cruising altitude of 36,000 feet. Our heading at the moment is directly west. There is a head wind and we're expecting a little turbulence, but we should arrive in Denver on time..."

USDOT was sending Martin to a transportation engineer's convention in Denver and he'd decided to combine the work trip with a long vacation. One look at the map told Elsa this was her chance to get in contact with her mother's parents and explore the rugged mountains of Wyoming that had once been her mother's 'back yard'. Letters to Ted and Marie Peterson had gone unanswered, but Daddy had promised they'd search for them.

Elsa nibbled at the edge of a fingernail and closed her eyes.

Oh, God! Now that we're really going, I'm afraid of what we'll find when we get there!

⸺◦◦◦⸺

The plane landed after dark. After a long shuttle bus ride to get their rental car, the two weary travelers started north toward Wyoming. They didn't get far; Martin was affected by the jet lag more than he thought, so they slept in the car at a rest stop and were up before dawn.

After stretching out the kinks, Elsa freshened up in the restroom and changed from the dress blouse she'd worn on the plane into her dad's Sting t-shirt. Sting wasn't rad enough for her; that particular artist was more her dad's speed. But his "Fields of Gold" t-shirt was totally cool and made her think of Wyoming.

They grabbed a snack from the vending machine and resumed their journey up I-25. For miles, the landscape around them was a dark void. Then form began to rise from the void. Stealthy hulks emerged from the shadow and morphed into eroded columnar rock formations. They were approaching a massive bluff when the brightening sky revealed a huge black bison on top, waiting to greet them when they crossed from Colorado into Wyoming.

A closer view showed it was made of plywood. Elsa harrumphed and felt ripped off… that is until they rounded a wide bend in the interstate and saw a vast herd of the shaggy beasts, including many bison calves alongside their mothers, galloping along the low foothills east of the highway.

Stopping on the shoulder of the road, they took pictures and reveled in their first taste of the real west. The sun was just breaching the eastern horizon as they turned back to the car.

"Daddy look!"

Rugged, snowcapped mountains were aglow all across the broad western frontier. The rising sun painted them a soft, lustrous red.

For Elsa, it was love at first sight. She leaned her head on her father's shoulder and watched as light rolled down the mountains and across the high plains, revealing a vast panorama under a deep blue sky.

Breakfast was a different experience altogether. Country music and a swiveling squeak of counter stools greeted Elsa and her dad as they followed the waitress to a booth in the truck stop restaurant. Loud coughs drew her attention to where several long haul drivers sat guzzling their morning coffee and grinning broadly in her direction.

The spontaneous return smile forming on her lips froze when a warning tickled the back of her mind and then she felt their lecherous intentions. Red spread up her neck and across her face. Her dad was oblivious as he slid into the booth, but the waitress wasn't. She plopped the menus on the table.

"I'll be right back for your order dears," she said. Walking by the rough crew at the counter, she hauled back and slugged the nearest driver in the ear. He groaned loudly, hand to his head, while the rest of the group turned back to the counter and laughed.

Elsa could make out "She's just a child, what's wrong with you?" from the direction of the counter. The cruder trucker comments that followed were inaudible, but the response of the angry waitress wasn't.

"That's enough now, ya hear!" she said. "Y'all hit the road. C'mon... take yer coffee and git. An' I hope the road hits y'all right back!" They grumbled and complained, but slid off the stools and made for the door, coins ringing on the counter as they went.

"Sorry 'bout that dear," the waitress said, smiling warmly at Elsa as she returned with a cup of coffee and two glasses of water. "What'll y'all have?"

"Steak, eggs over-easy and hash browns," said her dad, still heedless of the dust-up at the counter.

Elsa hadn't read a word in front of her, so she said, "I'll have the same thing, but can you scramble the eggs with some cheese?" as maturely as she could and handed the menu to the waitress, whose smile widened. "Oh... and orange juice please."

"Certainly, dear. That'll be right up."

⸺⬥⬦⬥⸺

What a morning! Elsa watched the golden prairie through the car window. An occasional, rusty oil derrick seesawed on top of a hill. Cattle grazed in the distance, widely dispersed across expansive fields of yellowed grass, like flakes of pepper lightly sprinkled on a bowl of buttered grits. Splashes of white decorated the tawny coats of pronghorn antelope resting on a hummock.

Although they were heading directly west, the mountains they had seen early this morning were playing hide and seek; disappearing for long periods only to spring up when the car crested a high ridge, as if growing from the barren landscape. She held pictures in her mind, and hopefully in her camera, that were just as impressive as the ones in Bill Pendry's coffee table books.

Less pleasant thoughts of the incident at the truckstop had been banished. It had been almost two years ago when she'd reached the painful, but somehow exciting, conclusion that she was no longer a child, no matter what that waitress said. Her dad hadn't been much help with that, but the school nurse provided all the information she needed... and more!

I'm growing up... I'm almost as tall as daddy now. Jerks like them are just something I'll learn to deal with. Good thing I can see them coming a mile away.

"Hah," said her bemused father, "will you look at that!" He was pointing at a sign along the highway that read 'Entering Medicine Bow National Forest'. Looking out across the barren landscape, one could count the number of trees on a single hand. A mile or more away, small clumps of green sprouted among towering rocky escarpments. As they drove on, the greenery thickened slightly and eventually became an anemic imitation of a forest. Not like home, thought Elsa, where a forest meant trees covered everything for as far as you could see.

Twenty minutes later, Martin drove down Grand Avenue into Laramie, Wyoming. Father and daughter were thinking the same thing...

Now comes the hard part.

⸻◦⸺

"Here's another avalanche," Elsa told her dad. She was watching the back window. A billowing haze enveloped the back third of the car. Particles filtered from the haze and settled on the window. As the dust built, a critical mass was reached and the next bump sent a triangular wedge sliding toward a long, deep ridge of dirt at the bottom of the window. Every so often, a really big pot hole would shake enough dirt off the car to leave room for the next slide.

They had bounced along this dirt road for almost 10 miles, yet the barren track still rolled relentlessly on through a sea of sage brush, with no end in sight.

A quarter-mile later, they took a right fork in the road. That led them to a barbed wire fence, split by a cattle guard where a small sign read 'Peterson Ranch'. Below it was a much larger sign-

Private Road
NO TRESPASSING
You will be prosecuted

Beyond the fence was a weathered ranch house surrounded by dust, tumbleweeds and sage, all kept in constant motion by the relentless wind. The road passing it continued on diagonally toward the mountains. A porch, covered in warped, sun-bleached planks, was tacked onto the front of a house that looked like it had been blown down and then shoved back into place like a pop-up book. Two rough posts held up the roof of the porch and the single horizontal rail nailed between them cried out for a horse to be tied there. Shadows embraced the porch, striped by uneven threads of sunlight streaming from gaps between the boards above.

Martin drove across the cattle guard, pulled up in front of the house, stepped out of the car and looked across to the porch.

In the shade was an ancient rocker holding a man who must have bought the chair new when he retired a century ago. A frayed straw boater graced with a faded red, white and blue band sat atop the old codger's head. The corn cob pipe sticking from his mouth completed the turn of the century tableau. When Martin asked for the Peterson's, the old man proved it all wasn't a simulated historical display by raising a bony finger and pointing down the road.

<hr>

Ted Peterson scowled as the plume of dust drew nearer. *Damn it all! I didn't answer a single letter and still they come!*

His furrowed, wind-burnt face shook in disgust. Peterson hadn't left the ranch since the siege at Koresh's Branch Davidian complex had ended less than two months earlier. In his mind, the deaths of eighty innocent, free people confirmed what he had said for years. The government was plotting to enslave or kill anyone that wouldn't get on board with their socialist, God-forsaken plans to ruin America. They were pissing all over the Constitution, and would try to destroy people like Ted who were willing to defend themselves, their property, and their rights.

At least the backlash from Waco had made it harder for them to make frontal assaults. Now they were trying to sneak in, using his estranged daughter's family for cover. Thank God for his contacts in town. They'd let him know that strangers were looking for him and asking about the Peterson ranch.

Ted was ready and his Wyoming Citizens Militia would show them Feds a thing or two. He went to the gun rack that covered the back wall of his living room and selected an appropriate welcoming instrument.

⸺⸰⸰⸺

Sunset was still an hour away, but Martin had created his own by driving into the shadow of the cliffs looming over their heads. The road became an undulating roller coaster that heaved itself up the mountainside. Cresting a ridge, Elsa spotted a sprawling structure far off, straddling the next shoulder of the mountain, and blending naturally with the landscape.

We finally made it. She leaned forward in anticipation.

"It looks like someone buried a castle in the mountainside!" exclaimed Elsa, as they parked and got out of the car. A semi-circular stone wall ran from corner to corner across the front of the house. The wall was six feet tall, crenellated at the top and blocked their view of the low house within. Martin opened the iron gate in the center and led Elsa into a large flagstone courtyard.

Martin thought the house looked something like a Spanish mission. Six deep, arched windows were set into thick, stuccoed walls, and they flanked massive double doors in the center. The doors were intricately patterned and appeared to be overlaid with hammered copper. All along the top of the front wall, vigas protruded from the stucco.

Heavy wooden benches abutted the stone wall around the perimeter and built-in 'bancos' were spaced along the wall of the house. The stonework of the courtyard floor included a variety of earth tones except for an expanse of lustrous black slabs that led to the front door.

Elsa took Martin's hand as they started down the black walk.

One of the double doors opened and a tall, gray-haired man stepped out, dressed in black jeans and a blue denim shirt. He closed the door behind him.

Martin grabbed Elsa's shoulder and pulled her to a stop when he noticed a shotgun nestled in the crook of the man's arm.

"We're looking for Ted and Marie Peterson."

"I'm Ted Peterson… and you're trespassing" said Peterson angrily.

"I'm sorry," he replied, "we just came out from Laramie and…"

"I know where you came from." Peterson was gruff and short to the point. "We've been watchin' your dust trail for 45 minutes."

"I'm Martin and this is my dau…"

"I know who you are, too." His voice was cold and unyielding.

"We just came up here because…"

"Listen," barked Peterson, "I know what you're going to tell me and I know the truth. Waco showed you Feds that you just can't run roughshod over free, stalwart citizens and get away with it. So now the FBI thinks…"

"Whoa," Martin was incredulous. He glanced briefly at thirteen-year-old Elsa and then held her hand up. "You think we're FBI agents?"

"You work for the government don't you?"

"Yes… for the Department of _Transportation_. And my job has nothing to do with why we're here. I'm on vacation for God's sake."

The door cracked opened behind Peterson and a female voice said "Ted, please."

"Shut the door," he said sharply, then stepped back and slammed the door shut himself.

"Gov'ment is gov'ment. They figure they can send you here like some kind of Trojan horse and undermine what we're doing." Peterson paused, "It. is. not. going. to. happen," adding stress to each word.

"Trojan horse?" Martin almost laughed, "What… you think my chest is going to open up and a team of FBI agents are going to come storming out?" He looked down at Elsa. "This is your granddaughter!"

Peterson patted the gun. "Mister, your chest will open up when I blow a hole in it with this shot gun."

"This is ridiculous." Martin felt Elsa tugging on his hand.

"I'm giving you fair warning. You are trespassing on my property and I want you to leave."

Elsa pulled hard on her dad's arm. "Daddy, let's go."

A stunned Martin Danforth allowed himself to be led out through the gate to the car. As he opened the door he heard the gate slam shut and Peterson call out fiercely…

"Don't come back."

The silence in the car was uncomfortable as they drove off the mountain. Martin wanted to talk with Elsa about what had just occurred. But how could he, since he didn't have a clue. No matter how he ran the encounter through his head, it still seemed like some insane, dark comedy. All he knew was that Elsa had been counting on making a connection with Anne's parents and now that wasn't possible. He thought she'd be crushed.

Martin was the only son of John Brewster Danforth. Before he'd married Anne, he had been the disgruntled heir to a fortune. After the marriage, he was disinherited, poor and happier than he could ever have hoped. But both sets of Elsa's grandparents were estranged, and it looked like that wouldn't be changing. It was just him and Elsa against the world.

"Elsa," he began.

"Now we know why she left." Elsa finished for him and then paused for a moment. "Don't worry Daddy. I wouldn't have learned anything about Mom from that madman."

"His eyes didn't look crazy, but what was coming out of his mouth sure was."

"He really would have shot you, I think." Elsa gazed out the window.

They were nearing the ranch house by the cattle guard and saw the old man leaning on a cane by the side of the road. While one hand kept a gust of wind from stealing his hat, the other waved the cane around weakly.

Martin stopped in front of him. The wide brim of the man's hat cast a shadow that hid his face. After a few moments he tipped his hat back, leaned forward and put a hand on the door of the car.

"Didn't get much of a welcome up there, I guess." The voice was as dry as the air and as brittle as the yellow prairie grass. But it was clear... and there was friendly humor in it.

Martin looked up into a weathered and wrinkled face. The expression was kind and the bright, intelligent, green and brown eyes that looked down on him were Anne's.

"You must be the boy Anne married after she run off?"

Those hazel eyes held him mute; he could only nod.

"Well, I'm Branford Olsen." He bent down and looked across Martin's lap at Elsa. "And that means you must be my great-granddaughter."

Elsa's eyes widened and her lips twitched into a little smile, which grew and grew.

"If either of you can talk," a grinning Branford said, "you're welcome to come in and set a spell."

Elsa stood aside as a splotched, leathery hand dragged the sagging, decayed screen open.

"Go ahead, just give it a shove." Her great grandfather nodded at the front door. "It ain't latched."

It felt sturdy and substantial as she pushed. Crossing the threshold, Elsa stepped out of a drab, pitiless landscape painted in dry shades of brown and gray into a bright, exuberant and welcoming space. Spanning the center of the room was a massive black beam, supported in the middle of the room by a pale lodgepole pine, veined with seams of gold. It was complete with several branches trimmed to serve as coat hooks.

A rugged majestic mountain vista swept from wall to wall, carved deeply into the polished surface of the black beam. The influence of an artfully subtle shading reached across the sculpted surface. On the left, the first blush of sunrise touched the face of the mountains.

Moving her eyes to the right, Elsa was entranced as the peaks and valleys brightened and sharpened approaching the center and then, moving to the right end of the beam, fell slowly into shadow while a molten red sun set behind them.

A reverent Elsa sighed. "Glorious." Her father could only look on in silent admiration of the talent that had created the masterpiece.

Branford Olsen closed the front door, hung his cane on a hook and walked by them to the kitchen. "I'll rustle up lemonade for us. That wind can dry a body out right quick."

When they could finally pull them away from the mountain vista, their eyes toured the large Great-room. The carved beam held up a flat pine ceiling that had been whitewashed and lacquered. It glowed with the reflected light of two ceiling mounted light fixtures that had stained glass covers. The walls were faced with vertical slats of beveled tongue and groove pine; landscapes and wildlife paintings were generously hung throughout.

A braided wool rug covered the golden oak floor. The dark blue oval swirled and faded until it became a white border for the blood red center. A long sofa faced one edge of the rug; the thick cushions and padded arm looked heavily napped-on. At the right side of the sofa a battered nail barrel and tall reading lamp sat close by a Bentwood rocker with a red Indian blanket folded over it. A black raven design on the finely crafted covering was carefully centered between the arms of the rocker. Interconnected rings of water stains covered the top of the nail barrel. Beyond the rocker was a simple, handmade end table with a single drawer.

Complex piles of books towered over the tabletop; Card and Clarke, King and Koontz; hard c's supported important pillars of the ersatz Jenga stack.

All of this was oriented toward a fieldstone fireplace, topped with a rough railroad-tie mantle. The fireplace shared the front wall with the door. Looking out of place, antique crystal stem oil lamps perched delicately on each end of the coarse mantle. Between the lamps was a portrait of a strong and determined-looking woman whose elegance infused the painting. Much was familiar about the face and Martin thought that the crystal lamps must have been hers.

"That's my Hazel." Branford handed them Mason jars. The yellow lemonade transformed the jars' blue tint into an emerald glow. He shook his head sadly; the loose skin of his face stirred gently, like curtains at an open window.

"It's hard to consider. We were married thirty-three years, but now I've been without her for longer than that. She died the winter after Anne, our only granddaughter, was born. So many times I've wondered how different it would be 'round here if she'd lived."

He turned toward the back of the house. "Why don't we go sit in the kitchen? Hazel always thought talkn' should be done while sittin' round the kitchen table."

Branford pulled out two chairs, then walked around the aged laminate kitchen table and sat in front of his own emerald-tinged Mason jar.

Time passed and the Mason jars returned to blue. Martin took a little time, but Elsa felt at home with 'Bran' right away. He talked about life on the high plains; harsh winters, late springs, and glorious summers. Bran and Martin traded memories of Anne while Elsa listened attentively. Elsa talked about school and life 'back east'.

Bran asked them to stay for dinner. "I got a big potta chili in the fridge needs finishin' up."

Martin and Elsa found out that the delicious, sweet beef in the chili was really elk. While they cleaned up, Bran told stories about early days on the frontier he'd gotten from his father. Martin started to talk about their encounter with Ted.

"Don't spoil a nice evening talkin' 'bout that knucklehead," said Bran.

Light was fading and Bran turned on the kitchen light.

Martin talked about meeting Anne and their experiences in Bangladesh; many of the stories were new to Elsa. They explored the cultural differences between city and country life. Elsa especially enjoyed their exchange about shed collecting.

"You collect sheds!?" Elsa felt her leg being pulled.

"Yep," Bran replied with a sly twinkle only grandfathers have.

"So, you drive around in your pick-up and steal them out of people's yards?"

"Elsa, I'm hurt! D'ya think I'm a thief?"

"No. But I don't think you collect sheds either."

"Cross m'heart. Every spring when the snow starts ta clear; I strap on my snow shoes, trek ta the woods and find 'em lyin' 'round on the ground."

Elsa slapped him playfully on the shoulder, and then laughed in delight when Bran explained that moose and elk shed their antlers early in the spring every year.

"They're called sheds," he said. "Folks 'round here are mighty passionate when it comes ta collectin' sheds. For me, it's just an excuse to be out in the woods."

Martin didn't talk much. He sat back and enjoyed the back and forth as Elsa and Bran bridged seventy years and started bonding. He did mention to Bran that, besides the convention, this was an improvised two-week vacation. Martin had to be in Denver from Friday morning through Tuesday afternoon. Apart from those days, they were trusting fate to deliver their itinerary.

The hint was well received. Bran insisted they stay with him. Uncertain at first, Elsa's enthusiasm for the idea convinced Martin to accept the invitation.

CHAPTER 6

Saturday, June 19, 1993

Since it was failing miserably to keep out the thunderous mayhem of the passing train, the motel window threw in the towel and joined the raucous symphony, adding a timpani of rattling panes. Elsa tossed and turned on the lumpy mattress, then cast a peevish glance at the other bed, where her father's snoring competed gamely for a place in the orchestra.

When the hotel falls down, I'll have to drag him out, since even that won't wake him up.

Thank God it was only for one night. In the morning they would check out, pick-up some groceries, and head for Bran's.

The following days were filled with activity and adventure, with an occasional awe-inspiring, soul-shattering experience thrown in for good measure. An early morning, father/daughter run on the prairie started the day. Racing pronghorns, soaring eagles and the sun rising into a cerulean sky made each run special. The scent of sizzling steak, fried eggs, toast and jelly greeted their return.

Then Bran became their tour guide; the rest of the day's activities depended on time and weather. Climbing a mountain was a primary goal for Elsa, but on the first day, despite a bright sunrise, weather rolled into the higher elevations. So, on a cool, cloudy Sunday, Martin followed Bran's directions to a remote, forested canyon.

As Martin drove, Bran gave them quick tips on walking quietly; legs apart, heel-to-toe, be aware of each step, breathe slow and deep. Once parked, he brought out a box full of socks and two pairs of moccasins.

"Keep putting socks on until the moccasins fit," he told them. "The softer your foot; the quieter your step." He draped binoculars around his neck and crossed the road toward a steep, wooded flank of the canyon. "When I hold up my hand it means stop and quiet. If I lower it toward the ground, squat low as quietly as you can.

"Just like the movies," said Elsa.

"Yep, just like the movies. It ain't as important ta be quiet right now, but it will be when we get higher." Like a seal sliding silently into the ocean, Bran stepped into the forest.

What lay ahead was a mystery to Martin and Elsa. Their hearts beat faster in anticipation as they followed Bran, who worked methodically back and forth up the ridge. His feet touched the ground like a mother stroking her sleeping baby. To the silent stands of spruce and fir, he was a down feather, alighting for a moment here and there on the forest floor before being blown along. The stillness of the woods helped amplify every sound; Bran's passage added nothing. Elsa and Martin needed the practice, but watched their guide and improved quickly.

After an hour, they stopped at a rock outcropping amid the Lodgepole pines that dominated the higher slopes. Bran, in a whisper, told them to rest and wait for him to return. Then he disappeared over the rocks.

Martin, for one, was glad for the chance to catch his breath. The pace had been slow, but the air at nine thousand feet wasn't giving the flatlander much oxygen. Elsa's younger lungs seemed unaffected by the altitude. She looked down through the trees, impressed by the steep, long climb they had made. Out of the corner of her eye, she caught a flash of white. A large bank of snow hid in the lee of the rocks.

Snow! And it's almost July! Maybe Bran wasn't kidding when he said we couldn't climb today because it might snow on the mountain.

Elsa looked up into a low, capricious ceiling of damp clouds roiling among the treetops. Gusting wind swirled and feathered the mist into cool, pallid fingers of moisture that often settled on her shoulders or brushed her face.

She felt a tingle on her neck and turned to find Bran close behind, with Martin at his shoulder. Bran's expression was that of a parent who anticipated the opening of gifts on Christmas morning. Leaning close, he whispered.

"We been lucky so far. Moisture in the air dampens sound and the wind helps cover it. If you can be very quiet during the next climb and luck stays with us, we could see somethin' rare and amazin'."

"What?" an exasperated Elsa whispered, "What are we going to see?" But Bran had already taken his secretive smile and headed up.

Elsa froze as Bran's hand went up; when it flattened and dropped toward the ground, she quietly crouched as low as possible. He signaled 'stay' and crept forward. When he returned, he pointed toward a jumble of boulders to the right. Using hand signals, he directed Martin and Elsa to different notches at the top of the pile.

When she reached her spot, she had a narrow view of a dense, misty section of forest downhill from her perch. Once the elk moved her head, Elsa wondered how she had missed it. Less than forty feet away, it was lying on a thick carpet of pine needles and breathing deeply. Blinking her eyes, Elsa took stock of the amazing sight. The elk had two heads!

"Mmmeeeuuwww," the elk cow was in pain as it struggled to get off the ground. Elsa realized that she was watching an elk calf being born. Now standing, the cow twisted its head around and watched as the baby dropped further from the birth canal, front hooves tight under its head. The momma-to-be nipped at the white placental sac that was wrapped around her calf's shoulders. Momma knelt on her front legs while keeping her rump in the air as the calf slid further out.

Elsa's face was aglow with excitement, and she felt like she was on hallowed ground, watching a miracle. She could sense pain and expectancy in the mother elk.

Swoosh! Plop! Falling to the ground, the baby elk immediately shook its head and complained. Elsa was sure that the squeaking meant 'who dropped

me on my head?' Then 'hey, it's chilly out here!' came next as it shivered and
tried to stand. After a few attempts, it succeeded and wobbled precariously on
long thin legs as Momma licked her baby's head and face. She called the calf
to nurse with a high, nasally mew and the baby tottered between her legs,
lifted its head eagerly and began to suckle.

The misty ceiling and stately columns of pine made a shrine for the
bucolic scene.

Urgent, coughing barks from the cow resounded across the mountainside
as a menacing tawny blur broke the peace of the evergreen sanctuary.

Spinning to protect her young, the cow lashed out with her hooves as
the lean mountain lion made a darting attempt to seize the calf. A glancing
blow drove it back. Racing in a circle around the mother, the lithe cat flashed
between Elsa and the newborn. With a burst of speed it leapt in, grabbed a
leg of the calf, and began dragging it toward the rocks. As the baby squealed,
Momma bellowed and tried to charge the lion without stepping on her newborn.

Without warning, Elsa felt a dark force urging her forward.

Ignoring Bran's urgent 'stay down', she climbed to the top of the rock
and screamed.

"Stop! Let her go!"

A threatening growl rumbled from the mountain lion's throat; but instead
of releasing its hold, it began to drag the baby up the slope alongside the rocks.

Elsa heard a challenging response erupt from her own lungs. She jumped
to a lower ledge and picked up a large stone. A surge of adrenalin gave the
stone impetus and righteous anger informed its path through the trees.

With a hollow thump, the stone hit between the shoulder blades of the
big cat which yowled and allowed the calf to slip free. The angry feline took
a step back, lifted her rump and whipped her tail back and forth.

Glaring at Elsa, the mountain lion wriggled her haunches and prepared
to attack.

Elsa glared back and stood her ground.

Bran and Martin appeared on the rocks above, shouting and waving their
jackets. The big cat hissed, backed away, and scampered up the mountain.

"Elsa, no!" called Bran as the girl jumped to the ground.

The calf was on its feet and moving unsteadily toward Momma. Elsa
wanted to make sure the calf was ok and moved toward the baby.

Momma didn't like it. She hissed and charged.

Shock and offended at the lack of gratitude, Elsa stumbled back and then scrambled up the rocks when the mother elk kept coming. Hooves hammered against the rock face around her; one knocked her foot and she began to fall.

Hands caught her arms and jerked her up to the ledge above. Martin pulled Elsa close and squeezed tightly. Hugging back, she trembled as the adrenalin that had fueled so many foolhardy actions began to bleed away and her racing heartbeat began to slow. Gazing into her father's face, she saw relief, awe, and even a little pride.

Hissing, now accompanied by the sound of grinding teeth, continued on the ground below them. A distressed Momma stood between them and her calf, which was surprisingly frisky given the circumstances.

Sensing displeasure from a source other than the elk, Elsa lifted her head from her father's chest. With arms folded across his chest, a stern-looking Bran stood on the rock above their heads.

"We'd better get going," he said tersely, "that elk cow won't be happy 'til we're gone."

⌁⌁⌁

The bounce in her step was evident during their hike back. Although it may have been imprudent and risky, Elsa was proud of saving the elk calf from the mountain lion. She thought the displeasure she still felt from Bran was because she had put herself and possibly them at risk when she confronted the vicious lion.

As they walked along, she tried to draw him out; to let him know she was sorry. "I know it was stupid to do what I did and I'm sorry I scared you guys," she said to both her companions. "At least everything worked out in the end."

"You think so?" Bran retorted angrily. "You don't know what you've done."

"I saved that baby elk!" The offended tone in her voice was clear. "Why are you mad at me? I didn't do anything wrong!"

Bran stopped and turned back to face her, his countenance was grim.

"That calf may have been the difference between life and starvation for that lion, and the three cubs she has in a den beyond the next ridge. Didn't you notice how thin she was? She's desperate; otherwise she wouldn't have risked getting kicked to death. Now she might go off the mountain and get shot going after some rancher's calves. Then her cubs will surely die."

"I'm sorry!" Elsa was stung by her great grandfather's disapproval. "I didn't know!" she cried, "I'm so sorry!"

Martin put his arm defensively around his daughter as she began sobbing.

"Did you think letting Elsa see a newborn calf get eaten by a lion was a good idea?"

Bran dropped his head, chastened by the rebuke. He shook his head sadly.

"I thought that elk woulda dropped the calf days ago. When she wandered up here last week, I knew she was lookin' for a secluded place to birth. I also knew that mountain lion was likely ta get the calf." He rubbed his hand across his face.

"I thought we'd see the lioness feedin' meat to her cubs at the den. That's why I brought the binoculars, there's a good viewin' perch up higher. When I spotted that elk on the ground, I figured we'd least get ta see the elk give birth. Didn' expect ta see what we did."

Bran regretted his anger. He stepped toward Elsa. "I'm sorry. It was my fault. Birth, life and death on the mountain are things I've lived with all my life. I didn't think about how it might affect you. Will you forgive me?"

He stood quietly for a moment and then held his arms open.

Elsa thought about the dark anger that had propelled her. It gave her courage and strength that made her feel invincible. But she wasn't invincible... and this time, she wasn't even right.

She stepped up to Bran and gave him a hug.

"Maybe we can forgive each other." She briefly rested her head on his chest, and then looked up at him, amusement creeping into her voice. "What I want to know is..."

"Yeah, I know," Bran the tour guide smiled. "How am I ever goin' to top that?"

—————

And then he did.

Elsa felt literally on top of the world. A monstrously huge sun felt so close; she could touch it if only she could reach a little higher. Her soul felt like it was expanding, as if the rays were pumping helium through the top of her head, filling her body with a lightness that threatened to float her off into the crystal blue sky above Medicine Bow Peak where she stood. The vistas available to her eyes were mesmerizing. In every direction, the view expanded to the limits of her vision.

Over one hundred miles to the south, the snow covered mass of Long's Peak was a luminous beacon among a host of mountains that faded into the horizon. Almost that far, to the northeast, was Laramie Peak, a solitary pillar towering over the endless prairie of the high plains. Twenty degrees to the left of the peak, the Big Horn Mountains were a distant white smudge.

In the Southwest, the Sierra Madres seemed only a flying leap away. Far beyond them to the right, the Uinta Mountains of Utah ruled a cloud-topped domain. And, impossibly far in the northwest, like a faint, fairy-tale kingdom, bright tiny wavering spikes and darker hazy bulges danced on the horizon. This magical glimmer of the Tetons and Yellowstone stood more than three hundred miles away.

Contrasted with the burning heat pouring from above, a crisp, strong breeze was a welcome relief to the parts of her body facing the sun and chilling to those that weren't.

The majesty of the moment was so strong, and the beauty of the mountain so pure, that Elsa didn't hesitate when she saw two teenage boys toss their candy wrappers among the rocks.

"Hey! You can't do that!" She rushed over and bent to pick up the litter. "This mountain isn't your trash can!" She was off balance as she straightened. When the wind gusted, it took her over the side.

———

Her eyes fluttered. A blazing angel floated down and resolved into her father climbing down beside her. He was brilliantly illuminated in the sunshine, while she was lying in shadow.

"Oh, God! Elsa... Elsa... where are you hurt?"

Pain radiated from a dozen places, but as Elsa mentally examined each one, they all felt like scratches and bruises. She wiggled her feet and then her legs. She put her hands on the rocks and pushed herself into a sitting position as her father gently aided her. From a cut high on her forehead, blood flowed down the left side of her face.

"Try not to move," her father said, "I'll take care of that." Bran had insisted they take a first aid kit, even though the hike was only six miles round trip.

Now Martin pulled it out, cleaned the gash and applied Neosporin, gauze and tape.

"Where else are you hurt?" Martin had been horrified by the sight of the strong wind gust blowing Elsa like a ragdoll off the peak. He thanked providence the summit was rounded at the top, and she had only fallen a short distance down the shadowed side of the mountain.

"I hurt lots of places, but I don't think any of them are serious. Let me rest a moment and I'll try to get up."

"Take as long as you need," Martin replied. His daughter made him so proud. When she saw something wrong, she took action, no matter the consequences.

———

Bran watched as Elsa and Martin hiked toward him. His 87-year-old bones had wanted a day off, so he'd brought a book, set himself at a sunny picnic table, and sent them up the trail. The morning had been pleasant and he awaited an awed reminiscing of their experience.

As they drew nearer, he spotted the bandage on Elsa's head. Once they related the details, an apology was on his lips when Elsa, a deadpan expression on her face, said...

"Yesterday you almost got me eaten by a lion, and today I get blown off a mountain...

"So... what are we doing tomorrow?"

———

When Elsa woke up the next morning, she felt fine... until she started moving; then she discovered that the echoes of her fall were more exquisitely painful than the fall itself. Massaging, gentle stretching, and ibuprofen helped, but the planned whitewater rafting trip was delayed.

The day became one of reading, conversation, and short walks on the prairie. After breakfast, they sat around the table for a while. Bran asked about their running and they told him how important it was to both of them; it was one way they could hold on to a part of Anne.

Elsa told him how excited she was about entering the ninth grade in high school and her hopes for the upcoming cross country season.

"I think I can be pretty good," she said.

Martin laughed and told Bran that, while there was no pressure, he thought Elsa would be a star right from the start.

Whitewater rafting went off the next day without a hitch. There were no life threatening events, at least none that was unexpected. On Thursday, Elsa could run again, albeit gingerly.

After breakfast, they took the long drive into Laramie and did some shopping... window and grocery. Bran introduced Elsa to a quaint bookstore called Second Story Books, where they both found enough reading material to keep them busy while Martin was in Denver. Bran had voluntarily stopped driving three years earlier when his attention span had shortened and his reaction time had lengthened.

"Not a good combination for drivin'," he said. So, while Martin was gone, their travel would be limited to that which could be achieved with their own two feet.

Before they headed back, Bran took them to a real cowboy restaurant. The hokey joke books at each wood plank table, the cowboy boot glasses, the menu heavy on steak and wild game would have been tell-tale signs, if they had needed them.

They didn't. The Chuckwagon dripped with western ambience. So much so, that you could close your eyes, open your ears, sniff, and imagine yourself on the high plains around a campfire, with a fresh steak grilling on a cast-iron frying pan.

Every other male in the place was wearing a cowboy hat. Of those that weren't, most of them were gentlemanly cowboys who'd hung theirs on the hooks available at each booth. Along with the authentic atmosphere, the food was incredible. You can't serve a sub-standard steak to a ranch hand and get away with it.

Her father packed that afternoon for his convention trip. He said he would call every evening and be back late Tuesday night. Elsa asked him to be careful; he told her to do the same.

"And don't go wrestling any mountain lions while I'm gone."

CHAPTER 7

Saturday, June 26, 1993

Elsa slipped out of her bed while the sun was still slumbering. The darkness of the sky was lessening, but the moon, only days away from full, was shining brightly as it fell toward the western horizon. After dressing quickly for her run, she went to the kitchen and wrote a note for Bran.

Out for my run, I should be back around 8:00 a.m.
I'd like to help fix breakfast if you can wait that long
Love, Elsa

She stepped out the door, walked to the driveway and did some of her Karate limbering up exercises. Her twice-weekly karate classes were the only thing she missed from back home. A little looser, she headed down the road.

Musing about her martial arts classes merged into her thinking about this run through the pre-dawn darkness. The combination took her thoughts down a path that was rarely explored. Inside her mind was a dark place that held a massive amount of fear and anger. The reasons for those emotions were buried deep, and her father seemed to know that it was related to her mother's murder. When she was young, that anger had often caused her problems because she didn't have the discipline or maturity to deal with it. Like an injured lion, it was dangerous and uncontrolled.

Karate had helped to give her that much-needed discipline, and for years she kept that lion caged, locked down tight. As she advanced through the belts, her teachers began to realize she had a talent for martial arts and began to concentrate on her focus and power.

One day, when she was struggling in a match and a teacher was urging her to "reach deep", something clicked, and she did reach... to that dark place.

The result was dynamite. She learned that her deep, unresolved fear and anger were sources of power, something she could learn to use. Her lion could be harnassed.

Lately, her running had become more important than karate. High school was fast approaching, and with it, the first chance to see how far her running could take her. Now she was wondering if the same power that she pulled from within for her karate matches could be applied to her running.

Fifteen minutes into her run, Elsa's remaining kinks were gone and her feet touched the ground like light brushes of a feather duster across a table. Her efficient, relaxed form allowed her to move like a rolling river, or a current of wind. She passed so silently through the dawning day that she was almost on top of a herd of pronghorn before they were aware of her approach.

She split the herd. The group on the right side of the road bounded away into the prairie, but the pronghorn on the left were hemmed in by the fence that ran along the left side of the road. They trotted along the fence away from her, nervous about crossing the road in front of the strange apparition that had startled them.

Drawing carefully from that dark source of power, she increased her pace to keep them close. The beautiful creatures moved over the earth so effortlessly. Elsa wanted to move like them, be part of their graceful herd. The fleeing antelopes increased their speed and Elsa followed. Her fluid stride propelled her along the road at a velocity that was all wrong for the long distance run she had planned, but the herd was like a magnet that pulled her along.

The pace increased again as the group began to angle toward the road. Elsa let more of the "lion" out and found another gear. She was now at full speed. Just ahead, the leader was in the road and the remainder followed. The trailing pronghorn were even with Elsa, but came on to the road anyway, and then Elsa was running among them, one of the herd. Like heavy hail on a shingle roof, the animals thundered along the road. The excitement allowed her to hold the ferocious pace a moment longer while she reached out her hand and brushed the flank of her closest companion.

Like an arrow from a bow, the herd shot forward and then across into the open prairie. Bran had said that, in full flight, the pronghorn can reach seventy miles per hour. Elsa was able to watch a herd of truly fast animals flowing along the contours of the earth and disappearing over a ridge in the distance.

She slowed and rested her arms on top of her head, breathing deeply in, blowing out slowly. As the eastern sky began to glow, Elsa recovered her wind and gradually moved back into her smooth, economical stride. The miles whisked by under her feet, and she reveled in the mystical, powerful feeling of running on the edge of aerobic endurance.

Runner's high isn't illusion, imagination or artificial. Elsa had felt it before and relished the amazing natural lift it gave her. Her father didn't like her to run far on her young legs, but she did anyway, when she got the chance.

A long time later the sun breached the horizon, and Elsa looped around and headed back toward Bran's ranch. She had come to adore the glow of the mountains in the morning sun. Now she ran as though the sun pushed her toward them, a solar-powered runner. At the turnaround, ten miles had already disappeared beneath her feet. Glancing at her wrist, she checked her time. The calculations in her mind told her that she was running way too fast for the ten miles still to go. Her heart, her soul, and her legs said otherwise. Since the majority rules, Elsa let the lion roar once more… and reveled in the power. Those miles flew by.

<hr />

Magic graced the rest of the vacation. While her father was gone there were long walks on the prairie and treks in the mountains where she soaked up Bran's vast knowledge. A mother fox was a vixen and her babies, kits. Even in the dry season, you can find water if you know where to look. She saw jack rabbits so big and fast, they seemed to fly across the prairie like an eagle. "The biggest ones have antlers and we call them 'jackalopes'," Bran said. Then he winked and nudged her with his elbow. "Least that's what we tell them naive lowlanders."

Bran taught her to look ahead.

The pronghorn are always on the move, roaming across the wide valleys. They create narrow trails in the coarse grass that are almost invisible. When you're on them, you can look ahead and see the path clearly as it disappears in the distance. Take a step left or right, and they vanish in the needle-and-thread and buffalo grass, leaving you stumbling on the uneven ground.

"Life can be like that," he told her during one walk. "You need to be aware of each step, but your eyes need to be on the horizon if you want to keep the path ahead clear."

Soon the weepy goodbyes were upon them. Martin promised they would return, and Bran said he would hold them to it. They would write. They would never forget. When their car had raised a cloud of dust that obscured her last look at Bran waving from his front porch, she prayed earnestly that it would all be true.

<hr/>

The plane banked and Elsa watched the snow-covered Rockies pass out of sight. The trip west had changed her... and more changes were on the way. High school, boys, cars... life; they were all still out there waiting.

Elsa looked ahead, trusting the distant path to remain clear.

PART II

Racing Ahead

O ccasional slivers of brightness from the streetlights slipped through the trees, dividing the shadows on the bike path into a pattern of light and dark. It streamed across the black macadam and briefly sparkled on the rushing water to his right.

The rider was revealed in the flashes of light, like the image on a child's flip-card animation. But, in between, the rider was not invisible. Instead, it was in the shadow of the pattern that the image pulsed, as if drawing power from every moment of darkness; power that was muted when it came into the light.

Moments earlier he had swept by her, close enough he could have reached out and run his fingers through her golden hair.

Lights changed and traffic roared from the intersection behind her. A cyclist whipped by, gaining speed on the downhill slope into the park.

She reveled in the feeling of power that running fast gave her and the result showed in her face. In high school, her teammates called it "the lion's mask." When she competed, her father started a tradition of "roaring" instead of cheering. Soon all of the team's supporters were roaring as she raced to victory after victory. After hearing that sound, most of her competitors shrank from the challenge that it represented.

CHAPTER 8

Saturday, October 2, 1993

Elsa was again running with a herd, except this time she was leading, not following. She could hear her father roaring in the distance. Dropping into the first dip, she used the slope to accelerate into the next rise.

During the boy's event earlier she had watched the elongated mass of runners cross this same rolling portion of the course. It brought to mind the herd of pronghorn flowing across the prairie. The mental picture of the fleet, beautiful animals had helped her to relax.

This meet was the largest and most prestigious invitational on the East Coast. The starting line was a kaleidoscope of colors as eighty-three high schools from eleven states were represented. The first weekend in October always saw the fastest, fiercest, most competitive runners going head to head in an early season test. This particular invitational was considered a preview of the Eastern Regional Championship, from which only the most talented would qualify for Nationals.

When the high school team had started summer practices, Elsa discovered quickly that she was different from the other girls on the team. Running was important to her; she loved testing her limits. Most of the girls were on the team because it was a sport where boys and girls were together. By the time her father had picked her up after the first day of practice, the constant chatter about boys was driving her crazy. Elsa wondered how she could take it for a week; much less an entire season: 'Did you see Bobby's abs, ooo! Don't you love it when he wears those cut-off t's' 'That stupid slut Sonya actually asked Greg…'

How would she ever stand it! Some of the other girls worked hard because they were smart, competitive, and knew that hard work was needed to improve. But none felt the joy of running like she did… and it showed. By the end of the first week, her coach had her training with the varsity boys. The guys hadn't taken it well until they discovered how difficult it was to stay in front on training runs. Grudgingly, they admitted she was where she belonged.

The first few tri-meets had been easy and enjoyable victories, but not that challenging. She wished she could compete in the boy's races. Her coach didn't know her well enough yet; he tried to keep her from getting a big head by talking how tough this invitational was going to be.

But Elsa didn't run to win, she ran because she loved it. Her competitiveness was instinct, not a desire to show she was above anyone else. Her ego was almost non-existent and her approach to everything she did was, *'How can I do this better?'*

⸺⬥⸺

Coach had told her to take it easy early in the race, and as Elsa topped the next rise, she thought it was his booming voice echoing across the field…

"Relax! You've got a long way to go!"

He sounded upset, but Elsa smiled. 'Long way to go?' Geez! The whole race was only three miles. She imagined a pronghorn racing in front of her across the field and gave chase.

The course was charming and challenging; twining between ponds filled with lily pads and cattails; crossing a wide stone bridge and forging up a long, heavily wooded hillside thick with the scent of balsam and magnolia; bursting into the open atop a grassy, broad hilltop that revealed more woods, ponds and the finish line waiting in the distance.

Running comfortably, Elsa relished the view and started across the hilltop toward dense trees on the opposite side. From the corner of her eye, a long, brown, pigtail came bouncing into view as another runner drew along side. Arms driving hard, the girl worked to pull ahead of Elsa as they drew near the woods. Elsa noted the name of a northern Virginia high school on the back of the jersey.

"Nice job Virginia," she said, excited to have company. Then she yelped as the high meadow ended at a steep narrow trail through the dense trees. Stuttering her steps, she fell in behind.

Wow! Those are so long I could grab hold and let her tow me. The pigtails bounced in the wake of the thin runner like braided whips. Soon Elsa realized why pigtail girl had labored so hard to get in front; the narrow trail gave Elsa no room to pass and the constant braking of her speed began to wear her out.

As the trail widened at the bottom of the hill, she pulled up to the shoulder of pigtail girl, who responded with a slight increase in pace. They began a back and forth battle that brought forth a cheer from the crowd waiting at the finish a half-mile away.

Her adversary was pushing hard, breathing like a freight train, as they rounded a pond and pounded up a short hill that brought them onto the finishing straightaway. Elsa still had a couple of gears to use and admiration for pigtail's guts and determination wouldn't stop her from using them. Her teammates were roaring; the finished line called... and Elsa answered.

A long string of red, yellow and green pendants formed a broad arc in the grass that held back proud relations, friends, and teammates of the award winners. They faced a rectangular wooden stage. In the center was a white awards stand, the platforms of which were staggered. From number six at the bottom, they stepped up to one.

Pigtail girl was sophomore Alicia Hoffman, Elsa discovered as they announced the second place finisher.

"...and in first place, utilizing an amazing final kick to set a course record of 18:27.2, freshman Elsa Danforth."

The trophy was nice and Elsa liked the proud, silly, beaming look on her father's face. She smiled as pictures were taken, then bent down and gave Alicia a one-handed hug.

"That was such an awesome, exciting race," Elsa said, "You are so tough."

"Oh god, you were incredible!" said Alicia, "You made it look so easy."

"It wasn't easy." Elsa smiled, "But it sure was fun!"

Afterwards, they stood at the bottom of the podium and talked. Elsa could see her father among the crowd in the background smiling as he watched and waited. His gaze shifted and the smile became a look of concern.

"Alicia!" Elsa turned and saw a police officer escorting a man and a woman into the awards area. Wide, reddened eyes and pale skin showed the woman was almost in shock. The man's face was grim. "Alicia!" he called.

"That's my parents... something must be wrong." She gave Elsa a hug and a final 'congratulations' and rushed away.

Alicia's parents put their arms around their daughter. As they left the awards area and moved through the crowd, Elsa saw Alicia cry out and bury her face on her mother's shoulder.

After a two year hiatus, police announced this afternoon that a missing Northern Virginia woman, Andrea Hoffman, may be the ninth victim of the Harvester. The George Mason graduate student has not been seen since Friday evening, and was reported missing after failing to show up for a car pool to a Maryland sporting event. The 23-year-old Hoffman is 5' 7"...

Martin's knuckles whitened as he gripped the steering wheel. They were heading out to Ledo's in Lane Manor Shopping Center for a celebratory dinner when the announcement came over the radio. Clenched teeth held back his cursing.

"Oh, no! That must be Alicia's sister." Elsa cried. "Why couldn't the Harvester have been dead, like they thought?"

"He was probably in jail for something else," said Martin, "I wish he'd been dead, too!"

"You think they could be wrong? Maybe she just changed her mind about going."

"I doubt they would have put it on the radio if they didn't have some solid reason to think it was the Harvester." Martin said.

The Harvester's usual method of operation was to call a D.C. area hospital and either inform them of an incoming donor heart or notify them of a delivery already made. As a result, the F.B.I's Voice Identification Unit had established a program to train Academy cadets in forensic voice identification. These cadets would be on call to report to local hospitals when there had been a suspected Harvester kidnapping.

Using their specialized training and questions designed to elicit specific vocal patterns, the Harvester Task Force hoped to obtain voice recordings that could be used as an additional tool in their pursuit, capture and conviction of the elusive serial killer. Participation in the Harvester Auxiliary Detail was mandatory for second year cadets. The initials of the unit led to a simple complaint about the tiresome duty that many of the cadets considered make-work.

Paul Demerov was one of those cadets assigned to the Georgetown University Hospital; he received additional training so that he could adequately answer all incoming calls and forward them efficiently to the right parties. On the morning of Saturday, October 9, he had one foot out the door, already thinking about his bike ride with Sandra along the Rock Creek Trail.

Then he got the call. Years later, when Sandra was just a fond memory, and he had the career all cadets dream of, he would sometimes regret that he hadn't ignored the ringing phone.

But he did answer it. Then he made a call of his own.

"I'm sorry Sandra, I can't make it," he told his soon-to-be ex-girlfriend... "I've been HAD."

He had taken extra precautions to guard against atrophy. It had been a long time between harvests and he wanted to make sure there would be no mistakes. Not that he'd been completely inactive during his summers in Arizona. But it wouldn't have been wise to complete a harvest while he'd been away. It would have opened up too many avenues for his task force to explore.

His summer sabbaticals had been educational, even thrilling. Self discovery was an important part of life and he had discovered something important. He could do more than Harvest. He learned that he could Plant also. Oh, how he could Plant!

The police in Arizona would be the ones who would harvest what he planted, but that was just fine. He would do his harvesting here in D.C.

The Harvester Task Force, the name alone filled him with pride. For nine years they had been searching for him, trying to stop him. But they were no closer now than they had been after that very first Harvest... and he was so much better than in those early days.

Why had he been worried? His task force was only good for comic relief. Their feeble efforts would never stop him. This morning's taking had been flawless. If he dropped Andrea on some street corner right now, she would be no help to the police at all.

As he walked up along the steel surgical table, he ran his hand up her cool, muscular leg. It trembled. He paused between her legs and she squirmed. Continuing up, he delayed again as he gave her left breast a loving caress. He adjusted the flow through the IV into her arm before he reached her face.

He gently removed the tape from her eyes and looked deeply into them... they were so lovely. Not quite blue... not quite green... mysterious. They were wide open and frightened; she was seeing his face for the first time. With a care equal to that which he had used to uncover those remarkable eyes, he peeled the tape from her mouth.

Andrea screamed with every ounce of energy and volume that she possessed. It was a scream that should have shattered every glass container within miles. When it hit the room's sound batting, it died, as if a vacuum had sucked it all away.

"Very impressive," he said, "almost as powerful as those enchanting eyes. You'd have better luck calling for help with those."

"You bastard!" Andrea screamed piercingly, 'Let me go or I swear I'll come back from the grave and haunt you the rest of your miserable life!"

His amused laughter was soaked up by the room.

"This is delightful! No one has ever tried that before. Begging, bribing, cursing... I've heard some dreadful language, but no one has ever threatened me with haunting. Sorry dear. I'm certain your soul is much too pure for haunting."

He leaned close to her with his calm, handsome face. "But mine isn't." Then he pressed his lips against hers.

She let loose with another ear-splitting scream and tried to bite him. He pulled away just in time.

"Tsk. Tsk. That wasn't nice at all." He walked away from the table but continued to talk. "I should explain my new procedures, and how they will affect the rest of your life."

Andrea knew she was going to die. She had struggled for hours against the bonds holding her to the cold table, knowing what was in store for her when the Harvester returned. What she wanted was a small victory; to see those cold eyes react; to shake that even disposition; to somehow deny this monster his pleasure. She'd heard of people committing suicide by swallowing their tongue, but now she knew it was a myth. If it could be done, she'd be dead.

He returned with two syringes in his hand.

"Andrea dear, I'm going to remove your heart. Before I do that, I can inject you with one of these two syringes. This one, let's call it Curtain Number One, will render you paralyzed and unable to feel anything; you will still be somewhat lucid until loss of blood renders you unconscious... then you die."

Clinging desperately to her sanity as her body shivered uncontrollably, Andrea moaned and shook her head to the tiny extent allowed by the strap holding it tightly to the table.

"This one, which we'll call Curtain Number Two, leaves you paralyzed, but still able to feel every deliciously painful slice of the scalpel, every pinch of the clamp, every bit of suction as I siphon your blood away.

"Oh, God! No, please, no!" Andrea hated to hear the desperate pleading in her voice, but she could plead, or go insane.

"Wait, dear contestant. You haven't heard the terms. What is behind Curtain Number Two is absolutely, 100% free. No cost to you what... so... ever."

Andrea's moans persisted, but he continued with his offer.

"The cost, should you choose to accept it, for Curtain Number One, will take just a moment to explain. To do that, let me bring in my lovely assistant..."

Her eyes shifted frantically from side to side in search of the silent apprentice.

"... oh, wait. I don't have one." He laughed. It was dry and humorless. "I suppose I will have to do it myself." With his elbows on the table near her head, he brought his mouth near her ear. "I've never cared much for sex. It usually involves emotion, which always... ALWAYS, leads to problems. The heart is an organ; when not properly mastered... as I have mastered mine, leads one to destruction. But, you see dear, during my sabbatical, I developed tastes that I had not previously thought I could afford to... satisfy. Your help in satisfying them is the only price of Curtain Number One."

Her victory would be costly, Andrea decided, as the Harvester stood and did a flourishing drum roll on the steel.

"And Andrea's choice is..." He pointed her way.

"Curtain Number One," she said grievously. Tears slipped from her eyes, filtered through her soft brown hair and fell to the table, where so many had fallen before.

"Excellent!" the Harvester exulted, ripping away his surgical apron. Underneath he was naked... and ready.

He climbed on the table and bent to kiss her lips. She trembled at their touch, but did not resist.

"Oh no, dear, that won't do." he kissed her cheek and then her ear. He whispered sensuously, "You have to make me enjoy this. Kiss me." While he whispered these sweet nothings in her ear, his legs worked between hers.

She held her revulsion in check and returned his kiss when his lips came back to hers.

He probed for... and found what he desired. "Oh, yes" he moaned into her mouth, then kissed her again.

She bore down and when she felt the stream begin, clamped her teeth onto his lip.

There was a brief moment, as he first felt warmth on his hard manhood, when he thought she was enjoying it... until he felt her teeth on his lip.

Shrieking in agony, he pulled away and felt his skin rip. He jumped off the table. Yellow liquid spilled from between her legs and puddled on the stainless steel. He could feel her urine dripping down his legs, smell it on his skin.

"You DIRTY BITCH!" Blood splattered her body as he screamed in her face.

Andrea exulted in her victory. Her eyes blazed with a fierce abandon. She spit his skin and blood back into his face.

With a strangled cry, he grabbed the nearest scalpel and drove it through her throat over and over again.

As her life slipped away, she knew that he had seen her eyes...

Her bright, blue-green and victorious eyes.

CHAPTER 9

Saturday, October 2, 1993

For almost seven hours, he'd felt like nothing more than a glorified telephone operator, not a future F.B.I. agent. The phone rang and he answered... again and again. Then he'd gotten *the* call.

"This is the Georgetown University Hospital Heart Center. How may I help you?"

"Please transfer me to your transplant team." The voice was brisk and business-like.

By reflex as much as conscious thought, Paul Demerov sat up alertly. "I've been trained to help with any transplant questions."

"Good, this is Dr. Kauffman from the Washington Hospital Cen..."

The words triggered a mental alarm. Spinning through Harvester facts, Paul found the right one. This was the same name and hospital the Harvester had used in his first year. He jumped in.

"I'm sorry Dr. Kauffman. Can you spell that for me please?"

The impatience was clear; Paul felt that the voice sounded nasal, stuffy. He checked off items on his list as the voice spelled it out.

"I'm sorry again, was that one 'f' or two."

"Two f's" was the reply, and Paul made another check.

"Could you give me a call back number in case we get cut-off?"

"No, I can't. This is an urgent call. We expect to harvest an A+ heart from a deceased female donor in the next hour, and I need you to alert your transplant team. "

After the third year, the Harvester had limited his calls to one minute or less. Once he had relayed the blood-type, he disconnected within seconds. This was in the mistaken belief that it would keep the authorities from tracing the call. Paul knew it would be easy to find where the call originated, in fact, if this location had the equipment on site, the point of the call would have been known in seconds. Georgetown University had not been contacted previously by the Harvester and did not have that equipment. In fact, because of the two year hiatus, none of the hospitals were equipped this year. His desire to keep the Harvester on-line was so he could tick off all the items on his list. His timer was at 58 seconds.

"Why do you do it?" he asked.

"Excuse me?" the Harvester asked.

Paul smiled and checked another item. "I know you are the Harvester," he said, "I want to know why you butcher people."

"I don't butcher." Check, check. "I'm a skilled surgeon." Check

"But why?"

"I'm practicing," said the Harvester, "for when I take your heart." Check, check, check

Paul smiled grimly as the line went dead.

⁓

The twenty-four-year-old Demerov knew he should be counting his lucky stars. Right now, though, all he wanted was something to eat.

He was a hot commodity since becoming the first law enforcement official to converse with the Harvester. This temporary assignment to the Harvester Task Force could make his career at the F.B.I. His day since the phone call had been a blur of reports, meetings, and conference calls. It was approaching midnight.

Agent-in-Charge Ronald Grantham continued his briefing.

"The call was initiated at 4:18 p.m. from a pay phone in Alexandria. The timing is important. Only fifty-seven minutes elapsed from the call to delivery of the package. Our medical experts believe it would have been physically impossible for the Harvester to perform the extraction, package the heart, and reach Northeast D.C. in that time. It has been determined through forensic analysis that in all previous Harvester cases, the victim was alive at the time of the phone call. That is not believed to have been true in this circumstance."

"At 6:09 p.m. a package containing the heart of Andrea Hoffman was delivered by a refrigerated U.S. Foodstuffs truck to the loading dock at Georgetown University Hospital. Quick action by Agents Rudolfo and Jones resulted in the identification of the likely point at which the package was inserted into the truck. Unfortunately, that location was the only one at which security cameras were inoperable. It was determined that the package was inserted at approximately 5:15 p.m."

"The package included the victim's heart in the expected Styrofoam container. As usual, a slip of paper with the victim's name and age was included. Below the name and age, written in a manner that indicates it was added at a later time, were the words 'DIRTY BITCH!'"

"Many of the procedures instituted in previous years were discontinued after 1992 when there had been no victims for two years. Fortunately, one of the procedures continued was a program that had the corollary benefit of training future agents. The program worked as it was designed, and we now have our first clear recording of the Harvester."

Grantham nodded to an agent who had his finger on the button of a tape deck.

"And this is the cadet who took the call you just heard... Paul Demerov."

Paul repressed a grin as he stood. He was being introduced by the Agent-in-Charge at a briefing of the entire task force! He nodded his head and glanced around the room, then sat down. He had been too hungry to be nervous when he took his seat at the start of the meeting. But having one hundred and fifty agents staring at the back of his head changed that in a hurry.

"Cadet Demerov, could you stand back up again." Agent-in-Charge Ronald Grantham motioned him back to his feet. "We have a few questions for you."

Paul decided that he was glad there was no food in his stomach; it had twisted into knots.

"Yes sir," he said.

"Why did you break from your script?"

He felt like he should have a blindfold and a cigarette. Hoping that his nervousness wasn't evident, he answered. "The clock was at fifty-eight seconds and I knew he was about to hang up. Anything from the script would have been ignored. Studies have shown that many serial killers will take advantage of the opportunity to explain themselves." Paul shrugged and, a bit defensively said, "It worked."

It wasn't a smile, but Grantham's face become slightly less stone-like.

"Give us your general impression of the Harvester."

That question felt way over his head. "I'm sure there are people more qualified than me for that."

"Relax, Demerov. I'm not asking for a psychological profile. You're right; we've got plenty of experts. But you were the one on the phone." Paul thought Grantham was coming as close as he was physiologically able to a smile. "I'd imagine you've come to realize this could be quite a plum for you. Besides, it wasn't a request."

There were snickers from the room behind him.

"Yes sir." He hadn't been asked for any opinions earlier. Paul hoped the sweat beading on his forehead wasn't noticeable. "General impressions... I hope I don't have to justify these." He wondered how many knew he was stalling as he tried to get his thoughts together.

"One. I think analysis of the recording will confirm the accuracy of the psychological profile, and show that he is indeed male and in his thirties or forties." Laughter followed this small dig at the vague generalities in the Harvester's profile.

"Two. It's clear that the voice was altered by artificial means. Possibly some type of flat plate in the mouth, cotton stuffed in the nose.

"Three. I didn't detect any overt anger when I tried to bait him, calling him a butcher. His response was calm. But it seemed forced, as if it was just on the surface. I didn't think he would make mistakes caused by passion."

Grantham interrupted. "You said 'didn't think'. What do you mean?"

"I think he'll make mistakes. Staying on the phone was one. But I didn't think they would be ones caused by fear or anger or panic. I didn't think he'd make emotional mistakes."

"You think the 'Dirty Bitch' on the note was a mistake?"

"Yes sir," Paul replied, "but only a small one. What caused the added remark was the big mistake. I think Andrea... I mean the victim, hurt him somehow. Physically, emotionally, who knows?" He paused and lifted a hand to his chin. "I wasn't sure earlier... and I'm still not. But I felt as though there was something a little off with his dipthongs. Uh, dipthongs occur when a vowel is followed by another vowel. It could be that he has a lip deformity or injury. I'd say that if you have a list of potential suspects, I'd spend tomorrow checking them for recent visible injuries. I'm sure he'll think he can explain it away, he thinks he is smarter than anyone." Paul cringed at the weak stereotype. "Sorry, sir. I suppose that's true of just about every criminal."

Paul thought that Grantham must have fractured something, since his mouth actually formed a smile.

"You seem to have taken charge of this investigation pretty quick... for a cadet."

There was laughter as Paul stammered out an apology.

"Don't apologize, son. You have good instincts."

A question came out of the crowd. "What do think of his threat?"

"I'm glad he made it. It helped me complete my checklist." More laughter and friendly applause greeted the statement. "Otherwise, I think it was empty. He's a coward who kills vulnerable, single women. I hope he does come after me."

When Paul left the meeting early Sunday morning, he thought about how much he was going to love being an agent. But it would have to wait until after he got some food.

—

One week had passed and Elsa hoped that it had been long enough. She dialed carefully and held her breath as she waited. A man answered with a flat, emotionless 'hello'.

"I'm sorry to bother you. This is Elsa Danforth and I was hoping I could talk to Alicia."

"This is her father." He paused, and then asked, "Who are you?"

"I was in the race with Alicia last week."

"Alicia isn't feeling very well right now, I doubt if she'd want to chat about running."

"I understand. I didn't really want to talk about running. You see... my... my mother was Anne Danforth. She was the Harvester's first victim."

There was a long pause. Eventually Alicia's father spoke.

"What is it you want," he said softly.

"Every time it happens, it hurts and I feel so helpless. I thought I could spend some time with Alicia; maybe I could help."

After a shorter pause, he said, "Ok...Yes. That might help. But Alicia is sleeping right now. When were you thinking of coming?"

A good feeling came over Elsa as they made arrangements. Not a happy feeling, really. The kind of feeling that you get when you've been at the bottom and are starting to climb out, or even better, helping someone else climb out with you.

—◁◁◁◁◟◞▷▷▷▷—

Elsa sat on the couch of the Hoffman's living room and told them about her mother... and losing her mother... and learning to be happy again. There were tears, and Alicia came to sit beside her and held her hand. Elsa knew that was a very good sign. If Alicia could comfort, she could be comforted. It was too soon to talk about her loss, but the time would come. After a while they did talk of running. They scheduled some training runs together, and Elsa knew that Alicia would become her best friend. Something she'd never had before.

She was getting ready to leave the Hoffman's when the door bell rang. Mrs. Hoffman answered and opened the door to a young man dressed in a dark blue suit. He fiddled with a paper in his hand and looked very nervous. Elsa thought he looked like the youngest F.B.I. agent ever.

After introducing himself, Paul Demerov looked at Elsa and Alicia. His eyes locked on Elsa's face, and she knew he was connecting her face to her mother's. *Please don't ask. Please!*

Mrs. Hoffman asked him why he was there.

He stuttered a few times, eyes flicking often to Elsa.

"I apologize for not calling. This isn't official business. I'm the cadet who took the call from the Harvester. There is something I thought you should know. It isn't part of the official report, and I'm not sure if you were told. It's an item they decided to keep out of the press. But I thought you should know."

Paul fidgeted some more and glanced at Elsa again.

"You said you thought we should know." Mr. Hoffman stepped into the room. "Well... are you going to tell us?"

"As I said, it is an item they want kept out of the press." He looked at Elsa once more.

"I'm certain that, if the F.B.I. wants it kept quiet, everyone here would agree to do that."

When he looked at Elsa again, she couldn't take it anymore.

"Yes," she told him. "I am Anne Danforth's daughter. Just tell them what you want them to know."

Paul wasn't sure if there was something important here or not, but his training made him ask. "Is there some connection between the two cases we don't know about?"

"Not at all," said Mr. Hoffman, "Alicia and Elsa are both runners. They met at a cross country meet a short time ago. When Elsa heard about what happened, she wanted to help."

"That... that's admirable," Paul said.

"Please Mr. Demerov," Mrs. Hoffman said, "tell us what it is."

"I just wanted you to know that I, we... that is most of the agents on the task force, believe that Andrea hurt the Harvester in some way. Physically or emotionally or both, we don't know. I can't give you details, but I believe the damage was substantial. I'm very sorry for your loss. I think we will catch the Harvester someday, and that Andrea will be one of the reasons. If it was my wife or daughter, I think it would help to know that she hurt the bastard." His anger had shown and Paul blushed. "Sorry."

Paul took a last look at Elsa as Mr. Hoffman thanked him for the visit and walked him out.

Although his words were prophetic, if any of them had known the count of years and the number of victims before its fulfillment, they would not have thanked him. Nor could he have ever imagined the manner in which that prophecy would be fulfilled.

CHAPTER 10

Saturday, November 16, 1996

T ears mixed with the sweat pouring down Elsa's face.

She was considered the best female high school runner in the country, and had been number one ever since she won the Footlocker National Championship as a sophomore. Now a senior, The *Washington Post* had ranked her the number one female runner in the Washington area all season.

On this warm and cloudy Saturday afternoon in November, her ranking meant nothing; she was trailing twenty runners in the Maryland High School Cross Country Championships, on a Hereford course where she had been victorious every time she had set foot on it.

This would be the last race of her high school career and she wasn't sure how far into the race she was, or who she was trailing, because she was running on auto-pilot. That she was running at all was a testament to her incredible physical gifts.

Her mind was still keeping vigil at her father's grave. Eleven days earlier, on a Tuesday evening that would haunt the rest of her life, she was in the back seat of her father's little green Geo Metro. He had gotten off work early and was taking her out for a pre-race meal. The next day was the Class 4A South Region Cross Country meet.

At 5:15 in the afternoon, rush-hour was in full swing. An aggressive driver, frustrated by construction that was widening the Beltway, cut her dad off; he'd tried to avoid a collision by swerving into the next lane. Their small car had been crushed between a tractor-trailer and a minivan. For ten hours, surgeons had worked valiantly to save her dad.

By dawn the next morning, Elsa was alone.

She spent three days in the hospital, but a broken radius in her right forearm, deep bruises, minor cuts, and a serious concussion were the extent of her injuries.

A few rusty leaves still clung to the skeletal red maple trees beyond the hospital window. The grounds were carpeted with fading colors. Elsa sat on the edge of the bed and waited for a wheelchair. Walking wouldn't have been a problem; her legs had survived the accident in better shape than the rest of her, but she wasn't given the choice.

As the orderly wheeled her into the waiting room, they passed a newspaper rack; the headlines screamed – "Harvester Claims No.12". "Full Dozen for Grim Reaper" was a more macabre offering.

Bill Pendry couldn't know that the tears she shed on the ride home were for far more than her dead father. Each time the Harvester struck, it was like losing her mother all over again. Elsa's own heart was ripped from her chest every year.

Elsa was released under leaden, gray skies on Friday afternoon. On a cool, rainy Saturday, she stood at graveside while the person she had loved most in the world was lowered into the ground next to the mother that was taken from her so long ago. Few high school students looked upon any parent as a friend, but Elsa had. Her dad had always encouraged, not pushed; advised, not ordered; listened, not ignored; cautioned, not condemned. As the rain poured down, she felt as though her life were washing away.

She needed Bran, but there had been no one in the aftermath of the accident who had known to notify him. His lonely ranch house on the prairie didn't have a phone. She'd only thought to have Bill Pendry send a telegram after she'd left the hospital. Bran still might not know.

The night before the funeral, her body had spent a sleepless night in Bill's guest bedroom while her heart roamed the empty house next door, crying for her father.

As her father was lowered into the ground, Alicia put an arm around her best friend's waist. Elsa, more than anyone, had helped her through the period after her sister's murder with the fewest possible scars. Now she would provide the shoulder on which Elsa could cry.

Her intense sorrow was too close; the pain too deep, for Elsa to acknowledge Alicia's support, but that buttress against the storm of despair made all the difference. When the arm around her waist was joined by Bill Pendry's around her shoulder, she realized that she wasn't really alone.

———◦◦◦———

With circumstances being what they were, and as a result of lobbying by coaches from around the state, the ruling body for athletics granted her a waiver. She would be permitted to run in the State meet even though she had missed the Regional qualifier while in the hospital... provided she had a medical clearance. Although her heart was broken, Elsa knew her father would have wanted her to run. If the doctors cleared her, she would be allowed to compete.

She spent the week after the funeral with Bill Pendry, who did what he could to allow her room to grieve while still being available as a surrogate father when she needed one. As she lay abed in the guest room, she considered the future.

It was hard, but she was taking the first steps out of the crater that her father's death had blasted into her life. She had no idea what lay beyond the horizon. There were too many questions to be answered and decisions to be made. Where would she live? Did she want to... was it even possible, to stay in the house where she had been raised? Insurance would pay off the mortgage, but she wasn't yet of legal age. The disposition of the house and years of accumulated belongings would be a major task. A decision about college was fast approaching. These critical decisions made each step burdensome. Oh, how she wished Bran was here!

Bill's familiar long, plodding stride echoed from the first floor as he crossed the hardwood to answer the door. In a tone she had begun to think of as 'Cautiously Cheery', he called up the stairs.

"Elsa, you have a visitor."

She swung out of bed and walked to the top of the stairs. Her mood lifted as she saw Alicia at the bottom. This was the second time since the funeral that her best friend had made the two and a half-hour drive from Philadelphia to be the rope that helped her out of the crater. She'd gotten a full scholarship to one of the most storied running schools in the country. Someday, Elsa expected Alicia to write her name along famous 'Nova track alumni such as Eamonn Coghlan, Marty Liquori, Sydney Maree, and Marcus O'Sullivan.

The memory of the race that clinched Alicia's scholarship flashed through Elsa's mind as she descended.

Her friendship with Alicia had blossomed as the sorrow of her sister's death had faded. Although it was a friendship built mostly on phone calls and occasional weekend visits, it had grown strong nonetheless. In the summer before Elsa's junior year, they began to meet every weekend. Often it would be at a rail trail or one of the many large parks or national forests.

When they first arrived, they would catch up on the week's happenings as they loosened up; Elsa's incredible SAT scores; the pleading college coaches that had called Alicia; the awful date with the quarterback of the football team; and the surprisingly less-than-awful date with the nerdy captain of the math team. Sometimes they didn't need to talk... and enjoyed that, too.

Then they would start to run. Evenly matched, they rejoiced in an unparalleled feeling that is as close to flying as a human can achieve without mechanical help. They pushed each other over mountain trails and through forested valleys. Grinning fiercely, they delightfully chicked every guy that had the temerity to run with them.

When the summer was over, the result was record-breaking. They breezed through their respective cross country seasons piling up victories that were almost effortless. In a replay of the first race against each other, Elsa won again, this time by a lean at the tape. The course record, which Elsa had broken again the previous year, was destroyed by an unfathomable seventy-three seconds. College coaches around the country saw the times and assumed a typo was responsible.

Until San Diego.

Traveling coast-to-coast with Elsa's father as an escort, the two co-favorites arrived at the Footlocker National Cross Country Championships in December. Alicia and Elsa ran away from the field, battling shoulder-to-shoulder through-out. Elsa knew that Alicia would be hurt if Elsa gave anything less than her best. So she did. Elsa was bursting with pride and joy when she looked up at her friend on top of the podium. This time Alicia won the lean at the tape. Second felt wonderful!

Since they had witnessed the record-breaking performance in person, coaches from around the country fell all over themselves to talk to Alicia after the awards ceremony.

Footlocker was at the start of Christmas break so, on the return trip, Martin took the girls on a vacation to Wyoming. Christmas at Bran's was magical. Bran charmed Alicia from the start and Elsa... well, her relationship with Bran was like a favorite cashmere cardigan sweater that she could only wear on special occasions. It was warm... soft... rich... and she slipped into it with ease.

Elsa reached the bottom of the stairs and was surprised that the memory of the last Christmas she'd spent with her Dad was more warm than sorrowful.

Alicia smiled in admiration as Elsa stepped into her arms. She looked much better than she had on Monday; more alert and more determined. Then, she had been broken and listless. Elsa had barely been aware of her presence. Now Alicia could see the spark of recovery in Elsa's eyes. She hugged her tightly; time to pull on the rope some more.

⚬

A week after her release from the hospital, on the day before the State meet, she had another exam. A severely concussed head is no trivial matter and the exam was thorough. The doctors checked her EKG and gave her a cat scan; they gave her numerous visual and physical tests to check for possible neurological damage. She brought her finger to her nose from a dozen different angles. So many doctors flashed their lights in her eyes that she developed a headache, and the doctors worried about that.

When all was said and done, they decided her head was O.K. But they wouldn't sign her medical clearance. The doctors felt that her deep muscle bruises had not healed enough for her to run; there was still a risk of blood clots. While lying in bed that night, she had told herself that she was going to run anyway, for her parents.

The race officials were watching her as the teams had gathered at the starting line, each in their own little groups. While her teammates stripped away their sweats and got ready, she pretended that she was just there to cheer on the team. The uniform manager and Elsa took the sweats and stood back as the athletes approached the four-inch stripe of lime. Each team was allowed eight feet of line where their four fastest runners prepared to start. The remaining runners on the team lined up behind them. Once the race was under way, over one hundred runners had the length of the field to fight for position as the grassy course narrowed down to about ten feet wide.

When the starting gun went off, Elsa dropped the clothes in her arms, ripped off her pull-away sweats, and started after the pack. Officials on both sides of the course began to converge on her, but she quickly caught up with the main body of runners. After a huddle, the officials decided they couldn't pull her out without interfering with the rest of the race.

At the first step, pain had washed over her, and it took all her will to maintain a semblance of her normal running stride. Her broken radius, with its lightweight cast, was the only part of her body not complaining. The constant aching helped her focus on the race, keeping all other thoughts out of her mind.

Several minutes into the race, the course passed the main section of spectators along a sweeping curve; this gradual turn led to a ridiculously steep drop into a feature of the race with a deceptively mild title, "The Dip". The cheering was enthusiastic as the mass of athletes moved past the red, white, and blue streamers holding back the crowd. But the cheers became a roar that rolled through the crowd as they noticed Elsa in the pack, moving steadily towards the front.

Elsa moved by runner after runner, grimly fighting the bone deep ache that throbbed with every footfall. The roar shook her concentration, overwhelmed her, and the scene before her blurred; pain became unimportant.

She knew that, for the first time, her father was not there leading the roar. This time, he would not be waiting for her to emerge from the finish chute. Tears fell from her eyes. In her mind, she found herself at her parent's graveside. There she remained while her body blindly followed runners into the crevasse and onto the backside of the course.

Elsa's coach stood atop a short steep hill, glancing at his watch as the approaching leaders came out of the heavily wooded loop on the back of the course. Back and forth his eyes went, from his watch to the runners as they fought up the challenging incline and headed out into "The Maze". Here, the course snaked back and forth across a hillside that was dotted with small fruit trees. In this part of the race, you could clearly see what your position was in relation to the other runners. More importantly, it was here the eventual winner often made the decisive move.

When she emerged from the trees, the coach checked his watch again and moaned. Elsa was more than a minute behind with just over a mile to go! This was an impossible gap to overcome. Besides, bruised and dazed, Elsa looked terrible as she hit the bottom of the slope and began stumbling up.

"Elsa," he called. Even louder, he yelled over and over..."ELSA! LISTEN TO ME!"

A third of the way up, she looked numbly at him.

"You don't need to do this! You don't have anything to prove."

Elsa shook her head and cleared some of the mournful mental haze in which she had been running. No! Her father hadn't raised a quitter! She had never dropped from a race, ever. Blinking back tears, she tried to rally. She embraced the increasing pain; it was a sign that her pace was improving as she weaved through the apple, pear and cherry trees.

Rotten, un-harvested fruit cluttered the ground around the base of the trees and, in some places, had fallen into the runner's path. Her muscles felt like the slimy brown goop beneath her feet... mashed by the tough course and the unrelenting pace.

Coming out of the maze, she got a glimpse of the leader far ahead and already well into the dip. It was then she realized her effort was futile. She knew the course better than anyone; given the leader's pace and distance to the finish, she didn't have a chance. It was hopeless.

Each step now seemed harder. She continued along a ravine that fell sharply off to her right, choked with trees and undergrowth.

Ahead, a hardy spectator had braved the ravine and was standing alongside the course. Tall and elderly, he looked familiar; then her heart skipped a beat before leaping in her chest; the funny boater hat, the cane. Her legs followed the leap of her heart and she raced into Bran's arms. He'd finally gotten the telegram and didn't hesitate to go wherever his great-granddaughter needed him.

"Lord, girl! Whatever are you doing?" Bran said. The feigned impatience barely covered the powerful emotion hidden behind his words. "I came all this way to watch a race. You can hug me later." Along with an encouraging smile, he gave her a short fierce hug that said all the things that were really important. Then he shoved her back onto the course.

"Now go catch those girls."

When the lives of Anne and Martin joined, they produced a daughter with the heart of a lion. Now, that heart swelled and the lion roared with new life. Elsa soared over the edge and into the dip. She wasn't sure where the pain had gone, all she knew was that there were runners ahead of her, and she was going to catch them.

Thunderous cheers echoed through the ravine as the crowd above caught sight of Elsa ascending from its depths. She pumped her arms strongly, forcing her legs to lift up and over the crest of the hill.

She was seventeen. A long, exciting life awaited her as long as she had the courage to face the hard times and challenges along the way. Rays of sun broke through heavy, turbulent clouds, and illuminated a lion that was running toward an uncertain future.

CHAPTER 11

Wednesday, February 11, 1998

The sound was clear, despite the crackling and popping from the logs in the fireplace.

"Brrrinnng, Brrrinnng,"

Elsa slipped the flap of the dustcover into the book to mark her place. She glanced at her great-grandfather, and then chuckled as she got up from the sofa; he was looking all around with a surprised expression. Bran realized what the ringing was at the same moment he heard Elsa's amusement.

"Don't you laugh at me, young lady!" His tried to project an offended air, but gave up and laughed along with Elsa. The phone had been installed when Elsa moved in almost fourteen months ago. It didn't ring often, but they both thought he should be used to it by now.

"Brrrinnng, Brrrinnng,"

"You better get that," Bran said. "This rocker doesn't want to let me go."

Elsa smiled as she headed for the kitchen. He would be ninety-three in May and still moved around pretty well. The getting up and down had gotten harder, though. Besides, who would want to leave the glow of that blazing fire? It was an unforgiving twenty-five below outside and the wind was howling. The kitchen stayed comfortable enough for working, but felt chilly after the warmth of the sofa.

Leaning around the corner, she snatched the handset from its cradle in time to prevent another intrusive 'brrinng'.

"North Pole" she answered and Bran let out a short bark of laughter from the living room.

"Ha, Ha," said Alicia, "We're in the middle of a spring tease here. I was out in shorts and a t-shirt today. It felt wonderful!" She rubbed in the 'wonderful' as hard as she could over one thousand eight hundred miles of phone line.

"Alicia!" Elsa walked back to the warm living room and sat on the edge of the sofa. "It's so good to hear your voice, even if you are teasing me."

"Well you deserve it for moving to that barbaric wilderness," Her voice was playful.

"I'll have you know we are about to become an official part of civilization."

"How's that going to happen?" asked a skeptical Alicia.

"They're building a Wal-Mart in Laramie, should be done mid-summer."

"From the sound of it, you might not be thawed out by summer!" Alicia laughed and Elsa joined in. Then they spent some time catching up. Elsa glanced at the dark mantle over the fireplace. There sat the second-place Footlocker trophy she'd won in her junior year of high school; the only trophy she'd brought with her from Maryland. It reminded her of the closeness she felt to Alicia.

"I've got a big, huge, monstrous favor to ask," said Alicia. "Please, please say yes!"

"Don't I get to hear what the favor is first?"

"No. I want you to say yes. If I tell you first, you might say no. If you say no, I'll have a lot of people mad at me."

"Uh oh, wouldn't want people mad at you… at least not anymore than usual."

"Good, I'll take that as a yes," said Alicia.

Elsa could hear her friend take a deep breath and worried that the request might be as big a deal as Alicia was making out.

"Two girls have dropped out of the Olympic development 10,000 meters at Penn. They haven't found anyone serious for either spot, and I talked them into giving one of the spots to you."

"Oh, god!" gasped Elsa. *She's gone off the deep end. The Penn Relays is the most prestigious track event in the country. They've been running it for over one hundred years! The top distance runners in the country will be there.*

"Are you crazy!?" said Elsa, "I haven't run a track race in over two years! Why do you want to let 115,000 people watch me embarrass myself?"

"Please, Elsa. I want to see you so bad."

"Then buy me a ticket, and I'll come watch! You can't think I belong in that race."

"I know you've been running, even in that god-awful cold out there on the plains. You know you can do it."

"It's not the same," argued Elsa, "besides; I'd rather watch you run."

"Can't... I'm one of the drops." Alicia sounded glum.

"Oh Alicia! What happened?"

"Stress fracture. The team doc says I have to take six weeks off."

"That's awful! I'm so sorry."

"So... you see you have to come run. Otherwise I'll be here all depressed and moping and feeling like I want to jump off a bridge or something."

Alicia could manipulate with the best of them.... and she was only getting started.

"Ok, Ok," Elsa said. A quick surrender would save Alicia an expensive phone bill.

"All right!" Alicia squealed. "This is so awesome! I get to see you in April!"

"But you know you'll have mud all over your face when I get lapped out."

"Like that's going to happen. But hey, if it does...I could use a facial."

Bran was enjoying the friendly banter, even if he was only hearing one side of the conversation. When she was on the phone with Alicia, Elsa was more animated and sounded the way an eighteen-year-old young woman should sound. As much as he loved having her around, life in a lonely cabin out on the prairie with a ninety-three-year-old wasn't what she needed now.

After her father's death, Bran had stayed in Maryland long enough to help with the disposition of her father's estate, such as it was. Then he had brought her to Wyoming. The beauty of the mountains, the peace and the solitude of the prairie were things that helped her cope with being on her own. There were still people in the world that loved her, but now there was no one responsible for her.

What happened in her life from here on out was completely up to her.

The receiver clicked onto the hook. Elsa returned to the sofa, pulled the scrunchy out of her hair and tried to shake out all the twists and tangles she'd created by playing with it while she chatted on the phone. As she ran her fingers through her hair, she filled him in on Alicia's side of the conversation.

"That sounds exciting," Bran said, when she described the race she'd been beguiled into running.

"Bran! I'm going to get slaughtered!"

"Well sure," he paused for effect, "but at least you'll have a nice audience for the execution."

"Why, thanks! I appreciate the vote of confidence." Elsa beaned him with the scrunchy.

———

Thursday, April 23, 1998

"Aarrrgh!" Alicia slapped the ancient brick in frustration. "You can be so stubborn!"

She crossed her arms over her chest and leaned against the wall of the narrow brick alcove she'd just assaulted. Only a step away, female athletes of assorted sizes, shapes and colors surged and swirled through a dim, narrow passageway. They were generally in groups of four that snaked through the crowds in a line. Each quartet could be identified by distinct matching uniforms and coordinated hair styles. Seen from above, the long curving concourse looked more like a psychedelic, subterranean tunnel filled with sleek, undulating caterpillars.

It was Thursday at the Penn Relay Carnival. Girls Day: when high school, college and professional athletes from around the country competed in the most thrilling event most would ever run. Although the meet is primarily comprised of relay races, there are individual events of such high quality that American and, occasionally, World records are broken.

Elsa kneaded her midsection, trying to untie the knot in her stomach. Soon she would report to the Clerk of Course and enter the bullpen; from there it would only be a matter of time before she would be called to the track for the start of her race.

She leaned over and glanced through a passageway at the track. Bill Cosby was near the finish line, shaking hands with the anchor legs after they crossed the finish. It was one of the quirky features of Penn. Cosby was the number one fan of the meet; he spent a large portion of the three days encouraging, greeting and interacting with the athletes.

Alicia was acting as surrogate coach for Elsa. She and her only athlete had been arguing race strategy. Elsa wanted to use one that would keep her from getting embarrassed; in other words, not to finish last.

"Come on, Elsa," Alicia insisted, "You know if you wear your 'lion's mask' you can keep up with anyone."

"But if I go too hard, I'll die" said Elsa. "Then I won't get to shake hands with Bill Cosby; he'll be long gone by the time I get to the finish."

⸺⸻⸺

Standing one step back from the starting stripe on the far end of a long line of competitors, Elsa considered the mind-numbing twenty-five laps of the track ahead of her. The announcer was introducing the field; eighteen of the top women distance runners in the country split between two alleys. After one and a half laps, the two alleys merged and the runners would continue the race together. When the announcer got to number nineteen, and announced her name, Elsa was certain she could hear thousands of voices whispering 'Who?'

She'd never in her life felt like such an underdog. Just as the starter called them to the line, Elsa thought about her conversation with Alicia and decided... 'What the hell, let's go for it.'

Craaack! The starter's pistol released them. Elsa shot away as if the sound had been the retort of a cannon blasting her down the track. Races of this level normally have a 'rabbit' whose assignment is to set a quick pace for top runners. The rabbit will usually drop out after pushing hard for a mile or so. Knowledgeable spectators shook their heads disparagingly as they assumed Elsa was the rabbit and going out much too fast. As the two alleys merged, the unknown girl with her blonde hair billowing behind was already ten meters ahead. In the main pack were experienced runners, some had world championship and Olympic races under their belts. They all smiled inwardly, confident that this unknown prima donna would soon be regretting the suicidal pace.

Elsa moved toward the rail with the knowledge that she had reached, and went slightly beyond, the anaerobic threshold, the point at which her body's processing of energy began to produce lactic acid. Elevated lactate was the major contributor to fatigue. The world's best milers, through years of intense training, could force themselves to last for approximately that distance... one mile, while running just above the anaerobic threshold.

She eased into a more comfortable pace that would allow her to last longer than a mile. The pace was still too fast and would eventually cause her muscles to fatigue to the point where they would begin cramping and soon thereafter, quit completely.

All this Elsa considered as she cruised around the huge red oval, time after time. She blocked out everything and ran within herself, monitoring her body...

...carefully dipping into that dark source of power.

Her heart rate and respiration soared; dehydration and fatigue took their toll. She was barely aware of the cheering crowd, the magnificent old stadium, or her competition. Even the overly-excited public address announcer had little impact on her concentration. After fifteen laps, a remote part of her awareness began counting runners as she passed them.

Roaring waves crashed around the stadium. The air itself vibrated as thousands of rabid fans used their stomping feet to telegraph approval through the concrete stands. Alicia's skin tingled with anticipation as she watched the exciting drama on the track. She glanced briefly at the jubilant host of people, all on their feet cheering. Her eyes were drawn to the brilliant pennants that crowned the top of the horseshoe-shaped stadium. They whipped briskly against the back drop of a shimmering blue sky.

The soft 'pffft, pffft, pffft' of her feather-weight shoes sweeping across the track somehow penetrated Elsa's senses. The stadium thundered. Up ahead, two competitors were disappearing into the next turn. They seemed too far ahead to catch, but along the track and in the stands, the roiling mass of people seemed to be looking at *her*, urging her to try.

Elsa responded, but her muscles were close to failing; teeth clinched against the pain.

I've hurt worse than this and survived.

Sub-consciously, the count of laps had been registering, and she thought she had less than two laps to go. She followed the runners off the next turn and, after the two ahead crossed the line, the lap counter flipped the large placards from 'two' to 'one'. Only four hundred meters left to make up fifty. Light-headed and weakening she gave everything she had to over-taking the leaders.

She was gaining slowly, but her consciousness was also fading. Frantically, Elsa clung to the hazy vision of her feet flying over the track. Her pain had bled into a body-wide numbness that resisted every effort to go faster. Nonetheless, she drew closer with each stride.

They were so close! Coming off the last turn with only one hundred meters to go, the finish was like a wavering mirage. Throwing caution to the wind, she opened the door in her mind wide, only to find that her dark source of power was drained. She grimaced as her muscles began to give way and she tried to fight off a cramping hamstring, then a collapsing calf. Her smooth form deteriorated as she stumbled toward the finish.

When she saw the runners ahead continue into another lap, her last thought was, *I miscounted, I still have one lap to go!*

Her body fell across the finish line as her consciousness drained away.

Elsa stumbled along a faint, winding trail through a dark mist.

Ahead was a fork, with two distinct paths cutting through the fog. Along one path she saw a husband, a family... and vengeance for her mother.

The other held fame and glory and Olympic medals.

Was it a dream... or a clear look at her choices? If she strayed but a step off either path, it vanished, leaving her struggling toward a far different finish line.

A light beckoned. Elsa heard a voice as she fluttered toward it.

"I'm having trouble finding a vein, she's so dehydrated... I'll try one more time."

A sharp poke inside her right elbow made her eyes blink open, and she tried to swat away the stinging. Her left arm was heavy and it tingled, as if she'd fallen asleep on it. Then she noticed that her whole body had that same dull, disconnected feeling.

"Don't do that. I'm having enough trouble as it is. *Hold still!*"

Befuddled and amazed, she stared as Bill Cosby tried to stick an IV needle in her arm.

The EMT noticed her staring and looked annoyed. He gave up on the IV and slapped it on the folding table next to the cot.

The room was swimming as she tried... and failed to push up onto her elbows.

"You're Bi..."

"Don't say it! He'll bite your head off!" Elsa recognized the amused voice as Alicia's. She was somewhere among the dizzy waves that rippled the white tent.

"What is the matter with your eyes?" 'Bill' used a cotton ball to swab an antiseptic solution on the numerous holes on the inside of her arm. "Cosby is at least thirty years older than me and we don't look *that much alike*!" He ripped open a bandage and clapped it on her arm.

"Now that she's awake, she'll just have to drink her fluids like everybody else," he grumbled as he stalked out of the tent.

Alicia couldn't help but giggle. "He sounds and acts more like Cosby when he's upset about being mistaken for Cosby!"

Elsa hoped the swimming room might be finishing a last lap in the pool as her friend leaned down and helped her to a sitting position. Alicia produced a bottle, twisted off the cap and held it to Elsa's lips.

"We need to get a lot of water into you, so start guzzling."

Like a sandy beach soaking up waves, the cool fluid felt as though it absorbed into her body before it reached her stomach. It also washed away some of her numbness.

When she'd seen how well Elsa's stomach handled the water, Alicia opened a bottle of Powerade and placed it in her friend's hand. While Elsa drank it down, Alicia started gushing about the race.

"... I'm still getting goose bumps just thinking about it. You were flying around that track like the roar of the crowd was pushing you on a magic carpet." Alicia took the empty bottle and put some salty pretzels into Elsa's hand. "You need some salt, too."

"Some magic carpet." Elsa said softly as she chewed the pretzels. "I was trying so hard to catch those girls that I couldn't even finish the race!"

Alicia started to laugh, but then stopped and studied her friend's face. "You're not serious!?"

"What?" Elsa wasn't sure what she meant. "I kicked hard because I thought I was on the last lap... almost caught them, and then passed out just when I saw there was still a lap to go."

A happy look of astonishment spread across Alicia's features. She closed her eyes and shivered as she thought of that last lap.

—◁◁◁⫘▷▷▷—

"Phenomenal!" The announcer's voice erupted from the stadium speakers, only to be swallowed by the roar of the crowd. "Ladies and gentleman, you are witnessing an amazing feat. This young unknown from Laramie, Wyoming is pulling away from the defending national champion and the national record holder. With less than one lap to go, the youngest contestant in the race, Elsa Danforth, has lapped all but four runners and is on a pace that could demolish the American record."

The crowd accomplished a seemingly impossible task and got even louder.

—⁓—

"What is the matter with you?" Elsa said. "You look like you've been smoking something naughty."

Alicia took Elsa by the shoulders and gave her a gentle shake.

"I never thought an American record holder could be so dense." Elsa's stunned head rolled lightly on her shoulders as her friend rhythmically shook her in unison with her words:

"You... won! You... silly... amazing... goof. You... won..."

During her return flight to Wyoming, Elsa began to think about moving back to Maryland. It wouldn't be so she could train and run; she'd decided that the gold medal around her neck was enough. Running had never been about the glory... or the medals.

A husband, a family, and vengeance for her mother would be the path she'd follow.

CHAPTER 12

Saturday, September 11, 1999

He loved the summers in the Washington, D.C. area. Certainly the heat and humidity were brutal at times. But it was the uncomfortable temperatures that made even the most modest of women peel down to a wonderfully revealing amount of skin, so much marvelous fruit from which to select. The long, leisurely days and warm, dark evenings gave him all the time he needed to choose a firm, ripe, delicious fruit for harvesting.

When he had first started, so long ago, only the purity of the heart and the love it held had been important to him. Harvesting was all that mattered. It wasn't enough anymore. A perfect heart in an exquisite package was what he sought now. He had noticed that since that dirty bitch had scarred him, his desires had become incrementally darker, more violent.

Pride caused his chest to expand. He was still in complete control. She was no longer a DIRTY BITCH! He had reduced her to small letters. Plastic surgery eliminated the physical scar, and he had come to accept, even embrace, the emotional one.

Every Harvest since Andrea's had led him to seek more than just a pure heart to harvest; more than a delectable body to satisfy his perverse desires. Every woman was now required to surrender, to give him a victory. It was worth waiting for, and he had enjoyed some very long, fulfilling victories.

After wiping the sweat from his brow, he once again grabbed the handle. With a lift and a scoot he moved forward a step. He paused and watched while, three blocks away, Jillian Cassidy locked the front door of her lovely Federal-style brick home. She followed the sculptured concrete walk across her immaculate lawn, and got into her dark blue Crown Victoria.

Lift and scoot.

On every second Saturday, she left home at 8:30 a.m. for a thirty-five minute drive to Baltimore, where she and friends from her college days volunteered at a shelter for homeless families. Although she was well into her thirties, he found her immensely attractive.

Lift and scoot.

The personal trainer, spa treatments, and stylish clothes all combined to create a very alluring package. As she left her driveway and headed in his direction, he decided that she was his first choice. Lifting his hand carefully off the walker, he waved feebly. She showed him her dazzling white teeth and waved merrily back. He returned his hand to the walker and carefully moved forward.

Lift and scoot.

Early in June he'd watched her stop her car, exit in her designer dress, and help an elderly man pick up groceries that had fallen from his torn bag. It was the elegant curve of her neck and her sensual way of bending over, as well as her generous spirit, that initially attracted him.

Jillian smiled as she admired the old man in the rearview. He looked like he was at least a hundred, yet, even in the awful heat, he was still out getting his exercise. And he always waved.

Lift and scoot.

He increased his pace slightly now that she had passed. Eventually he would reach the van and move on to check the other women he was considering for this year's harvest; though he was already envisioning a delightful victory over Jillian.

⎯⎯⎯⎯⎯⎯

Friday, September 17, 1999

Elsa controlled the dark anger that had tried to escape when she'd entered the restaurant and come upon the tense scene. Then the darkness evaporated and she relaxed when she understood what was happening.

Indignant and confused, the hostess flinched as the angry hands weaved a blur in front of her. When she began to turn her head toward Elsa, the right angry hand snapped its fingers in her face, and then rejoined left angry hand to re-weave the blur.

"But I don't understand you," the hostess said in the slow, patient voice reserved for small children and geriatrics with hearing aids. "Why don't you write on this tablet?"

The young man with the blurring, angry hands was obviously adept at reading lips. He stomped his foot and pushed the tablet away. Then he began an elaborately slow and scathing hand-formed imitation of the waitress' condescending voice. An observant person would see that his facial expressions told almost as much as his hands.

Elsa's stifled laugh turned both their heads, so she stepped forward and offered to help. She'd enjoyed an introductory sign language course, so she'd taken two more. Though far from fluent, she enjoyed the intellectual challenge of speaking with her hands.

In her classes, she was taught American Sign Language, or ASL. She struggled with the unusual grammar and syntax, which made the challenge of learning it even more rewarding. But, even now, her mind tended to "translate" ASL into Standard English. Therefore, his "I speak manager" became...

"He's asking to speak to the manager," Elsa said.

"Speak? Christ! If he'd speak we wouldn't have this problem." the hostess said. "Besides, the day manager's gone and the night manager isn't here yet."

Angry hands began to blur his words again and Elsa raised her hands in surrender. Carefully signing back, she told him;

("Sorry, I'm new at this. Please sign slowly.") Elsa watched attentively as Angry Hands, deliberately but without noticeable disrespect, signed back.

("Please tell this insulting woman that I want to know why this establishment doesn't have an employee who is able to communicate with the hearing impaired.")

While he was signing, Elsa couldn't help but sense that Angry Hands wasn't really mad; he seemed to be putting on a show. When he had finished, she looked in his eyes and confirmed it; there was lively amusement dancing in them.

She relayed the message to the waitress, who was less than polite with her response.

Forestalling another blurring of hands, Elsa asked him if he would like to patronize a different restaurant.

("Both of us?") he signed. She nodded. ("Yes, absolutely.") he replied.

Elsa turned to the waitress as Angry Hands walked toward the door.

"Now you've lost *two* patrons because you couldn't be polite to the hearing impaired."

※

While they waited for their food, Elsa delighted in an entertaining display by her dinner partner, Benjamin Kendrick. He was signing out an elaborate, hilarious, and self-deprecating story of his experience trying to get service for his car. His strong, subtle hands painted an artful picture. Occasionally, she would make a small questioning gesture with her hand, and he would re-phrase or spell out the signing that she hadn't understood.

She couldn't help but notice that they had become a focus of attention in the restaurant and was surprised that she didn't mind. His face was expressive and open, and she was bursting to ask why he was pretending to be deaf.

They had only been in the booth for a few minutes when she realized that Ben was playing out some elaborate ruse. There was a slight narrowing of his eyes at the clatter of broken dishes from the kitchen or laughter from a nearby table. His eyes rarely left her face. Her teachers had been hearing-impaired and their eyes were always moving; gathering visual information to offset what they couldn't hear.

The food arrived and they continued to find out as much as they could about one another without being too obvious. Her acute perceptions were of enormous help.

She asked him how long he had been deaf, and smiled politely when his hands gave her the misleading answer that he had been signing since he was two years old.

He watched patiently as she worked through signing that she was an 'old' freshman at the University of Maryland. If she was stuck on a word for which she didn't know the sign, he had her spell it and then suggested appropriate signs. She told him she was majoring in physics with a minor in astronomy, and that she hoped to work in cosmology. That word stumped him; they playfully took turns suggesting silly, elaborate gestures to represent a discipline that blended theoretical physics and astronomy with hefty doses of mathematics and philosophy in an effort to discover the scientific underpinnings for the creation and structure of the universe.

Then his hands weaved a statement that made her blush.

("So... not only are you prettier than Natalie Portman... you are smarter, too!")

Elsa had long ago come to terms with her appearance. Her face was too long and thin, her body... the same. Wiry was sometimes a complimentary term for a man, never for a woman. But she was comfortable in her body, since this was the price she paid for being a long-distance runner. Her embarrassment came from the fact that he seemed sincere in his compliment.

She quickly responded and hoped he was looking at her hands, and not her red face.

("She can't be that smart. Queen Amidala isn't exactly a thinking woman's role.")

His dark, full eyebrows arched in grudging respect. ("You keep surprising me. I didn't think you would be a 'Phantom Menace' type of girl.")

("Let's just say that I'm very interested in exploring the universe.")

("Is that what you do in your spare time?")

(With what little I have... Yes!")

The mysterious smile that accompanied her playful answer intrigued Ben, but Elsa didn't give him time to follow-up.

("And how do you spend your spare time?")

While her dinner companion related his love of off-road cycling, Elsa listened politely with half of her attention. The other half thought of a risqué method to prove he could hear. It also should give her the chance to see *him* blush.

("I'm going for a ride tomorrow. Maybe you'd like to come?") Ben asked.

Silently, she looked deep in his eyes; they were like burnished copper, and gave her a quivery feeling she'd never experienced. She cast a brief glance around the room, hoping that no one was paying too much attention. When she looked back at Ben, he smiled and signed at her.

("What are you thinking?")

She took a drink of water and held the glass in front of her mouth with both hands so that he couldn't read her lips. Trying to keep her voice low while still speaking clearly, she said...

"I've been wondering how those sexy hands would feel on my body."

That he had clearly heard every word was evident. Ben's jaw dropped while his eyes did an excellent imitation of milk saucers, and a deep red spread from his neck to the top of his forehead.

Elsa reddened a little herself; surprised that she made such a provocative statement to a man she'd just met.

Regaining his composure, his hands asked,

("How long have you known?")

Playing along with the charade, she signed instead of speaking her answer.

("Almost from the start. My teachers were hearing-impaired. There are subtle differences. Why are you doing this?")

Benjamin Kendrick thought for a moment and then his hands spoke.

His older brother had been born deaf. Ben had started learning sign language as soon as he could talk, maybe even before. Carl was the best big brother anyone could have. As Ben got older, he realized how hard it was for the adult Carl to deal with insensitive people.

("There are six *million* hearing-impaired people in the U.S.") Ben told her. ("This area has one of the highest concentrations because of Gallaudet University. Businesses should make more of an effort to accommodate them. I do this to make people think. Are you angry?")

("Not at all. I like signing; this has been fun. I wish my signing was better. We can say whatever we want and no one else can understand a thing.")

("I wish you had signed that 'sexy' remark. You shocked that old couple behind you.")

With a mischievous glint in her eyes, Elsa signed her response.

("I've been wondering how....") She paused and then grinned as his eyes began to get that saucer look again, (... you sign when you're biking.")

CHAPTER 13

Saturday morning, September 18, 1999

After studying the long turn in the road for months, he chose the perfect spot. This area of deep, wooded lots was upscale long before the term was used to describe communities of bare, postage stamp lots with big, gaudy homes that would someday bankrupt their owners. The residents here never worried about money. Even the small retirement development nearby housed the wealthy. People who lived in these homes jealously guarded their huge, old-growth trees, their manicured lawns and hedges, elaborate topiary... and their privacy.

He glanced ahead at the small chalk mark. From that exact location beside the road, there wasn't a single home offering more than a glimpse of its majesty through the trees. With a lift and scoot a little further around the turn, he would see Jillian backing her car out of the drive.

A morning shower was predicted, but that didn't disturb Jillian's warm, contented mood. The shelter was drab and depressing, but at least they kept it clean. Besides, volunteering with Jenny and Corrine was a blast, and she loved shopping at the Inner Harbor and lunching at the Power Plant afterward.

Her smile came automatically when she saw the old man shuffling along the road. She wondered if he would finish before it rained. All at once he was down, tangled awkwardly in his aluminum walker. She pulled alongside, put the car in park, and rushed around to help.

The old man was tsking and muttering as he struggled to get untangled.

"That was quite a fall! Are you hurt?"

"Just my pride. Damn fool thing to do... stubbed my toe and went down like a two-year-old." Although deep and gravely, Jillian thought his voice was clear and strong for someone of his apparent age.

"Let me help you." She took his arm. As he rose to his feet, he winced.

"Blast it!" he said, "think I twisted my knee."

Jillian loved being a good Samaritan, and immediately offered to drive him back to the seniors village where she assumed he was from.

"That is very sweet of you, dear. I accept your gracious offer."

She opened the front and began to help him in, but he grasped the top of the door while pushing the walker toward her. "Could you put this in the back seat for me?"

Jillian smiled and did what the old man asked. When she turned back to help him in, the elderly, arthritic stance was gone.

A strong hand gripped her elbow and a wet mist hit her face.

Jillian was the one who was helped into the front seat as drops of rain began to fall.

⟞⟝⟞⟝

"Ouch!" Elsa grimaced as she swung off the seat of the bike. "My butt is killing me."

Ben made an exaggerated leer. "That's strange; your butt's making me feel pretty good."

Her squawk was most un-ladylike, and the punch she delivered to his shoulder was going to leave a bruise.

He moaned and rubbed. "I guess that'll teach me to be more sympathetic, huh?"

"You took the words right out of my mouth." She grinned and leaned against his Honda hatchback to stretch. An early morning shower had freshened the air and left the towpath free of dust for their first date... a bike ride along the Potomac.

As she massaged her hamstrings, Elsa admired the view of Ben lifting the bikes to the rack on top of the car. Mud was splattered on the back of his tight riding shorts and colorful form-fitting bike jersey. Sweat was dripping from his chin and his hair was a mess of dark brown waves and spikes as a result of the bike helmet.

He looks really good, she thought.

Life had conspired against her when it came to guys her own age. Her first crush hadn't been able to handle getting beat, especially by a freshman girl. A budding love had been quickly forgotten when her father died and she moved to Wyoming. There had even been someone in Wyoming that she dated a few times during the summer; she'd liked him well enough, but it didn't feel like anything special. Her only real male friends were Bran and Bill Pendry—ninety-three and eighty-nine. She knew some girls who liked older men, but this was ridiculous.

Why can't I find someone who makes me feel comfortable like they do?

Then she realized that she already had.

I feel as comfortable with Ben as I do with Bran; and it happened just as quickly.

"Ben, I'm going to be sore tomorrow if I don't run some of this tightness out. Do you think we have time for me to go for a short run?"

"Sure," he replied, "Turnabout is fair play, right? I'll change and go with you." Ben knew Elsa liked to run and figured that he should be a good sport and give it a try. He could run in his padded bike shorts, but went to the back of the car and changed out of his clip-in bike shoes. He had chuckled a little when Elsa had shown up for their ride in running shoes, shorts and a t-shirt. The fact that her butt was sore was no surprise to him.

When he walked back around the car, Elsa spun away from him, bent over at the waist and began to cough dramatically. He walked up beside her and patted her on the back.

"You ok?" he asked. "Did you swallow a bug?"

Vigorously shaking her head no, Elsa pointed down at his canvas deck shoes, no socks. In a moment she was on the ground, convulsed in laughter.

Ben felt his face starting to burn; then realized the turnabout had already started.

"Right, I get it." He thought she even looked good rolling in the dirt and smiled tolerantly. "Enough already, you've made your point."

Elsa stood up and kissed him on the cheek. "You look so cute."

With hands on hips, Ben extended his foot, heel on the ground, toe pointed in the air; modeling his footwear. "I take it you don't think these are appropriate."

"If you were planning on boating up the river beside me... they're perfect. Not so much if you want to keep up with me on a run."

"Oh, ho! That sounds like a challenge!"

She quickly turned serious. "No, really it wasn't. Please don't be the kind of macho guy that can't stand a girl beating him at anything."

Ben even liked her serious look. He put his hand over his heart. "I'm not, truly I'm not!"

"That's great." Elsa beamed and nodded at the roof of the car. "I'll get started; get your bike back down and try to catch up."

After the unfamiliar motion of peddling a bike, her muscles were saying 'this is more like it' as she gradually worked into a faster stride. It was a good sign he brought her to the C&O Canal. So many precious memories of her father were made along the beautiful Potomac.

For 185 miles, the magnificent river drifts, meanders, rushes, and occasionally crashes down from the mountains of western Maryland on the way to the Chesapeake Bay. The towpath of the C&O Canal National Historic Park twists and turns as it follows the river. In the first half of the nineteenth century, using the primitive, labor-intensive technology available to them, workers endeavored to make it as straight as possible. Obsolete before it was finished, it has been a treasured recreational resource for generations.

As the canal makes its way south, tributary streams, encroaching cliffs, and wide turns in the river create pleasant curves in the towpath. With its stone aqueducts, a border of tall trees and wild flowers, the shady dirt path allows walkers, cyclists, and runners to imagine that D.C., and its crowded suburbs, are light-years away.

Elsa's father began running soon after his wife's murder. Anne had loved to run and Martin told Elsa that he felt closer to her mother when he was out running. As a child, Sunday mornings were spent on the canal while Elsa peddled merrily along beside her father.

Striding along, she revisited those memories. Then Elsa remembered what day this was. September eighteenth. Her birthday was usually a mournful affair because of the horrible day with which it shared an anniversary. 'Yeah, baby... hit it,' was the response from her muscles when she increased the pace another notch, trying to derail any negative thinking. The knowledge that Ben would eventually be catching up helped accomplish that task.

I think I really like this guy... hope he asks me to dinner.

Ben rode hard as the first falling leaves of autumn swirled red and yellow in his wake. He had been pedaling furiously for much longer than expected. His odometer clicked three miles as a freight train was pulling slowly past him on the other side of the canal. Then he saw her.

"God... bless America!" he said. It looked to Ben like she was trying to beat the train. The elegant, dynamic ease with which her body covered the ground made his pulse quicken.

When, up ahead, Elsa slowed and made a wide loop on the towpath, Ben did the same with his bike and peddled slowly as he waited for her.

"Where have you been?" Elsa pulled alongside. "I thought you were going to catch up."

"Hah! Right... and I thought you were going for a short run." He glanced at his speedometer. "Three miles, with three still to go; that isn't short in my book."

"Sorry, I get a little carried away sometimes."

"Yeah, well you made me late for lunch. I'm starving. You can treat me to a deli sandwich to make up for it."

"Hold on there, sport." Elsa grinned, her day was developing nicely. "You stuck me on a bike for two hours and gave me a big pain in the butt. I returned the favor by saving you from running your feet into a bloody pulp. And for that *I* have to buy *you* lunch?"

"Since you put it that way, I suppose I could make up for it by taking you to dinner tonight."

They were both having the same thought.

Yes, the day is shaping up very nicely indeed.

PART III

Tumbling Down

He recognized her smooth, effortless stride easily. The same was true for the confident tilt of her head when she sparred. A stirring image of her firm breasts as they brushed the grass during her morning pushups came to mind and caused a predictable result. Watching her for so many months had triggered a need from which he couldn't turn away.

Even at this distance, a glimpse was all that was necessary to identify his prey, to make his desire for her grow. Although she was still far away, the anticipation of her arrival was sweet.

Enough miles had flown beneath her feet to activate the pituitary gland and send endorphins streaming through her blood stream. This produced a near-euphoric state that made her feel faster and almost invincible.

When a cyclist trying to pass her rang a warning bell, it produced a strong reaction.

She surged forward and left the ringing behind.

The bells also prompted an even stronger memory.

CHAPTER 14

Saturday afternoon, September 18, 1999

Elsa had imagined Ben thinking 'What a dump!' as she'd led him across the wooden bridge, passed the battered antique gas pumps toward the ugly building with the chipped green paint that revealed gray concrete block beneath.

She thought of the place as a well-kept secret and hoped to surprise Ben. The last time she had been there was with her father, a long time ago. Inside was the friendliest service and most generous deli sandwiches anywhere along the one hundred eighty-five mile towpath.

Familiar bells jingled as she led Ben through the door of Kerrigan's. The greeting she received was exuberant.

"Elsa!" Two stocky men rushed from behind the counter and surrounded her with hugs.

"Hi, Gerry," She kissed the grizzled chin of the balding black man on her left.

The man on her right could have been Gerry's twin, except for the white skin and extra hair on top. "We've missed you around here," John said.

Elsa pecked his cheek. "I've missed you guys, too."

Before she could introduce her companion, Gerry and John both said, "Hi Ben," and headed back behind the counter.

Hiding her disappointment that her surprise was spoiled, Elsa turned to Ben with her hands on her hips and huffed, "So you were just playing along, huh?"

"Of course!" He turned to Gerry and John. "Hey! Don't I get a hug? I thought this was my special place."

"Sorry, Ben," said Gerry. "Elsa was coming here with her dad ten years before you showed up."

Elsa stuck her tongue out at Ben before she noticed that a somber mood had overtaken both of the older men.

"We were real sorry to hear about your father," they said in tandem.

"Thanks guys," Elsa said. "He loved coming here because we could always find a smile and a delicious turkey and provolone with those sweet, home-grown garden tomatoes... on whole wheat, of course." She tried to jumpstart the good feeling that had driven the day thus far.

"So how about some of both!"

Minutes later they were handed a brown-paper bag filled with the Dag-wood-sized sandwiches. As they were leaving Gerry reminded Elsa about the old-fashioned playground around the corner where her father had brought her as a child.

"No one uses it much anymore," he said, with a glint in his eye. "Very secluded. Great place for a private lunch for two."

The playground lawn was lush and green. Many years had passed since children dragged their shoes to create ruts under the swings. Long, heavy chains supported the thick, oak seats on which Elsa and Ben swayed gently while they worked on their sandwiches. Later, Elsa relished each touch of Ben's strong hands on her shoulders as he pushed her high on the swing.

Warm sunshine chased shadows across the playground as Elsa and Ben talked through afternoon. They each let their inner child enjoy the day while the attraction between two adults grew stronger.

The sun glinted off the burnished handles of the metal merry-go-round as they pushed it faster and faster. Side-by-side they straddled the outside bars and locked their legs around the posts. They released their hand hold; letting the spin lean them backward. Wispy clouds, blue sky, sunshine, and tower-ing red oak trees spun over their heads. Hands touched, then fingers laced, and their heads pulled together; their lips touched in a whirling, giddy first kiss.

SsshhhhhhhhhhhwishCLUNK! .... (tap... tap...tap)
SsshhhhhhhhhhhwishCLUNK! .... (tap... tap...tap)

Jillian is standing naked in the midst of an enormous space. The air is still and threatening. A cool, antiseptic scent compounds her fear and she starts shivering. A dense, oppressive shadow surrounds and mimics her every effort in slow motion; she feels as though she is trapped inside of a huge, black, quivering Michelin Man.

In the distance she hears a faint tapping. A hidden door opens quietly to reveal brilliant sunshine, and a tenuous path of light reaches across the vast floor. A soft whooshing sound echoes through the stillness as the door closes with a loud clunk, leaving her in utter darkness. The tapping repeats and the distant door opens again. Groaning under the effort of moving her cumbersome legs, Jillian lumbers toward the light.

SsshhhhhhhhhhhwishCLUNK! Pitch black returns, but she continues on a few steps before becoming disoriented. The tapping is renewed and seems to come from behind. Her bloated, Michelin Man body executes an ungainly pivot on a single black pillow foot. From a crack of light, the metal door opens to reveal a path to glorious freedom that is as far away as ever.

Her slow, bouncing effort begins once more; again the darkness; again the tapping from an unexpected direction; again the taunting door opens to offer life-saving brilliance. Over and over she shambles back and forth across the nebulous concrete plain.

Finally the door stays open! As she draws closer, a cold steady rain begins falling out of the darkness. The dazzling light from the door remains, and as she shuffles toward it, droplets glitter through the air, splashing little particles of light as they strike the hard floor.

The black, billowing mass surrounding her begins to dissolve. It liquefies and flows into small channels in the floor, which has become shiny and metallic. She's excited and can move faster now; running through the chilling rain, and she's getting so close. Her hand reaches toward the bright rectangle of light when her feet fly out from under her and she floats down to land gently on a chilly, damp, metal surface. She tries to get up, but her body won't move... she can only gaze longingly at the brilliant light that shines down upon her.

SsshhhhhhhhhhhwishCLUNK! .... (tap... tap...tap)

SsshhhhhhhhhhhhwishCLUNK! .... (tap... tap...tap)

Shivering violently, Jillian awoke from a dark dream into something much worse. Hypothermia had advanced from moderate to severe and addled her mind. Excruciating cold dulled her senses and made her limbs feel numb and swollen. She was naked on a wet stainless steel table; glistening drops of water on her body reflect the large, rectangular light above her head. Her legs were secured, spread purposely, her knees at the edge of the table, and lower legs dangling off. Water drained through channels along the perimeter of the table to a basin at the end. Wide, white straps sprouted from the surface of the table, and held her firmly across each leg and across her neck. Her arms responded sluggishly in an attempt to fold them across her exposed chest. Numb hands rubbed her arms in a useless attempt to warm her body.

SsshhhhhhhhhhhhwishCLUNK! .... (tap... tap...tap)

The sound came from the shadows at the border of the light. Her teeth chattered as she turned her head toward the sound. Reflecting the light was a skeletal steel computer desk, half in the fluorescent pool and half in the dark. An obscure figure reclined at the desk. His hand extended into the light, absently withdrawing the empty keyboard tray. After three deliberate taps, his forefinger flicked it back into place.

.... (tap... tap...tap) SsshhhhhhhhhhhhwishCLUNK!

Her jaw ached from the cold as she opened and closed her mouth without a sound emerging. With an effort she focused and expelled a weak, "Huh... huh... Help... mmme, pplease."

.... (tap... tap...tap) SsshhhhhhhhhhhhwishCLUNK!

Her plea was ignored.

"Pppplease... huh help!"

The incessant tap and clunk stopped, and a man wearing a luxuriously warm fur robe walked into the light. With his hands in his pockets, he came to the right side of the table by her head. His calm, unremarkable face smiled, and his tall, erect bearing seemed familiar.

"How are we doing?" His voice was solicitous. "Are you cold?"

Jillian's head jerked spasmodically up and down. 'I don't want to be cold anymore' was the only thought that could penetrate her stupor.

"Would like me to warm you up?"

Desperately, she nodded her head. "Yyyess. Ppplease." She envisioned the warm fur draped across her bare skin.

With an energetic motion, he pulled his hands from his pockets, clapped them together, and rubbed vigorously.

Jillian thought the warmth radiating from his hands on her stomach was heavenly. He massaged her mid-section briefly and then his right began moving down between her legs. She tensed and the warmth was abruptly pulled away. Her moan was despairing and weak.

"You want me to stop?" he asked her, his face a mask of questioning concern. "Or do you want to be warm?" The mocking caricature of an innocent smile was abruptly flashed at her.

The chill she felt was soul deep and had nothing to do with the temperature. But there was no resistance in her shivering voice as it replied.

"Waa…Warm."

He rubbed his hands together again and placed them on her body. This time, his left hand unfolded her arms and cupped her breast while his right hand slid smoothly down her stomach, across her pubic arch and began to finger her with a slow, rhythmic stroke. The moan that escaped from her lips was an anomalous mixture of shame and relief.

The left hand spread sublime warmth across her upper body, and then lovingly caressed her neck. Her hands sought the radiance of his skin and were carried along as she held his arm.

Meanwhile his right hand sought to produce a deeper warming.

A profound revulsion churned in her head, but blood flowed only where his probing hands roamed. Nothing was left to fuel the process of thinking. Instead, her body responded instinctually; deliriously seeking to generate more heat.

Her cold flesh was warming, and his fingers became slick with her moisture. When Jillian's hips began to rock in urgent response to his attentions, he developed an urgency of his own. He removed his hand and began to climb on the table.

The movement brought her mind into focus, and she pushed him away. She clenched her teeth against her desire for warmth.

"N-n-no!" She raised her head and dropped it against the steel again and again. "No! No! NO!"

He got off the table. She would break eventually; this was only her third time through the treatment. But there was a trace of disappointment in his voice as he repeated his earlier question.

"You want me to stop?"

The pounding had helped clear some cobwebs from her brain. Had she been through this before? Enough cobwebs remained to cloud her memory. "Yes! I want you to stop!" She was grateful for the small, but evident, strength in her voice.

"Whatever you say." With a resigned patience, he walked back to his chair and sat down.

Jillian found that she could concentrate more, and that soon brought her to a disheartening conclusion. The last thing she remembered was that old man standing tall before her and spraying something in her face. Harvester warnings had been all over the news during the last week: she had thought she was being careful; avoiding secluded, unfamiliar areas; and not going out alone after dark.

Now look at what being a good Samaritan had gotten her!

Anger was starting to build: at herself for being so stupid; at that monster for what he was doing; and at the hopeless feeling that was growing stronger every moment. The anger helped warm her more, and she pounded her fists on the table.

The Harvester reached up, grasped a chain above his head.

Jillian's fury finally unfroze her tongue. As he pulled on the chain, she gave voice to her anger...

"You freaking basta..."

Water poured out of two nozzles at each end of the light fixture above the table. She was immediately soaked; her body convulsing from the shock of the biting cold. The metal resounded from the drumming of her fists and her heals bruised as they kicked the underside of the table. Despite her exertions, the frigid water washed the heat from her body. Soon her only movement was an uncontrolled shivering. Still the shower continued as she yelled, and cursed, and cried. Eventually she tired and turned to the torturing maniac who controlled hot and cold, wet and dry, and most importantly, life and death.

"S-S-Stop it!" she screamed, "P-P-Please t-t-turn it off!"

He pulled out the keyboard, flicked it back... and ignored her screams. SsshhhhhhhhhhhhwishCLUNK! .... (tap... tap...tap)

―――⟶⟿⟵―――

The half-moon was high above them as night drove the sun from the sky, leaving only a field of burning embers scattered on the horizon. While the sun was high, the day had been pleasantly warm; now cold air moved in, and a restless mist surfaced from every stream, pond and grassy expanse.

But the magic of the day lived on, too strong to let them part. Ben and Elsa coasted on their bikes from the distant parking lot toward his apartment building, passing through a waist-high mist that floated above the broad lawn. With the bikes secured, four flights of stairs were conquered before Ben led Elsa into his apartment.

The door opened into a moderately-sized rectangular living room. At the far right end, sliding glass doors led to a concrete balcony that was level with the treetops beyond the black wrought iron railing. Opposite the door was a wall that stretched half the length of the room and ended at a small open dining room. Free-standing book shelves had been strategically placed end to end to divide the dining and living rooms. Left of the dining area was the bare, Spartan-like kitchen. Between those two rooms was a short alcove with doors to a bathroom on the left, the bedroom straight ahead, and a small office to the right.

"Make yourself at home," he said, "I'll try to be quick." He dashed into the kitchen and left her standing in the middle of the living room. In a moment he reappeared and tossed her a granola bar.

"I don't know about you, but I don't think I'll make it to the restaurant without a snack first. Feel free to look around… be as nosey as you want." Ben headed for the shower as Elsa hurled a 'Thank you' at his back.

Munching on the granola bar, Elsa did a slow pirouette, studying the apartment; to her the room was comfortably neat. Single men lived like slobs; every girl she knew said so. Never having seen evidence of it, Elsa was skeptical. Bill, Bran, and her father had all lived much like this. Sure there was dust in places that didn't get much use, and a few books piled haphazardly on a coffee table that had worn slippers underneath. On the dining table sat a dirty bowl, spoon, and a glass with a layer of orange juice drying in the bottom. Maybe her standards weren't that high, but if she lived alone, she imagined her place wouldn't be any neater.

I've always lived with a man. That fact was obvious. Her father, then Bran, and now she lived in Bill Pendry's guest room while she went to classes at

Maryland. Although she had loved and been comfortable with all three, something was missing… *I've always felt lonely.*

Elsa began a methodical tour of the room while her sub-conscious considered the question- 'Could it be different with Ben?'

At his CD tower she found that alternate rock bands dominated his collection; Counting Crows, Better Than Ezra, R.E.M. But there was also an eclectic selection of classic rock, folk, blues, Celtic, world and new age titles. She pushed the play button on the stereo, and the sounds of Led Zeppelin's "Battle of Evermore" filled the room.

After lowering the volume to a background level, she moved to the bookshelves. An entire section was filled with history books, most related to the Industrial Revolution and transportation. So many of the titles were familiar, for a wistful moment, she was standing in her father's office, perusing his books. Although Ben didn't look at all like her father, Elsa had begun to notice small things that reminded her of him.

Her fingers swept gently along the spines as she moved along. They brushed across an expensive, red leather-bound copy of <u>The Lord of the Rings</u>. Asimov, McCaffrey… she was also acquainted with his selection of science fiction, much of it she had read, or re-read, during long winter evenings in Wyoming.

One of the shelves was devoted to pictures: Ben, and a taller man Elsa assumed was his older brother, standing on a rugged, snowy mountaintop; a recent Christmas picture with Ben, his parents, the man Elsa more confidently identified as Carl, and a much younger girl… his sister? There was also a picture of Ben with a group of older men standing around Maryland Governor Parris Glendening; they all looked very pleased.

When she spied the next picture, she laughed. It showed two small boys facing each other. From the angry grimaces and animated posture of their hands and arms, they could be fighting. But Elsa knew at a glance what it showed… Carl and Ben arguing in sign language. Carl's had one curved arm held high, the hand extended toward Ben while the other arm seemed to be sweeping across his body, hand flat. Ben's right fist was against his chin, thumb and pinky extended, the sign for 'wrong', his left was simultaneously making the sign for "NO!"

She brushed a thin layer of dust from the young Ben's face.

"I was only seven…"

Elsa jumped and put her hand to her chest. "God, Ben!" She took a deep breath. "I don't remember the last time someone startled me like that."

He smiled sheepishly, "Sorry. The people below me are real complainers, so I tip toe around a lot."

"That's OK. I *think* my heart is still beating." She looked back to the picture. "I know what you are saying, but what is Carl signing?"

"If I remember correctly, I think that is his version of 'go jump in a lake'." He laughed. "I really love that picture even though I can't recall what we were arguing about."

He then used the Christmas photo to introduce his family.

"My parents Albert and Laney, brother Carl, and little sister Emily." He gave his head a rueful shake. "I'm only twenty-four and life is already going by too fast. She's a senior in high school; it seems like last week she was a half-pint pest begging for rides on the back of my bike."

"What about that one?" She pointed to Ben and the Governor. The picture looked new. "You aren't planning to be a politician are you?" He had told her that his work for the Washington Metropolitan Council of Governments involved encouraging mass transit and alternative commuting options: he lobbied against road construction projects on his own time.

"This past Wednesday, a group I belong to lobbied Governor Glendening to stop the Inter-County Connector." Ben's enthusiasm was evident. "It worked! He is making the announcement Tuesday that he's rejecting the Transportation Solutions Group report that recommended construction." He shut his mouth and slapped himself. "Sorry… didn't mean to get carried away… but it was kind of exciting for me."

Elsa laughed. "I don't mind, but why don't you tell me over dinner?"

Ben gestured to the door. "Shall we go?"

CHAPTER 15

Saturday evening, September 18, 1999

J illian's mind lost the ability to distinguish between her nightmares. In
one, she suffered and was cold. In the other, her suffering was different...
and warm.

She chose the warmth.

In the end, his victory was quite enjoyable. Well worth the wait. She wel-
comed him with open, thankful arms, desirous of his heat, and accepting of
his violation. Her arms slipped inside his thick robe and sought the warmth
of his body, clutching and caressing. Spreading the robe about their coupled
bodies, he dispatched her cold most strenuously.

He much preferred harvesting a warm heart.

Once victory and harvesting were complete, he yielded to a desire for even
darker activities.

He was sure Jillian wouldn't mind.

⊷⊶

As she rushed upstairs to change, Elsa chuckled. She'd just given Ben the
same spiel he gave her at his apartment. "Make yourself at home, feel free to
look around." He wouldn't find out much about her, though, since it was Bill's

house. Her high school picture was on a shelf; but unless he snuck upstairs while she was in the shower, he wouldn't find anything of hers.

When she returned, she found him in Bill's old easy chair with *The Majestic Rockies* open on his lap.

How did he do that? She'd loved that big photographic book since she was a three-year-old. It was probably the only item in the room to which she felt a personal connection.

"I hope it's alright I got this out." He got up and returned the book to the shelf. "The mountain my brother and I climbed is in here."

Elsa gave him a warm smile.

"It's fine." She took his arm and led him out. "It's just that, with the thousands of books Bill has, I come down and find you looking at the one that I love the most. It is way too weird."

———✦———

Candlelight glowed from the lace-curtained windows and Ben grew worried that he had chosen a place that was much too romantic. He'd only known Elsa for a single day, but his feelings for her had grown stronger every moment of those twenty-four hours. Why did he assume she felt the same way? He was sure she enjoyed his company, but now he was afraid he might be getting ahead of himself.

"I hope this place will be ok," he said as they crossed a stone walkway toward the tiny restaurant. It was supposed to be a French provincial cottage. With white clapboard siding and black shutters, it looked more like a home than a restaurant.

Elsa watched his eyes widen as she signed her response. She loved those copper saucers!

("It looks charming! Do you mind if we sign during dinner… like last night?")

His broad smile was all the answer she needed.

The candle burned down, and the conversation became less animated… more intimate. They used more looks and fewer words. Long, quiet moments passed as they studied each other. Her eyes were drawn to the curve of his chin; his dimples when he smiled; and the unruly locks of hair that curled from behind his ears.

He was entranced by the left corner of her mouth when she gave him her small, private smile; the way her wide, delighted grin set her entire face aglow; and her eyes - always those hypnotic hazel eyes.

Fingers intertwined across the table in a more direct sign language.

Elsa drew back her hands to tell him...

("For the first time since I was three years old, I have truly enjoyed my birthday.")

She loved how his beautiful copper eyes opened so wide when he was surprised. The reflected glow of the candle made them look golden.

("Birthday? We've been together all day and now you tell me?') He gave her a clown's sad-eyed frown. ("Now it's too late for me to get you a present")

("That's ok. I only have one birthday wish.")

Elsa speared him with a sensuous gaze that started Ben's heart pounding. He lifted his hands. ("What is it?")

She leaned close and signed as if whispering in his ear. Her hands were intimately brushing lightly across his as she formed the words...

("I want to find out how those sexy hands would feel on my body.")

⁓◍⌁

Gravel crunched under the tires of the car as it moved slowly down the boat ramp at Greenbelt Lake. Ben eased to a stop after the ethereal fog, lying heavy over the lake, consumed the front half of the car. The half-moon was turning orange and hung just above the trees across the water. Its spectral light gave the mist a supernatural glow. An easy listening station was playing Andy Williams' Moon River on the radio.

"This just keeps getting better and better." Elsa whispered as she leaned toward Ben, "you must be some kind of sorcerer." She kissed his neck, then his ear, "because you have definitely put me under your spell." She reached his lips and surrendered a part of her soul that had been unclaimed far too long.

Ben closed his eyes and immersed himself in a kiss that was beyond anything he had ever experienced. It felt as though their very essence became as entwined as their tongues. Awash in a sea of emotion that required no thought to enjoy, he barely had the presence of mind to begin fulfilling Elsa's birthday wish.

Her lungs had no need to breathe; her mind no need to think. All she needed was his lips on hers and his hands on her body. A part of her loved and appreciated how much a gentleman he was being, but after a while, a stronger need took over.

Elsa framed his face with her hands and pulled reluctantly back from the kiss.

"This is the way I see it," she said as calmly as her highly aroused emotions would allow. "We've been together for about eighteen hours. By my reckoning this is more like our ninth date instead of our second. I believe you're entitled not to second base, but a grand slam. I know I'm shameless, but will you stop being such a gentleman and get me in the back seat?"

His grin was as eager as any virgin boy's, but he didn't care. He leaned his seat all the way down, crawled into the back and dropped the rear seat. The hatchback had plenty of room. This whole crazy, romantic day was like a dream, and he just hoped some cop didn't come snooping at the wrong time and wake him from it.

"All ready." He leaned over the seat and saw Elsa was sitting motionless with tears dripping down her face.

"What's the matter?" He scrambled to the front. She covered her face with her hands and sobbed.

"Elsa, please tell me, what did I do?"

She dropped her hands into her lap, then reached over, and turned up the radio.

"... these ambiguous circumstances, Mrs. Cassidy was not reported missing until late this evening. Police officials say that this resulted in a disruption of the normal Harvester protocols. Mrs. Cassidy is the fifteenth Harvester victim. Maryland, Virginia and Pennsylvania governors and the D.C. mayor, have scheduled a joint news conference for tomorrow where they are expected to criticize the F.B.I. for the lack of any progress in apprehending the Harvester. Whether by awful coincidence or gruesome plan, Saturday, September 18, 1983, was the date that the first victim, Anne Danforth, was murdered.

"Tune into our sister station for complete..."

Ben snapped the radio off. "Anne Danforth... was your mother?" Elsa responded with a small, sad nod. He thought a moment, and then shook his head. "I can't imagine how terrible that must be for you... every year holding your breath, dreading the moment when you'll hear something like this."

Elsa threw her arms around him and put her head on his shoulder. "I'm so sorry. You made this a perfect day and I've ruined it."

"You haven't ruined anything, Elsa," he said gently but firmly. Ben held her tight and realized... holding this woman was what he wanted to do for the rest of his life.

—⚍⚎—

Saturday, April 8, 2000

It was a cool, wet morning and the crunch of the gravel under their shoes competed with the patter of the rain drops on the canopy of bright green leaves above the two runners' heads. Their heavy, rhythmic breathing produced clouds of vapor; ghostly reminders of the steam locomotives that once chugged through these forested hills.

Elsa was loving life as she cruised up the North Central Rail Trail just south of Monkton, Maryland. The temperature, in the low forties, was perfect for running and the light, steady rain had kept the normally crowded recreation path north of Baltimore almost deserted. Her best friend was at her side, and Elsa was bursting to tell the news that she had been holding inside for the first fifteen miles of their twenty mile run.

She cranked up the pace and surged a stride ahead. A short distance later, Alicia had adjusted her speed and pulled back alongside.

"You're feeling frisky this morning." Alicia was breathing hard as the speed took its toll.

"Sorry, Ali... can't help it," Elsa puffed. "I'm so excited... hard to hold back."

Rather than climbing over the rolling landscape, the North Central Railway cut through the hills between Baltimore and the state line. When the railway was abandoned and eventually became a rail trail, the cuts provided deep, shady canyons for runners, walkers, and cyclists throughout the region.

The pair was making a gradual climb northward through one of those cuts. At end of that dark tunnel of trees, a break in the clouds revealed the path bathed in brilliant light. Alicia glanced over to see a glowing smile lighting up the rain and sweat on Elsa's face.

"Better tell... what's got you excited," Alicia blew a drop of moisture off her nose and forced the words between labored breaths. "Maybe I can be excited too... not have to work... so hard to keep up."

Her friend leapt in the air and raced into the sunshine as she answered, the words echoing down the narrow canyon …

"I'm getting married!"

When Alicia finally caught Elsa, they joyfully chattered about the wedding as they chased the patch of sunshine north toward Monkton.

Soon, low rumbles, like the sound of a phantom freight train, interrupted their conversation. Glancing back, they found that they were also being chased.

A warm front was waging a violent campaign northward, and they were in its path.

———

Hail drummed on the metal roof of the old, red brick building as the skies opened up. Competing with the loud pattering was a deeper growl of thunder that Alicia and Elsa could feel through the soles of their soggy running shoes. They pushed through the heavy, wooden door, laughing in relief at having escaped the violent storm.

Ten minutes later, a frightened Elsa looked out on the deluge while she cuddled a mug of hot chocolate. Alicia sat next to her and watched her little Toyota get pounded by popcorn-sized chunks of ice. As if shot from a popper, they bounced off and joined thousands of others that covered the parking lot with a rough white carpet.

Elsa shivered, but her body, cooling down from its exhausting effort, was only part of the reason.

On sunny days, the tall windows of the historic industrial building made the interior bright and welcoming. On this day, the expanse of glass allowed the dark skies to augment the creepy feel of the empty store.

They were sitting at a small, wrought-iron table inside the combination convenience store, fudge shop and souvenir stand that served the Monkton trailhead where they had started their out-and-back run.

Wet tracks were still visible on the hardwood. The tracks wound through the widely-spaced racks of snack food, t-shirts, wall plaques, postcards, and the like; evidence of the two girls' roaming as they searched for someone to serve them. After calling for several minutes, they'd still only received echoes in reply.

Drawn by the smell, Alicia had left shoeprints that led behind the counter to an electric cook top where a pot of hot chocolate sat unattended.

Contributing to the eerie mood was the chorus of an I Nine song playing over and over in the background:

... it'll shiver you down
Your body's bare and the feeling is abounding,
I feel it abounding.
Where do you go
When the dark calls you out...
Beckons by name?
Where do you go? Where do you go?

At the end-cap of one aisle, a small puddle showed where Elsa had paused to look at some exquisite, bandsawn wood name plates, neatly aligned in alphabetical order. The rich, darkly-patterned grain of the walnut and the quality of the craftsmanship would have enticed her into getting a small gift for her future maid-of-honor and maybe her fiancé... but for two facts.

First, there seemed to be no one from whom to make a purchase.

Second, the slots that should have held what she wanted instead had little signs that said 'Sorry, we are out of... Alicia' 'Sorry, we are out of... Ben'. Out of more than one hundred slots chock-full of name plates, she noticed only two others that seemed empty.

She felt an unnerving chill when she noted that one was Anne. Kneeling to check the other barren slot; she slipped on the wet floor and stumbled forward, catching the edge of the shelf with her hand just before she would have planted her face between the plentiful Marks and Matthews. Instead she found herself at eye-level with the last empty space...

Martin.

At the moment she looked down the slot, a violent gust of wind slapped the branch of an oak tree against one of the tall windows.

Then she saw that the slot wasn't empty after all.

An unnatural fear gripped Elsa as she saw the name plate that was inexplicably resting in the space where her dead father's name should be.

Benjamin.

Compiled from the Harvester Task Force
Archives — January, 2000

On November 1, 1999 Ronald Grantham was relieved as Special Agent-in-Charge of the Harvester Task Force. F.B.I. Assistant Director Alexander McDonald, a 27-year veteran, took direct charge of the task force. Agent Paul Demerov was named Assistant Special Agent-in-Charge, at the age of 30, the youngest ever promoted to that position. ASAC Demerov was responsible for developing the lead that resulted in the F.B.I. making the first significant progress in the investigation: leading a team that spent four intensive weeks reviewing security camera footage of the day in question, from throughout the region. Demerov identified the victim's car at a time and location which indicates it was, at that moment, being driven by the Harvester. Agents later developed further information which allowed the F.B.I. to project the Harvester's base of operations to lie within a 30-mile radius of Linthicum, MD.

Addendum C: Page 34

Advances in chemical analysis have allowed F.B.I. technicians to identify three specific chemical compounds that the Harvester used during his abduction and murder of the victim Jillian Cassidy. Although relatively common in the medical and veterinary communities, it is believed that this is also a significant development.

CHAPTER 16

Wednesday, July 12, 2000

Claude laughed loudly as another muscular, macho guy landed with a loud thump on the mat. He had tried to warn them, but Elsa had the same problem he had, people always underestimated how much power could be delivered by focus and determination alone. At 5' 9", slim, a wiry 160 pounds, and with a distressingly feminine-looking face; his opponents on the mat always miscalculated his strength and ability. It was one of the reasons his World Martial Arts School was struggling for members, despite his titles.

Several rapid slaps were followed by the crunching sound of an elbow to the celiac plexus and a painful 'oompfhh'. The 200-pound bull of a man fell back on his butt like a toddler.

"Do not underestimate your opponent!" Claude screamed. "This woman can kill you if she chooses!"

Surrounded by her three remaining opponents, Elsa swayed as if dancing to the beat of the Brazilian music that blared from the speakers. In fact, the beat did inform her movements since some of the bizarre mix of martial arts she employed was Capoeira. It was a fighting technique that originated in colonial times among escaped slaves in the jungles of Brazil as a means of defeating the Portuguese slave hunters. One of the primary advantages of this martial art was its usefulness against multiple opponents.

In modern times, it has become more theatrical and acrobatic. It is rarely incorporated into combat. Claude's school was one of the few that taught Capoeira Regional, the more martial method that stressed attack and counter-attack.

He had known, from the moment Elsa had first stepped through his door, that she would be a formidable fighter. It was obvious that her long, well proportioned limbs and tall, muscular body could become well-trained. But he sensed a strong and well-balanced energy and intensity lurking inside her that would make her dangerous.

'Crrrack!' He watched the heavily-tattooed young Hispanic gasp and grab his arm. They had all signed what Claude hoped were iron-clad liability waivers; Elsa had most likely broken the man's humerus.

At their first meeting, she had asked for a match, testing him. He had bested her in relatively short time, but only because she expected him to underestimate her. Instead, he surprised her with an immediate, aggressive assault, not holding back anything. He knew that he had delivered some very painful blows that would leave deep bruises, but she had smiled as if she'd hit the jackpot.

Since that day, she'd developed into the Mozart of martial arts. She could replicate any throw, block, punch, kick or sweep from any martial arts discipline after only a single demonstration; then she would incorporate it into a rhythmic Capoeira that was beautiful, fierce and intimidating. Certainly, if restricted to a one discipline, there were masters who could defeat her. But in unrestricted martial arts combat, he did not believe a single person could beat her.

His attention was drawn back to the mat.

Elsa was flat on her stomach with 430 pounds of sweaty muscle holding her down.

"Match" he called. The two men rolled off and Elsa jumped to her feet with a grim countenance. She bowed to each of the six opponents, four of whom were gingerly nursing various parts of their bodies.

She stood stiffly in the center of the mat until all six had left the room. Then she marched purposefully toward Claude, anger flashing in her eyes. He smiled calmly when she stopped directly before him.

"That can't happen!" she said, as if her being defeated in a combat with six larger men was his fault.

"This isn't the movies, Elsa." It was a phrase he had used often with her. Unfortunately, her hypnotic, dance-like fighting style made it hard for him to believe. Sometimes it appeared as though Elsa was really a mythical Greek goddess, a modern Athena, dispatching opponents like so many movie extras.

She let the anger and adrenaline recede and took a cleansing breath. "I know it isn't the movies," she said. "In the movies, you would have said "cut" instead of "match". But if it was real, you wouldn't have been there to call match, either. I'd either be dead or having unspeakable things done to me. You have to make sure that can't happen."

"Even you are not invincible. But..." Claude held up his hand to forestall Elsa's interruption, "...you can do better."

Metal clattering echoed through the empty training room as Elsa opened her locker. She picked up the band of gold and slipped it over her finger. Immediately she relaxed and smiled. Every session, it felt as though she stored her regular Elsa persona in her wedding ring and let the angry lioness come out for lessons and matches. While changing, she thought of how fortunate she was.

Life was becoming so happy and full of purpose; Ben was her perfect match. He treasured her the way she was, yet challenged her to be better. Constantly giving of himself, but always needing her and desirous of everything she offered. He weaved so many magic moments into their life that it really did feel like a movie fairy-tale.

Friday, September 8, 2000

"Ben, come on... please don't make a big fuss out of this." Elsa was loosening up for a run, while he stood near the door with an angry look on his face and his arms folded across his chest.

Ben was discovering that sometimes it was hard to have such an independent and self-reliant wife.

"Please Elsa! You should know better than anyone why I don't want you running out there by yourself." He waved his arm vigorously toward the world beyond their door. It's September... you know what that means."

"Yes, Ben, I do know." She softened her tone. "I know you're only acting like this because you love me. But I need to run, and I'm not going to let some maniac keep me from doing it. You've got your meeting... which I won't let you skip... so I'm going to run by myself. Besides, I hope he does try for me. You know I'll rip him to pieces."

Elsa had taken Ben to her last training session. He'd almost called a halt to it before it started. Six fierce looking guys standing in a threatening circle around his wife. Claude had put a restraining hand on his arm.

"Just wait," he'd said as he started the video camera. Then he pushed a button on the CD player on the floor by his feet. The Samba-like music started Elsa swaying. Before any of her adversaries had a chance to move, she struck like a cobra. A hybrid cobra with four frightening paws. Before Ben could really process what he was seeing, all six men were writhing on the mat, and Elsa was stomping toward Claude.

"That was pitiful!" she growled. "They weren't ready!"

Claude shrugged his shoulders. "I warned them. I challenged their manhood. What more can I do?" He held out her wedding ring.

"Show the next six," She pointed toward the camera with her left hand and used her right to snatch the ring from his hand, "this video." Then she slipped the ring on her finger.

Ben flinched slightly when she turned toward him. Then he saw that her face had gone from lion to pussycat in the blink of an eye.

Elsa was dismayed to see her husband recoiling from her. He held up his hands in mock surrender... and grinned.

"I promise... I'll never leave the toilet seat up again... never... ever."

Now he had to fight against the instinctual desire to protect his wife.

I don't know why I'm standing in front of the door. If she wants to go out, she could just use my head for a battering ram.

"Ben?" She was standing in front of him, her hand resting gently on his crossed arms, staring lovingly in his eyes. "Please?"

He stood reluctantly aside and opened the door. As she started to leave, he held out his hand.

"Just don't kill anyone," he said as she dropped her wedding ring in his hands.

"No promises," Elsa growled. Then she ran down the steps and into the night.

Ben's nervousness was not improved when he watched a program later that evening. It was something that had become an unfortunate part of life in the D.C. area - a broadcast that marked the start of Harvester season. The local T.V. station was showing a very serious-looking young agent who was conducting an F.B.I. news conference.

"I can't stress this strongly enough," Paul Demerov looked directly into the cluster of television cameras and spoke forcefully, "we have not divulged a pattern because there is no pattern. In the seventeen years since he first struck in 1983, this criminal has taken women using four different methods that we know of." He ticked them off on his fingers, "He has used car-jacking at least twice; he has snatched women off a street or trail multiple times; one or more times he has used false pretenses to lure women to a screened location and taken them; and we now believe that he took the ninth victim, Andrea Hoffman, from her basement apartment. In some cases, we are still unable to pinpoint a method. He has taken women as young as nineteen and as old as thirty-five. Many, but not all, of the women had long hair, many, but not all, were blonde; many, but not all, were Caucasian."

Paul paused to sip some water from the paper cup on the lectern. He waved down the reporters shouting for the chance to be the next to torture him.

"I'm not quite finished answering the previous question. All of the women would be considered somewhat light-skinned, BUT... I'll tell you this, no matter the age, tone of skin, the length or color hair, if it were my sister, daughter, wife, girl-friend or mother; I would make sure that every possible precaution is taken until this criminal is apprehended. We cannot warn you any more clearly than that."

"Last question," he drained the cup, and then pointed to a reporter waving from amid the fifty or more that packed the conference room. There was only one reason that he was in front of the cameras instead of Alexander McDonald, the head of the task force. McDonald wanted Demerov to be the face and name people remembered if there was a screw-up like last year.

"What are the odds of you catching the Harvester?"

"Odds?" Paul came close to throwing the paper cup at the reporter with national television recording the action. He barely held his temper, and hoped his anger didn't show too clearly. "I'm not a handicapper, people's lives aren't something I would choose to bet on. It is September eighth. It is likely that sometime in the next eight weeks, this criminal will attempt to claim another victim. The F.B.I. is doing everything in its power to prevent this. If the kidnapping is not prevented, we will do everything in our power to rescue the victim. If this criminal kills again…" Paul tried hard to keep his frustration from showing. "The F.B.I. is committed to stopping this reign of terror. We *will* apprehend this criminal." He slapped his notebook closed and walked out of the room.

CHAPTER 17

Friday, November 3, 2000

The fall nights were getting cold. Paper jack-o-lanterns, skeletons, and ghosts still decorated apartment doors throughout the complex, even though it was November. A frost earlier in the week had persuaded most of the trees to shed their colorful cloaks and surrender to a rapidly-approaching winter.

For Elsa, the best running weather was just beginning. The low forties, even the upper thirties were perfect and tonight's forty-one degrees felt great as she cruised out of the neighborhood. She was planning a fast fourteen-miler on a course that would take her all the way to Greenbelt and back.

The route wound through quiet communities and parks, away from the congestion that plagued most of the Maryland suburbs. Her planned journey also had an attraction, unique to Elsa, of passing near two locations from which the Harvester had taken a victim.

She settled into the pace she wanted and let the miles roll.

Toby was just inside the park when he saw the two guys up ahead. They looked like trouble, so he threw down his cigarette, and stepped on it as he spun around and headed back. He wasn't sure why they were hanging around in the woods, but he didn't want any part of it. Thank god they hadn't seen him. It was a pain he had to sneak his smokes... he was fifteen already. Why didn't his parents just leave him alone? He left the park, and was most of the way home, when he saw her.

"Whoa baby!" Toby gave a low wolf whistle as the tall blond came cruising down the road. He would have been embarrassed if the woman heard him. She was really flying along toward the park.

Toward the park! Not a good idea. Not with those guys hiding in there.

"Hey lady" he yelled, "I wouldn't go in there!" She must have heard him, she wasn't *that* far away. "Hey lady!"

Then all that talk about Harvest season hit him, and he hurried home to call 911.

She heard the kid clearly. The adrenaline hit her blood stream and she made sure that it stayed under control. Easing into a relaxed pace, Elsa waited for her heart rate and respiration to slow.

When the man stepped into the asphalt path ahead of her, Elsa was ready. She stopped just out of reach. Leaves crackled as the second man blocked the path behind her.

"I can't believe my luck, a piece as luscious as you out alone; what with it being Harvest season and all."

His face was pock-marked and decorated with a Van Gogh beard. His voice was deep, slow, malicious, and he had made his intentions clear enough.

"You really don't want to do this," Elsa said, as she began swaying to the tune in her head.

"Yeh, bits," slurred the guy behind her, "weh really do."

Van Gogh rubbed his hands together. "Oh, baby... I'm going to do so much more than dance with..."

Elsa did the dancing, leaping forward and whipping out her fist, which broke his wind pipe. Then she spun into a low, quick kick at the leg of the man advancing from behind. As he fell toward ground, she caught his chin on her rapidly rising knee and snapped his neck. Spinning around, she saw Van Gogh staggering away down the path. He stumbled and fell to his hands and knees. She took several running steps to catch up, then leapt high in the air. A vicious kick to the back of his head saved him from suffocating to death.

Stepping carefully over the bodies, she returned in the direction from which she'd come. Quickly reaching her original pace, she headed for home.

"You will follow orders," thundered Alexander McDonald, "or you will be suspended pending your termination."

Paul Demerov knew that he had used up all the maneuvering room that past successes as an agent may have earned him. He buried his outrage and responded with the only answer that would save his job.

"Yes sir!" He spun on his heel and marched out of the office.

The Harvester Task Force had taken over the top two floors of an office building several blocks from F.B.I. headquarters. McDonald took an executive corner office on the tenth, while Paul chose a modest office at the hub of the action on the ninth floor. It was centered between the always bustling communications room and the huge area in the middle of the building where the investigating teams had their cubicles. He had cooled down enough when he reached his office that the slam of his door shook only the ninth floor and not the entire building.

The 911 call from the teenager in Greenbelt had brought an immediate response from the closest HRRT. The Harvester Rapid Response Team had arrived in Greenbelt Park simultaneously with local police and taken charge of the scene without any of the normal cross-jurisdictional jealousies. When it came to the Harvester, for the first time in history, everyone really was on the same team.

The bodies of the two men were identified within twenty minutes as Brad Tolin, thirty-five and his half-brother Jason Peters, thirty-two. In 1990, at the age of twenty-five, Tolin had been convicted of third degree rape for which he served twenty-seven months. That term ended in August of 1993 and coincided with the cessation of Harvester activity. Peters was borderline mentally retarded and had never been incarcerated despite dozens of assault charges. Their father and two other half-brothers were being held for twenty-four hours as 'persons of interest' in the Harvester investigation.

In the hour since the bodies were identified, no evidence connecting Tolin with the Harvester had been uncovered. Despite that, Paul was being ordered not to discourage local news media from reporting that the dead brothers were suspected of being involved with the Harvester murders. Based solely on Tolin's coincidental jail term, and their deaths during what was, in Paul's mind, most likely a failed rape attempt, McDonald was willing to allow the public to jump to the wrong conclusion.

Not only that, but Paul was the one who would be in front of the cameras at a news conference now just twenty minutes away. His instinct told him that this entire incident had nothing to do with the Harvester, and that any decline in vigilance by the public or the F.B.I. could be deadly. He couldn't let it happen! Now all he had to do was prevent this mistake in a way that didn't involve destroying his career.

In the end, Paul decided the simplest solution was the best; a note to the right reporter who he picked for the last question of the news conference.

"Agent Demerov, do you believe that the two dead men found this evening are related to the Harvester serial killings?"

Paul didn't like the re-wording of his planted question, but it did give him his opening. "The F.B.I.'s Harvester Task Force will thoroughly investigate all leads from tonight's incident. My personal belief is that the evidence we collect will show that this incident is completely unrelated. In my opinion, the criminal responsible for fifteen murders is still at large and continues to be a very real threat."

The reporter called for a follow-up as he was about to end the press conference.

"Of the previous Harvester episodes, the latest occurred October twenty-second. If this incident is unrelated, do you believe that the Harvester threat for this season has passed?"

McDonald, over Demerov's strenuous objections, had been planning to scale down HTF operations for the year beginning on Monday, November sixth. This evening's developments had given him an excuse to cut back even sooner. Unless it was carefully phrased, Demerov knew that his answer to this question could put him on very thin ice.

"The F.B.I. will continue to respond appropriately in our continu..." *Hell with it, I'm tired of walking on thin ice.* "No, I don't. This criminal is intelligent, adaptable, and disciplined. The public and the F.B.I. must remain on guard. If we don't the result could be deadly."

As he walked out of the briefing room, Paul wondered how long it would be before he was called on the carpet for that performance.

<hr />

Is the Harvester's reign of terror at an end? Stay tuned for that story and more, next on...

"Elsa..."

"I heard. I'll be right in." She left her laptop and text books on the table, walked into the living room, and snuggled next to Ben on the sofa.

"Do you think it's possible?" he said as they waited for the commercials to end and the eleven o'clock news to start. "That monster has been around for so long. I know how much it would mean to you for him to be captured or killed."

Elsa was afraid she knew what the news might be and worried about her husband's reaction. When she was still just his fiancée, Ben had understood when confronted by her propensity to react violently under certain circumstances. But tonight's incident was on a much higher level.

Her own emotions had been on a roller coaster all evening. After the initial exhilaration of victory in a life or death battle, she had fallen into a period of guilt and despair for having taken another human life. Reliving that brief, violent encounter only provided a temporary relief from that dismal state of mind.

Their malicious intentions had been clear and the threat, palpable. She gradually faced down her guilt by accepting the reality that those two animals would have continued to prey on vulnerable women if she hadn't stopped them.

"I'm sure everyone wants to see this nightmare over with," was her cautious answer. "We can only hope."

There have been some startling developments in the long-running Harvester investigation. Two men... Brad Tolin, 35 and Jason Peters, 32, both Beltsville, MD residents... were found dead this evening along a pathway in Greenbelt Park near the intersection of I-95 and the BW Parkway. Tolin was a convicted rapist who was in jail for a twenty-seven month period from May of 1991 until August of 1993. This period coincided with the hiatus between the Harvester murders of 1990 and September, 1993. Speculation from anonymous sources suggests that Tolin may have been the Harvester. Bringing you more on this story is our correspondent, Cynthia Stoker, reporting from Harvester Task Force headquarters where a news conference has just concluded.

Thank you, Brian. The news here is conflicting. Anonymous sources have confirmed that substantial HTF resources are being shifted to the investigation of Tolin and Peters. Both men have lengthy criminal records. This news conference was primarily devoted to confirming information concerning tonight's apparently foiled attack...

Excuse me, Cynthia. I'm sorry to interrupt, but you said 'apparently'. Can you explain?

Yes, Brian. A young woman was seen running in the area, and this woman has not been identified or located. While there has been no missing persons report so far this evening, police are still anxious to speak to this unknown runner. Fifteen-year-old Greenbelt teenager Toby Hansen made the 911 call to report suspicious activity in the park. This clip is from our exclusive interview with Mr. Hansen.

After the clip, the news continued with a report that contradictory information seemed to indicate a conflict within the investigation. A clip of an F.B.I. agent clearly stating his belief that the Harvester was still a threat allowed Elsa to breathe a sigh of relief. As soon as the attack had begun, she'd known they were just twisted men... common rapists. It would have been a heavy burden if somehow her actions made the Harvester's murderous mission easier.

Ben had stiffened when the news referenced the young woman. Elsa knew that he was struggling for the right words to discuss it with her. But the news ended, and they went to bed without him uttering a syllable.

The glow of the street light through the blinds spread alternating streaks of black and white on the bedroom ceiling. They brought to Ben's mind an image of prison bars... with Elsa penned behind them.

He lay with his hand laced behind his neck; sleep an impossible task until he hashed-out the conflict in his mind. That Elsa was also awake and patiently waiting for him to accomplish this, was a certainty.

Among all the thoughts that were racing through his head, one stood out, and brought a rueful smile to his lips. Countless women throughout history had lain next to men who had blood on their hands; men who, either with or without cause, had killed... or were capable of killing, another human being. But how many men had ever been in his position? For him, those roles were reversed.

In the cold, rational light of civilized thought, his reflexive liberal tendency would lead him to reject condemning even the basest criminal to death without a trial. But, in the real world, where dark forces became a threat to the woman he loved, those liberal tendencies were checked at the door. Regardless of the fact that she was intentionally putting herself at risk, Ben believed that what had happened earlier this evening was self-defense.

Now, Ben's only thoughts were of his love for Elsa and his desire to protect her. Not a second would he waste mourning the deaths of Tobin and Peters. But the authorities were looking for Elsa now. He turned to face her.

Spooning herself into the warmth of Ben's body, Elsa waited.

He kissed her neck and then spoke softly in her ear.

"If anything ever happens to you..." he squeezed her tight, unable to consider further that horrible possibility.

Elsa thought she knew what he wanted to hear. "They never had the chance to touch me. After they made it clear what they intended to do, it was over in ten seconds." She lifted his hand from her stomach to her lips and kissed it firmly. "I'll never take a chance on letting someone hurt me."

He brought his hand to her face and lifted it so he could kiss her cheek. "I know you can take care of yourself. That anyone who tries to hurt you is likely to end up in the hospital, or hell, doesn't bother me. If the authorities find you, your ability to defend yourself lethally could be used against you. I don't want to spend time visiting you in prison."

The consideration of prison made her shudder. She'd never allowed her thoughts to go that far, though now that Ben had spoken of it, she realized it could happen.

"You're right. I hadn't considered where all this might lead." She took his hand and brought it to her lips, kissing tenderly. Then she pulled it under her cheek, using it as a pillow as she thought about her next words.

"I'll work on my control and try to avoid any repeat of what happened this evening... until I find the Harvester."

Time passed as she lay in his embrace, letting the tension leach away.

"Besides," she shifted in the bed to face him. "It would be very selfish of me to end up in prison and put you through that." She pushed her husband onto his back and crawled on top. "Although I understand they do allow conjugal visits." Various parts of her body began an earnest effort to move their thoughts into a more pleasant realm.

"Maybe we should practice."

Tuesday, November 7, 2000

It was mid-morning and a light, chilly mist was falling on Willa Brenham's shoulders as she trudged up the hill. She always waited until after the morning rush to take the walk down to her local polling place.

"God help us if that Yale frat boy ever gets elected President" she muttered, as she returned home having proudly done her civic duty.

The handsome man with the umbrella and clipboard was still waiting by the sidewalk. On her way down, he had nodded politely and handed her a brochure about the exit poll he was conducting. His face was familiar, but she couldn't quite place it.

"Do you mind?" He gestured with the clipboard. "I haven't had much luck so far. Morning voters are always in a hurry to get to work." He was standing in front of a tall white Sprinter van with doors open to reveal a comfortable padded bench in front of a large desktop.

"That's too bad," Willa said, "I was hoping you could tell me how the vote was going."

"I'm not supposed to discuss the numbers, but if it'll get you in the van, I'm sure we can work something out." He gave her a conspiring wink and gestured toward the door.

She laughed with delight. "I'd love the inside scoop!"

Compiled from the Harvester Task Force
Archives — December, 2000

The Tolin/Peters Case resulted in the dismissal of Alexander McDonald. This third change in leadership in three years resulted in Paul Demerov's appointment as Special Agent in Charge of the Harvester Task Force. In response to complaints from public officials in the greater Washington area, concerning Demerov's youth and lack of experience, F.B.I. Director Louis Freeh released the following statement. "Paul Demerov's experience with this case and his commitment to apprehending the Harvester are unmatched. Among a string of deplorable failures, his successes and insights have been the sole shining light. The challenges that face us are monumental, our foe is formidable. However, I have complete confidence that under the leadership of Paul Demerov, our task force shall prevail."

Willa Brenham, age 36, became the oldest victim of the Harvester. Her abduction was not reported until her husband returned home from work on November 7, and found her missing from their Manchester, MD home. Although her abduction took place on November 7, her heart wasn't delivered to INOVA Fairfax Hospital in Virginia until 2:00 a.m. on November 10. Forensic analysis on heart tissue indicated her death occurred at approximately 9:00 p.m. on the ninth. This marked the first time that the abduction and murder did not occur within a twenty-four-hour period. It was also the first time the Harvester had struck on a weekday.

CHAPTER 18

Tuesday, May 29, 2001

Heads turned when Ben angrily slapped the frame of the doorway on their way out of the hearing room. The Prince George's County Planning Board had just rejected a proposal to create separate bike lanes along Route 1 into the District. In addition, they had also rejected other proposals that would have made the existing on-road bike lane safer.

"They plaster those 'Share the Road' signs everywhere, but don't do anything that would actually make that road safe enough *to* share. All the injuries that have happened along that stretch, and yet they refuse to spend a few thousand dollars to make it safer. Then, they turn around and approve millions of dollars in road construction that will just continue to make the area's congestion worse. It's insane."

Elsa could do nothing beside provide a sympathetic ear. She'd attended numerous of these hearings throughout the area this spring, and knew that the constant string of defeats was starting to wear on her husband. And she knew that the news he'd gotten from a fellow mass-transit activist earlier that evening could worsen his mood even more in the long run.

Commemorating their first anniversary over the previous weekend had proven to be a wise decision. Although the past year was filled with love and happiness, they would not have felt much like celebrating after this evening's disappointment.

The Inter-County Connector that he worked so hard to stop wouldn't go away, it just would not stay dead. Money that could be used to expand Metro, improve the bus system, and add bike lanes around the region was still being held hostage, so that new life could be breathed into this bad idea. The only plan that ever received enough funding was one that resulted in more and bigger roads... and more congestion.

She understood why he was so infuriated. All the way home, she massaged his tense neck muscles. When they got home, she worked on other muscles; eventually she found the right one and got his mind off work.

⎯⎯⎯⎯

After five months in charge of the Harvester Task Force, Paul Demerov's patience had run out. He stood at the head of the table and checked his watch. The timing had to be perfect.

Blam! His clipboard crashed onto the polished surface, scattering papers, and making the thirteen male and three female agents around the long mahogany conference table jump. Most had laptops, legal pads, and Starbuck's cups setting in front of them. Those closest to the young head of the Harvester Task Force grabbed protectively for their coffee; it had been a long meeting, and now it looked as though it wouldn't end anytime soon.

"Damn it! This crap is going to stop right now!" His fury wasn't faked, and now he didn't have to worry about holding it in. Intensity oozed from every pore as he looked each agent in the eye. Everyone in the room was his senior in both age and time served in the F.B.I.

The meeting had been going on for two hours and progress had been minimal; contributions had come from only three of the agents. The rest had been no better than warm-blooded statues; he knew they were alive only because they occasionally raised a lukewarm coffee to their lips.

"Some of you are waiting for me to fail. You're steamed... you don't think I've earned the right to this position. For my part, I think all of you are competent agents, which is why you are sitting in those chairs. But consider this fair warning, I'll see you assigned to mail fraud in Topeka if you don't start contributing!"

After a perfunctory knock, the conference door opened and all of them leaped to their feet. Paul had known the Director was planning to visit HTF this afternoon and had staged this interruption as carefully as any stake-out. He was a favorite of the Director and after months of resistance to his leadership from elements of the task force, he'd finally decided to play this card.

"Gentlemen... and women! Good afternoon. Please, sit, sit!" The Director waved them down. "I was in the area and thought I'd pop in, and let you know how critical I regard the work you are doing. This bastard needs to be stopped and I know Paul..." He paused and looked carefully around the room with an unspoken threat that caused many a spine to shiver, "... and all of you feel the same. While we are all working toward ending this horrific streak in 2001, I want everyone here to understand that I believe this task force needs consistent leadership, and Paul Demerov will be heading the HTF until that monster is apprehended."

"If any of you aren't up to the effort required, I can see that you are trans-ferred to a more appropriate position."

"I'm sure you can count on all of us," Paul extended his hand and the Director took it in both of his and shook it aggressively.

"I know I can count on you, Paul." His aide opened the door and the F.B.I. Director waved as he strode purposefully from the room.

Demerov turned back and found that the faces around the table had changed. They were all completely and earnestly attentive.

With exaggerated enthusiasm, he rubbed his hands together.

"I believe we were looking for a possible, deeper significance to the period during which the Harvester has been active. Any thoughts?"

Paul smiled as sixteen hands were raised.

"Let's work our way around the table."

The resulting discussion was constructive. Paul thought an important corner had been turned. With a determined eagerness he looked forward to a busy and productive summer.

—⟨⟨⟨⟨⟩⟩⟩⟩—

His instincts were well-honed and warning klaxons blared throughout his nervous system. The dark blue car rolling up the street screamed unmarked law enforcement. As it pulled to the curb at the end of the block, he knocked the hub cap onto the tire and began jacking his car down. He watched the

F.B.I. agent start up the walk toward Flores, who was standing near a realtor's for sale sign in front of the sprawling rancher on the corner lot.

After stowing the jack and flat tire in the trunk, he got in the car. For a few moments, he watched the attractive, raven-haired woman as she spoke with her dark-suited visitor. Then he started the car, and drove slowly past. Turning the corner at the end of the block, he saw Nina pull a small handgun and a piece of paper from her purse.

⎯⎯∾∿∾⎯⎯

"Ma'am, I'm sure that gun makes you feel safer. Two of the Harvester's victims also owned guns and felt safe." Agent Ward watched her put the gun and license back in her purse. He was a rookie assigned to the HTF; part of a new unit that had been unkindly dubbed the 'babysitters' by F.B.I. veterans. Their assignment was two-fold: one- constantly patrol their assigned area and warn any at-risk women they spot; two- use their imagination and training to develop scenarios under which those same women could be taken against their will.

He was constantly amazed that, with sixteen women already killed by the Harvester, there were still so many willing to be out on the streets alone.

"I sell real estate in a very competitive market. Showing houses is something I must do to make a living. I shoot at a range twice a week; believe me, Agent Ward, that asshole messes with me, I'll blow his effing head off." Nina Flores tossed her head fiercely and glared.

Ward couldn't believe how stubborn people could be. In these cases, he felt compelled to demonstrate that such confidence was a mistake.

"I can see you're well protected." He gestured toward the house. "How long has this been on the market?"

The saleswoman's eyes lit up. "Only a few weeks... Are you looking for a house?

"My wife and I are expecting, and our apartment is so small. I probably shouldn't be doing this while I'm on duty, but could we take a quick look?"

"Oh, absolutely! It would be a beautiful starter home." She pulled the house keys out of her purse as she walked briskly up the sidewalk.

Opening the door, she led Agent Ward into the house. He followed closely and slammed the door shut at the same moment he ripped the purse from her hand. She screamed and tried to run from the room, but he forced her into a corner.

"Calm down, ma'am." Ward held up his hands. "I need to make several very important points that I hope will save your life."

After she stopped screaming and looked warily in his direction, he continued.

"First... You didn't ask for I.D., *always* ask for I.D. and then confirm that it is legitimate. Second... Every victim of the Harvester has been alone. You should find someone to accompany you when you are showing houses. Third... Even though it is only August, you shouldn't stake your life on the Harvester keeping to an arbitrary schedule. Fourth... that gun is only useful if it is in your hand... and that probably wouldn't be good for sales."

Then he left the house, hanging her purse on the door handle on his way out.

Ward had just reached his car when he heard Flores calling from the door...

"Does this mean you aren't interested in the house?"

⸺◦⸺

That self-conscious 'my slip must be showing' sensation had caught hold of Carla again. She brushed her hand down her soft, cotton skirt and then moved forward in the checkout line.

It was silly, but she was certain someone was watching her.

That damn Stop the Harvester campaign had turned every one of her friends paranoid, and now she'd caught the bug, too. She felt stupid, but looked around the store. She didn't find any prying eyes, but she didn't feel stupid anymore. Every other woman in sight was doing the same thing.

The ride home wasn't comfortable either. Twice she turned the radio to avoid one of the 'YOUR safety is in YOUR hands' public service ads. After it started up on a third station, she gave up.

When the landscaper arrived at the house a half-hour after she got home, she was mad at herself for being suspicious of that. Then the same feeling she'd had at the mall hit her while she was sitting at the kitchen table... except it felt more like 'there's an axe murderer waiting behind the door'.

She wandered through the house to the living room window, and watched the man who'd done their yard work all summer with a nervousness she knew was irrational. He'd done a wonderful job. Charlie wanted to use him on the weekends during the fall. And her husband wasn't one who trusted easily.

Carla couldn't help the way she felt. The man was too neat; too reliable; he looked honest and trustworthy; just the type who would be successful killing women for all these years.

Charlie would just have to do the work himself.

—⠐⠐⠐⠐⠐⠐—

"No problem," he said. "I think I over-booked myself anyway. At least I've got things in pretty good shape for you. Shouldn't be too hard to keep the yard looking nice this fall."

"I'm sorry," Charlie said. "My wife's gotten squirrely... must be Harvest season, huh?"

"Tell me about," he said. "They're all getting squirrely."

The Harvester kept a smile on his face as he loaded the wheelbarrow on his pick-up. After he drove away, it became a grimace. He'd worked long and hard to develop that target. The HTF was really becoming a pain in the ass.

—⠐⠐⠐⠐⠐⠐—

The look of pent-up desire and frustration on Ben's face was adorable, and Elsa couldn't help but laugh. She'd suspected his plan from the start and knew it had little chance of success.

They were standing atop Medicine Bow Peak. Although it was August, they were being buffeted by a stiff, cold wind. Despite the conditions, a number of other climbers had made the trek; some were arriving, some leaving... which was the source of Ben's angst. He'd had hopes of joining the 'mile-high club' here at the summit of Medicine Bow.

She wrapped her arms around him and kissed his cheek.

"We're still young. The mountain isn't going anywhere. Let's go someplace where you can warm me up without getting arrested."

Instead of making the long drive back to Bran's ranch house, they got a room at the Old Corral Hotel in the historic town of Centennial.

Elsa was warmed up sooner than expected.

The afterglow was delicious and she lay in the hotel bed, thinking of the unrelentingly wonderful summer that was nearing an end. Every weekend had been an adventure.

On their hike in the Blue Ridge mountains of North Carolina, they'd climbed through fragrant pine forests and stood atop the same peak used in *The Last of the Mohicans*. As the moisture rose from the surrounding valleys, the distant mountaintops became islands of green in a misty white ocean.

They had picnics beside cascading waterfalls that reminded Elsa of Cunningham Falls State Park; frequent bike rides and runs along the C&O, and a trip to the beach at Stone Harbor, New Jersey.

On the sandy ocean shore, Elsa learned to truly relax as she lay on a beach towel with a good read and soaked in the warm sun. When the humid heat finally got the best of her, she would race into the ocean with Ben at her side. They would float, hand-in-hand, in the salty water, and then body-surf the surging waves into shore. As they crashed around her, thundering in her ears, Elsa felt nature's power and wondered if it was as strong as the love she felt for Ben.

Then she would lay back down on the beach, take up her book and start the process all over again.

Now they were vacationing in southeast Wyoming and she was showing Ben the mountains, canyons and prairie that she loved. Bran accompanied them at times; he was still hardy for a ninety-five-year-old. But he didn't do much climbing anymore, so it was Elsa who led the way into 'Lion' canyon. They sat in a shady niche on the mountainside and watched through Bran's binoculars, as the regal feline that she had once confronted trained her latest litter of cubs in the fine art of stalking.

She hugged herself and smiled at all the wonderful memories she and Ben had created. Those treasured scenes had begun to crowd out many of her unpleasant memories of the Harvester. Autumn was no longer a time to be approached with dread.

Fall classes would be starting next week, and Elsa was excited about advancing her knowledge of cosmology and the origins of the universe. She felt like the entire universe was expanding... if only to contain her happiness, which kept growing and growing.

The dark April morning when she'd felt that cold premonition... seen the names Ben and Alicia linked with those of Anne and Martin, her dead parents, was long forgotten.

"Was it that good?" Finished with his shower, Ben walked naked from the bathroom toward the bed with a big grin, rubbing his head vigorously with a towel.

Although a teasing remark was on the tip of her tongue, her emotions were too strong to deliver it. Her exuberant nods and glowing face were more expressive than any words. He jumped across the king size bed and landed with his face on her firm belly. She ran her fingers into his hair.

"I feel as good as you look," He pressed his lips against her soft skin, "and that is too deliciously scrumptious for words."

Kissing his way up to her face, he found it shiny and wet. Her eyes, and then her lips tried to show him how she was feeling, it wasn't enough. She pushed him up so that her hands would have room to express emotions so powerful her voice failed.

She signed, ("My love for you... and the happiness I feel... are too much for my heart or even the universe to hold.") With both hands she pointed to the tears that continued to spill down her cheeks. When he leaned close to kiss those tears away her hands were trapped and she freed her tongue to finish.

"... the rest is leaking out"

—◦◦◦—

Paul's gut told him this was the year... the Harvester was going down.

Cooperation from the media had been excellent. Every manpower request for the Harvester season had been met. They had new procedures in effect that would allow the increased number of Harvester Rapid Response Teams to be on any crime scene in minutes. The 'Babysitters' had been his brainchild, and it was evident they had been effective. During the last week he spent hours cruising the metropolitan area and he had not seen one unaccompanied woman who was even remotely at-risk. Even the lonely grandmothers seemed to have teamed up. He was certain the HTF finally had the upper hand.

The auditorium was filled with motivated agents. They displayed a positive energy never seen at the start of other Harvest seasons. He walked toward the podium and applause built throughout the packed room. The serious look on his face helped quell the outburst.

"I understand where that was coming from, and I do appreciate that we are all feeling good about what has been accomplished this summer. But there will be no celebration, no congratulations, no rest until the Harvester is in on death row."

More than a few eager agents couldn't keep their hands from agreeing, but Paul waved them quiet. He briefly reviewed the summer accomplishments of the HTF, and some of the kidnap scenarios that the 'babysitters' had developed. The scenarios allowed Demerov to establish a number of sting operations using highly-trained female agents as bait. He noted that the increased manpower had allowed them to cover the entire area much better than previous years, but that gaps still remained. Then he lauded the impressive number of agents that had volunteered for unpaid overtime to fill many of those gaps. Applause again started weakly, but then exploded when he joined, instead of waving it down.

He smiled briefly when the applause died down.

"I guess this *is* supposed to be a motivational speech. And all of you deserve to be acknowledged for the great work you've done so far." He waited out another wave of applause.

"Starting today we'll have twenty-five percent of the HRRT's on duty around the area. One-hundred percent will be on the ground and ready for action; along with instituting all Harvester procedures on Tuesday, September 11…"

CHAPTER 19

Tuesday, September 11, 2001

H er Tuesday classes didn't start until eleven, so Elsa used the crisp, clear morning to get in an extra long run. Because it was Harvest season, she hadn't seen another unaccompanied female during any of her runs lately; which was what she wanted. If she was the only target, some day her path, and that of the Harvester, would cross.

She'd starting taking along her cell phone at Ben's insistence but hadn't used it once, so she was startled when her Brazilian Samba ringtone began trilling. Easing up on her pace, she pushed the receive button.

"Good morning," she said brightly.

"Elsa, its Alicia…"

"Hey Alicia! I'm out on my run…

"Elsa, listen! I knew you had your phone… You were the first person I could think of. I can't get hold of my parents, so I need you to give them a message."

She doesn't sound good, Elsa thought.

"Of course, Alicia. I'm sure everything's…"

"I love you Elsa, but please just shut up and listen!" The fear and desperation in Alicia's voice stopped Elsa in her tracks.

"The plane I'm on has been hijacked. We've heard that other planes have crashed into the World Trade Center in New York and maybe the Pentagon."

To Elsa the sky seemed suddenly darker, the air thicker. There was a stillness... as if the entire planet was holding its breath.

"People on the plane think the hijackers are going to crash us into the Capitol or the White House. Elsa ... my Dad works at the Capitol!" There was a pause; Elsa could hear frightened voices in the background.

"Alicia what..."

"Elsa, a group of us are going to try and take the plane back. And I think a Navy fighter is shadowing us. I'm sure they'll shoot the plane down before we get anywhere close to Washington... I hope they do."

"Oh God! Alicia..."

Alicia was sobbing into the phone. "S-s-say goodbye to my Mom and Dad for me, tell them how... much I love them... I'm sorry I can't hug them one more time. Let them know that I'm not scared and... that I'll die fighting."

"I love you Alicia!" Elsa cried desperately, "you were always the toughest..."

"We're going now, Elsa." A calmness and strength grew in her voice that contrasted with the rising clamor in the plane. "I love you, too. Tell them... be brave."

"I will... I promise." The phone went dead, slipped from her hand and broke apart on the concrete. Her legs slowly gave way until she was sitting cross-legged on the ground. The world had turned grey, ugly and threatening.

Irrational fear broke upon her, along with a memory of four empty slots. She jumped to her feet and started to run.

Ben worked downtown...

Paul fought against the awful, mind-numbing depression that threatened to make him useless. The fact that everyone faced the same burden didn't make the fight any easier.

Twenty people... that was all they could leave him. All the group heads... senior agents... HTF was gutted. Even the twenty that were still with him wanted to be hunting down al-Qaida; as did he.

Twenty wasn't nearly enough. It was ludicrous. He wasn't bitter toward his superiors; the task facing the F.B.I. now dwarfed anything in its history. But it didn't help him deal with the knowledge that the Harvester had been within his grasp. It was now likely he would kill again with little risk of Paul being able to prevent it.

Friday, September 14, 2001

The housing market and real estate agents everywhere would be taking a big hit in the coming weeks and months. That was what all the insiders were saying. Who wanted to think about buying houses when the stock market had been closed all week, and was expected to crash when it finally did open on Monday?

When the call came in, Nina Flores was grateful for the possible sale. But Agent Ward had put a good and lasting scare into her. She got a call back number and then arranged for Tim Cowry, the lone male agent in the office, to go with her when she met the prospective buyer on Saturday. The return call was picked up immediately, easing her mind. She didn't think mass murderers normally gave out their phone numbers. Nina had her pick of male companions; Tim had been fun on the couple of times they'd dated. Maybe if she got an offer, they could celebrate by christening the plush carpeted floor of the den... or maybe the kitchen counter, if Tim was feeling kinky.

As she left work, Nina smiled for the first time since Tuesday morning. With a possible sale tomorrow and vacation starting Monday, things were really looking up.

Ben's hand was a lifeline that kept her strong and Elsa held on fiercely. She had hardly let go since that terrible day when she'd struggled home to find him waiting anxiously at the door of their apartment. Sent home early, he'd placed call after call to the cell phone that lay broken and forgotten miles away. Like the rest of America, they had spent the rest of that chilling day watching the planes hit the tower again and again and again.

It had been a long and emotionally exhausting day. And today had been another. They were looking forward to reaching home. Although Elsa had been able to relay Alicia's last words to her parents by phone, they had been stranded in Kansas City by the ban on airline flights immediately after 9/11, and only arrived back in town this morning. She and Ben had spent the day in mourning and remembrance with them. The awful reality that a funeral might be weeks or months away had not made the day any easier.

Alicia's phone call still haunted her, and reliving it for her parent's had been an excruciating but necessary experience. Moving beyond fear and sorrow would take time; getting past the anger even longer. The process had started and, with Ben at her side, Elsa knew that she would get through this.

—◆—

He was certain that Nina was pleased with the showing so far. All the right questions had been asked and satisfactory answers given. Her delicious curves were easy to follow from room to room. They were in the kitchen now, checking the appliances.

"The refrigerator doesn't seem to be working," he said. "That's strange, neither is the microwave."

"It's probably just a breaker," said Cowry, who volunteered to run down to the basement to check. His moment presented itself exactly as planned.

The spray hit her beautifully-surprised face moments after Tim disappeared down the stairs. One hand over her mouth kept a weak cry from escaping, and a strong arm behind her back lowered her gently to the floor. After retrieving the gun with which Nina had spent so many long hours target shooting, he slipped the beautiful silver scarf (so sexy with her jet black hair) from around her neck and walked toward the steps.

"No , that's not it," he called, and wrapped the scarf around the gun as he walked down the steps. "Let me see if I can help."

Tim Cowry stood in front of the breaker panel looking clueless. Clueless became frightened when he turned and saw the barrel of a gun wrapped in silver silk in front of his face. The first shot assured that Tim wouldn't get the chance to christen the kitchen counter. There was little splatter from the tiny hole between Tim's shocked eyes - or any of the other holes that resulted from the gun being emptied into Tim's head for that matter.

He removed Tim's car keys from his pants pocket, turned off the light, closed the utility room door, and returned to the kitchen. From Nina's purse he obtained her keys and took one of the remotes from the kitchen counter, went to the garage, opened the overhead door, and brought both cars in before closing it again.

After Nina was safely ensconced in the trunk of her car, he clicked the remote and exited the garage. As he watched it close, he considered how smoothly everything had gone.

No one would think to report Tim Cowry missing until Monday morning at the earliest. He was young and actively single, so it could be much longer. The decimated Harvester Task Force wouldn't care about a male missing person report, anyway.

Backing out of the driveway, he thought that Nina was lucky. She was about to go on a vacation that would last the rest of her life.

———————

Monday, September 24, 2001

At sixteen minutes and fifty-nine seconds after eight o'clock on Monday morning… for one brief moment, Ben thought he would survive; then the driver swerved further and clipped his front tire. While he was airborne, and before he was pinned between the careening vehicles, he was surprised by how much time he had for regret. He regretted that the greedy, short-sighted jerks that controlled the purse strings hadn't seen fit to make this road safer for cyclists. Then he regretted that he hadn't ridden the bus this morning. Near the end, he regretted not giving Elsa one more, no… three, no… a thousand more kisses before they'd parted this morning. Finally, he deeply regretted the pain his death was about to cause her.

———————

The mysterious empathy that had existed between a young Elsa and her mother was something that twenty-two-old Elsa had never expected to experience again. But, with each passing day since she had met Ben, a tenuous connection had grown into a palpable reality. At first she resisted; denying the strengthening bond, afraid that it would end in the same, soul-crushing manner. In the end, she was wrong.

It was much worse.

Elsa's world shattered on Monday, September 24, 2001. The scream that marked that shattering came shortly after the start of her Condensed Matter,

Physics 385 class. Her shocked classmates did not notice that the scream was attempting to fill a black hole which, at that moment, consumed her entire life.

By the time Elsa's cell phone rang, and the ER nurse pulled it from the jacket lying on the end of the hospital bed, Elsa had been at the University Health Center for twenty-three minutes. The emergency contact number in her purse, which was her husband's cell phone number, had gone unanswered. The nurse was surprised when she answered the phone to find another nurse on the other end of the line. After the initial confusion, the nurses were unnerved to discover the news that each had to deliver. According to her professor, Elsa Kendrick cried out and went into a catatonic shock at 8:17 a.m. According to EMT's on the scene, Elsa's husband, Ben Kendrick was killed instantly when he was crushed between a dump truck and a pick-up. Time of death was set at 8:17 a.m.

———

Before Bran maneuvered his walker into the hospital room, the attending physician explained to him that Elsa had been unresponsive for fifty-three hours. There were no indications that her catatonic state was the result of any physical causes. Unless there was a change in her condition, they said, she would be transferred to a more appropriate, mental health facility before the end of the day.

As soon as he saw her laying there, her ferocious spirit broken, his eyes began to blur. When he got to the foot of the bed, he saw that tears were falling down her cheeks as well. Her hand lifted slowly from the bed and Bran moved to her side. He brought Elsa's hand to lips and kissed it softly.

"Oh honey," he said, "How can life be so cruel? I'm so sorry."

"Bran," her voice was weak and lifeless, "Bran… I can't stay in this life without him."

"I know how much you hurt, Elsa." Bran squeezed her hand and held to his chest. "Be brave. What choice does any of us have but to go on?"

Be brave. Those were Alicia's last words. Elsa hadn't been sure if they were meant for her or Alicia's parents.

I don't want to be brave, I just want to stop hurting.

———

Compiled from the Harvester Task Force Archives — November, 2001

On Saturday, September 22, 2001, real estate agent Tim Cowry's body was discovered by a prospective buyer at the house in which Cowry had been murdered the week before. The F.B.I. was not involved with the investigation until it was determined that Cowry had last been seen accompanying Nina Flores. The lack of manpower caused by the 9/11 attacks resulted in a slower investigation once the HTF entered the picture. Neither person had been reported missing. Cowry's history of unreliability had led ETS Real Estate to begin dismissal proceedings the previous week. Flores, a single woman, was not due back from vacation until Monday, September 24.

Flores was initially considered a suspect due to reports of a previous relationship between the two, and the fact that her gun was the murder weapon. This situation caused significant conflict between the Howard County Police, who considered Flores a suspect in the Cowry murder, and the F.B.I./HTF which considered Flores a potential Harvester victim.

The conflict was not resolved until Flores' heart was left in the customary Styrofoam container on the doorstep of a heart disease patient on the donor list.

PART IV

Coming Back

Pretending to be a sixty-year-old sitting on a bench should be simple. After all, he was sixty... and he was sitting at a bus stop along Viers Mill Road. But he was also in the kind of physical condition that would make most thirty-five-year-olds jealous. And he was having trouble controlling his excitement.

She was coming up the Rock Creek Trail toward him. Taking a chance like this wasn't like him. One more look in her face before he took her... that was all he wanted.

He stood and moved to the edge of the enclosure. She would cross the road right in front of him.

Timing was everything if she wanted to cross without breaking stride, so her eyes were on the traffic. At the last minute, the cold malignance from the man at the bus stop distracted her. She didn't see his face as she flashed by, but could feel his eyes on her.

Stuttering her steps at the last minute, she avoided the dump truck speeding down the road. The windy backwash buffeted her face.

It was a pale imitation of the Wyoming wind that whistled through her mind.

CHAPTER 20

Thursday, March 6, 2003

Elsa struggled north into the teeth of the cold Wyoming wind. It was an extended, continuous resistance workout that was slowly turning her muscles to jelly. She could only endure the bitter wind because of the layers of Under Armour winter gear, face mask, ski goggles, and thick mittens.

The only reason she *chose* to continuing fighting into the wind was simple; the effort took her mind away from darker things. Besides, the longer she ran into the wind, the longer she would be able to fly before it once she turned around.

The wind blew the crown of the dirt road free of snow, while filling and leveling the deep swales on each side. Scattered across the wind-swept prairie on each side of the road were oblong, aerodynamic masses of snow that developed in the lee of larger rocks and small shrubs. Behind her head and shoulders, and in the small of her back, piles of white had collected, snowflakes hiding from the incessant force.

There was nowhere for Elsa to hide, so she struggled on.

Struggling against the way of the world had become second nature for Elsa. For a while, during the bitter year and a half since Ben's death, she'd considered not going on. Having all that happiness only to see it ripped away had left her hollow and knocked off her path.

But the Harvester was still out there. Somehow Elsa knew that only she could remove that menace. The existence of that maniac shadowed her entire life. She'd become cold and hard. Deep inside, Elsa felt that only by killing the Harvester, would she be able to reclaim her life.

Only she couldn't decide if it was a life she wished to reclaim.

Then, she had dreamed of what her father had told the State Trooper so long ago.

"I've been trying to teach my daughter that, when you see something wrong, you should try to fix it. When you see someone doing wrong, you can't ignore it."

Martin Danforth had raised his daughter well. An avenger with the heart of a lion was needed. Bringing Hell's retribution down on the head of the Harvester would become her life's work.

Feeling as though the wind had been defied long enough, Elsa finally circled about. The winter sun was low and orange in the southern sky. She let the wind push her; an earth-bound kite. The fierce thrill of so much natural speed was the closest she could come to feeling like a pronghorn racing across the prairie. It became easier, with every day that went by, to let the power that running once brought... emerge again.

Elsa knew that this run had been a turning point for her. Though the life ahead of her was still bleak and dark, at least it had purpose.

⸻◦⸻

When Elsa came back to him, Bran felt his his heart lifted. First, he was simply relieved that she had returned. He had worried that she might not come back at all. Second, his more profound relief was a result of the spark of determination that once again was alight in her eyes; that spark had been missing for so very long.

⸻◦⸻

Saturday, October 18, 2003

"Goodnight dear," a protective Mrs. Whitman said, "thanks for checking in."

For almost two months, ever since she'd chosen to move away from home and closer to campus, her nightly conversations with her mother had ended the same. If her roommate hadn't dropped out last week, life would have been a lot easier... and safer.

Hanging up the phone, Tara wondered when her mother would stop thanking her for doing what any sane single woman her age would do, especially at this time of year.

When it came to the Harvester, Tara was serious about safety. She was one of the campus volunteers that led 'Staying Safe' seminars for incoming female freshmen. Her apartment came with an alarm system and her parents had paid for steel reinforced doors, both for the entrance *and* her bedroom. She *always* checked in, never went anywhere alone.

A lot of her classmates worried more, but did less than Tara to make themselves safe. The nervous conditions and sleeplessness during Harvest season had become a named disorder, Harvest Stress Syndrome.

Tara was not a victim of HSS. She did everything possible to be safe and slept just fine.

He'd come to enjoy her soft, almost melodic snore. To be honest... it turned him on; a recording of it would become part of his permanent collection. With a twist of the knob on the canister at his side, he sent an odorless mist through the wall and into her bedroom, making sure that she would stay asleep... and snoring... for a long time.

―――∽⊶⊷∾―――

Sunday, December 28, 2003

The screeching yowl of the female mountain lion echoed from the rugged canyon, and the herd of pronghorn lifted their heads in unison. First one, then more, soon all of them began trotting away from the mountains. They left a wide path of trampled snow and prairie grass in their wake, as they ran from the potential threat; soon they blended into fields dappled in white and brown.

Although the cat was miles away, Bran and Elsa turned toward the sound.

"Bit early for your lion to be going into heat," he said. The young mother lion Elsa had confronted when she was thirteen had become 'hers' in Bran's mind.

"Must be thirteen, fourteen years old now," he said, "won't be makin' that sound too many more years. Huh! I recollect that's how old you were when you met that lion."

"That's right, Bran." With sad eyes, Elsa studied his deeply lined and leathery face. "Did you know lion in Finnish is Leijona?"

"LAYo.. na." Bran pronounced the name slowly. "That's a mighty pretty name for such a ferocious animal. Where'd ya come up with that?"

"It's the name I'm going to use when I go back east."

Elsa hadn't forgotten the two men she'd killed… or what Ben had said about the possibility of prison. Her hunting and killing of the Harvester would be outside of the law. Using an alternate identity held out the hope that she might be able to have a life after the deed was done; if she wanted one.

Bran dropped his head and tried hard to hide his disappointment. He knew her mind was made up… he even understood why she was doing it. 'Vengeance is mine; I will repay, sayeth the Lord.' That was all well and good. But Elsa had waited almost her whole life for the Lord to take vengeance on that monster, the Harvester. Nineteen victims that evil man had claimed.

Elsa wasn't waiting any more.

He'd miss her, but Bran had lived alone for most of his long life. Something inside told him she'd come back to him before the end.

CHAPTER 21

Thursday, January 1, 2004

H e can feel it among the shadows… almost see it. Moving quickly between murky buildings, he searches in a frenzy. His vision, which is failing him, reveals *everything* in tenebrous outline. Turning one way, then another… he strains to find the clue. It is right there… need to get a little closer. Rushing ahead he reaches out and grabs it… can touch it with his fingers, turning it over and over in his hands. It is soft and silky and right in front of his face… but he can't see it. What is it? Damn it! WHAT IS IT? Whatever it is, it emits an increasing brightness that disperses the shadows and blinds him. Then it screeches and explodes.

Demerov's head jerked abruptly off the table. Frustration from his dream mixed with that from his waking life and made him growl. It was already fading, the dream, but something was there, and he could feel it. Sirens, car horns, and fireworks celebrated the New Year on the streets of Washington, D.C. With a tired push of both hands, he forced himself to stand on stiff legs, leaning on the folding table laden with files and charts.

The open file that had been his pillow was an exhaustive account of the last three months of the Harvester's nineteenth victim, a young blonde coed at Montgomery College. It attempted to recreate, day by day, hour by hour, every step she took: each conversation over a cup of coffee; every guilty donut during a late night study session. It was filled with long, boring summer class hours, hallway kisses, lab experiments, and sexual experiments - every summer sunset, starry night, bleary-eyed dawn that Tara Whitman experienced until she was murdered on Saturday, October 18, 2003.

It was assembled by a special team of agents that became retroactive stalkers. Any moments they could not rebuild from interviews, class attendance records, security camera footage, and other physical evidence; they created with clearly noted conjecture and imagination.

Paul had spent countless hours with the thick file. It had begun to influence his dreams.

Closing the file, he walked unsteadily past his cluttered office desk to the door and turned off the lights. The room became a maze of conflicting shadows. City light leaked through the blinds on the windows, and the glow of exit signs and night lights from the open area behind his door filtered through the shades of the window wall. For a moment, he considered going home to his bed. Instead, he lay down on the couch near the door.

The dream returned almost before his head hit the pillow. He was again racing shadows, *through* shadows, between shadows. Chasing, yearning for something beyond his reach; he stumbled among dark buildings... it was around the next corner, he was sure!

Shifting on the couch, Paul woke briefly, distressed that he was missing something important hiding in his dream. He buried his head in the pillow and dove back into the shadows.

When Paul turned the corner, it was waiting in the soupy miasma just ahead; his arms wrapped around... something that sucked him in and trapped him. Evil was very close, and it chased away the shadows. His nightmare was clear and bright.

He was in a colorful open space surrounded by modern office buildings; visionary structures of glass and steel; stark lines of black and white pacified by shades of gray. Planters with fresh pansies in deep purple, yellow, and blue were divided by slashes of red and white mums. Stone benches were dispersed throughout the plaza.

Moving easily, he wandered about until he was in front of a three-story glass building with a massive concrete awning that extended from the first floor. The walkway created by the awning was separated from the plaza by long narrow planters filled with trees and shrubbery.

Sitting patiently on a bench, he could sense that what he wanted was approaching. There were brief, teasing glimpses in the gaps between the planters; his heart fluttered in anticipation and dread.

Then she emerged from the shadows walking toward him; tall, with a lithe body that moved with such sensual grace... it filled him with an aching, terrible need. There was something familiar about her narrow face. When she brushed past, a charge of energy pulled him along behind. Her red hair was layered and short; he eased closer and wanted to run his fingers through it. As she walked confidently across the breezy, sun-drenched plaza, her thin cotton blouse and khaki shorts dissolved and drifted away.

The sight of her firm bare ass and long trim legs made him hard. He surged ahead, turned and waited for her. The answer he was searching for was right behind his eyes, the name of the evil was on his lips, but her body was all he could see; her perfect breasts, the smooth creamy skin of her belly, so much more pleasure waiting for him. A throbbing urgency pushed him forward. He floated against her, and then surrounded and ravished that tempting body.

Without warning, her angelic face filled his sight. The radiant smile that rested easily on her lips became a rictus of death. Her glittering hazel eyes burned to black, and were swept from their sockets by a howling wind. Then flames blazed from empty holes and ate away the delicate skin of her face, leaving only a grinning skull. The fire spread, consuming all the beauty that this unknown, blameless creature had shared with the world.

He woke, horrified and disgusted by the stiffness between his legs. Soaked in stale sweat, he sat up on the couch and massaged his pulsing forehead. If wallowing in the filth of this killer's mind was the cost he must pay to catch him, Paul would reluctantly do his duty. He only hoped that he could keep his sanity long enough to see the Harvester behind bars.

—∈∏⌠∭—

Tuesday, February 24, 2004

The committee report provided exactly the results Paul expected. He had 'primed the pump' in such a way that any other result would have been disappointing. The Historical Harvester Record Committee had been formed to review the Task Force Archives for insights into the criminal's identity based on twenty years of activity.

After an expeditious two weeks, the committee delivered the draft report; now it was lying on his surprisingly clean desk. In the past, that desk had always been cluttered with files, notes and other items related to the investigation. The customarily over-burdened folding table was similarly clean; the mountains of evidence files which would normally fill it had been relocated to the committee's file room. Even the large whiteboard had been wiped clean. All because of a report whose contents he could have recorded in the first minute after he'd woken up from 'the dream'.

It was the dream that had become a regular part of his irregular sleep; wandering a shadowy urban landscape desperately pursuing a tantalizing clue that was just out of reach. The dream shifts, and he is stalking the red-headed girl. Only this time he wandered along the outskirts of the plaza, beside the modern glass and steel buildings.

Glancing movement in the corner of his eye made him turn to the left; he saw his reflection in the mirrored glass. He turned and walked close to the glass, studying the man that certainly didn't look like Paul Demerov, F.B.I. Agent.

Wire-rimmed glasses, gray goatee, messy salt and pepper hair that grew over his ears and the collar of his tweed sport coat with leather elbow patches. Blue jeans and running shoes completed the ensemble.

This was Paul Demerov, college professor. The flash of recognition woke him from the dream, and for the first time in months, spared him the nightmare ending. But he couldn't go to his superiors and explain that he was about to commit substantial F.B.I. resources in the pursuit of a dream. So the HHRC was formed.

—◦◦◦—

"In retrospect, perhaps this possibility should have been considered at an earlier date. The Columbus Day 1986 murder of Gloria Strenfield, combined with the fact that all the remaining murders prior to 2000 had been committed on Saturdays or Sundays, were one clue; the meticulous and well-thought methods, another. Because of the technical nature of the surgeries he has performed, the Harvester has always been assumed to be a highly-skilled person."

"The experience of our 'stalker team' demonstrated that an enormous amount of time was required to develop the information used by the Harvester. Someone who had an entire summer free to stalk potential victims fits that requirement. And finally, serial murderers commonly select victims from their own socio-economic group. Two of the victims were college students; all of the others were college graduates."

Paul paused and took a drink of water. He sensed a confidence in the room that he hadn't felt in several years. For the first time he would be sending men out to search for a suspect that was more than just a shadow.

"Willa Brenham's murder on Election Day, 2000, along with the fact that she was herself, a college professor, has led us to the hypothesis that the Harvester is a college professor. You will be examining the employment records for every post-secondary institution in the greater Washington area.

"We will assemble a list of potential suspects; males age 35 – 65, to interview. Initially you will be examining their files with the intention of finding information that would definitively exclude them from suspicion. Be thorough. Make this the year we put the Harvester behind bars."

CHAPTER 22

Monday, May 17 , 2004

As Leijona West landed at Baltimore-Washington International Airport, she was relieved her long trip was over. Elsa Kendrick had started in Wyoming as a long-haired blonde with a single, easily forged birth certificate, and now Leijona arrived in Maryland with a short, red 'Jane Fonda' haircut and a portfolio of legitimate IDs and documents.

One more stop and her new identity would be rock solid.

⸺⸻⸺

"Can I help you?" a frazzled voice asked.

Leijona stepped up to the counter and looked over to the harried clerk sitting in front of the computer screen. "I need to apply for a social security card," she said.

"I'm sorry, but you've waited through the wrong line," he said patiently. "Name changes or replacement cards go to windows seven through fifteen."

"This will be my first card; I've never been issued one before." The surprise on the man's face was expected, and Elsa began explaining before the clerk could ask. As she spoke she passed him the appropriate documents that supported her story.

"I know this is an unusual circumstance. My name is Leijona West. My father is a Finnish diplomat, Aanos Westerinen, and my mother was a US. citizen. I was born in the U.S., but my parents took me to Finland shortly after my birth. I have dual citizenship. Although I spent a lot of time in the states when I was young, I was always part of my father's diplomatic party, and I was never employed here. My mother died last year and I've decided to live here, so I know that I'll need a social security card." With that she handed him her completed SS-5 application.

He was impressed. "That's the clearest explanation of a complex situation that I've heard in a long time." Leafing through the pile of cards and papers that had grown on his desk, he grunted as if disappointed. "It looks like everything is in order."

Leijona slipped the clean, new card into her wallet and passed through the revolving doors onto the streets of the Nation's Capitol. She looked out at the cars inching across M Street on New Hampshire Avenue. Men and women dressed for battle in the business and political arenas made their way down the crowded sidewalks.

Among them was a killer who had gone undetected, and unpunished for far too many years. At times, the task she had set for herself was daunting, but that task was all that she had. So many things that made life worth living, had been stolen from her, but she still had this. Bringing down the Harvester and avenging her mother might be a cold, cruel, violent reason for living, but it would be enough, for now.

⊸⊸⊸ஃ⊸⊸⊸

"It is private and has a beautiful view for a first floor unit." The property manager was considering turning the unit into storage space. It had been vacant for almost a year. He was giving the redhead his best sales pitch.

"And the first month... uh, I mean two months... are rent free."

The ground floor apartment of the Bethesda Towers was on the back of the building. It was "cozy and efficient" according to the classified ad; tiny and cramped would be more accurate, Leijona thought. But it had everything she required.

She would have privacy... and it was close to a cluster of locations from which the Harvester had snatched previous victims. Best of all, the apartment was a potential target. Three of the previous victims may have been snatched from their own beds in ground floor apartments.

"I'll take it." Leijona said.

—⟪⟫—

The sliding glass door opened onto a chipped and leaf-strewn concrete patio. Up a slight, grassy rise was the edge of a densely-wooded lot. Backed up to the door was the smallest truck U-Haul had available. Still, she hadn't come close to filling it during her shopping trip at the Goodwill Store in Silver Spring.

The living room, dining room, and kitchen were areas of a single room. Leijona unloaded a frayed couch, coffee table, and a tiny 13-inch television into the living area. A small round table with a single chair went into the dining space.

The bedroom may have been big enough to serve as a walk-in closet for some people, then again... maybe not. There, Leijona assembled the cheap metal bed frame. On it she placed the only new items from the truck, a double-bed mattress and box spring. Then she brought in the nightstand and lamp. In the efficiency kitchen, a box of second-hand kitchenware sat on the counter next to a couple of grocery bags.

A large, laminated map of the D.C. area took up most of the wall in the dining area. A selection of dry-erase and permanent markers lay on the table. Leijona used the red to mark spots where the HTF believed the Harvester had struck. Green traced a route north, then west to the C&O Canal. Then she used the black to plot out her early morning and late evening runs.

Keeping to a rigid, predictable schedule, she would run fourteen different routes each week. This would allow her to cover a wide swath of the Harvester's hunting grounds. They all passed through areas where she would be vulnerable to attack; wooded paths, lightly-used side roads, and dark underpasses.

The Harvester would find her sooner or later.

—⟪⟫—

"If I can only get it right, I know I can save her!" Paul shouted. "Give me more time!"

His HTF team leaders stood shoulder to shoulder around the table, as if at attention. They were watching him as he struggled to assemble a woman's face from the parts on the table. The hair was right, he was sure of that. And... yes! Hazel, the eyes were hazel. The nose was wrong, though. He ripped it off and tossed it aside. He frantically rummaged through the pile of noses on the table, searching for one from his dream.

The clock was ticking; time was running out.

Got it! He shoved the aquiline nose in place. It wrinkled and the eyes on the face widened in alarm. The lips next; no, not that one, a little fuller... natural, no lipstick... that's it! He put them on and they pursed, looking distressed; now there was fear in the bright hazel eyes.

"Tick... tock," one of the agents said. Paul looked up and saw that they were all staring at their watches and shaking their heads in unison. Then they looked at him and pointed at the big Mickey Mouse alarm clock on his desk; it had large silver bells instead of ears. The agent's black shoes tapped out the seconds of time speeding by.

"Teeth," Paul called out, "She was smiling... she needs teeth!" He reached across the scattered noses and flipped the lid off the box marked 'teeth'. He swept rejected eyes, ears and hair styles onto the floor, and upended a pile of teeth that began chattering about the table like party jokes. One set stood out because it wasn't dancing about. The teeth were bright, and strong, and even. Paul snapped it up and shoved it between her lips.

"Yes!"He screamed in victory. "That's her!"

Her eyes widened in alarm when the bells on Mickey Mouse began ringing.

"Help me, Paul" A softly accented voice arose from the assembled face on his desktop. "Please help me."

Then her eyes turned black and started smoking. Her entire face burst into flames and was consumed in an instant, leaving only the skull. The jaws worked open and from between the blackened teeth came the sound of her begging, "Help me, Paul."

CHAPTER 23

September, October 2004

It was the evening of the second Friday in September. Dozens of "Harvester" web sites had popped up over the years. According to most, this was the beginning of the period when 'The Surgeon Ghoul' would strike. 'Get ready for The Heart Reaper!' read the lurid headline on one supermarket tabloid.

Leijona was ready.

She strapped on the hip belt containing what she'd come to think of as her 'Harvester gift pack'. Stepping out her sliding glass door, Leijona remembered the nineteen victims. She was determined that it would not reach twenty.

⸻

The Harvester was eager for the evening's festivities to begin.

She was teasing him. Always alone, following a clockwork routine, using dangerous routes; she wanted him to take her.

Maybe she has a death wish. Or thinks she can beat me.

His black eyes glittered with amusement. Many had thought they were prepared; capable of defending themselves. After Anne, every snatch had been flawless. Tara's strict routine, Brenda's mace, Nina's gun; nothing had helped any of his succulent victims.

The redhead would be no different.

—⊶⊷—

Squealing tires and headlights that cast her shadow down Beach Drive told Leijona she was about to have company. She'd just turned off Georgia Avenue and was heading home. Another Harvester fishing expedition had come up dry.

The silver Buick LeSabre roared by much too close and sped out of sight. Once beyond the curve in the road, silence returned too quickly; like a key had been turned, an engine killed.

A thrill ran up Leijona's spine. She had a nibble on the line.

—⊶⊷—

He cursed as the car pulled to the side of the road. Lights were doused and the engine shut off. When the back door opened, and three shadows slipped out, the Harvester quietly retreated deeper into the trees.

Along the shoulder of the road, the redhead approached. The front doors of the car shot open and two more shadows jumped out.

Click! A flashlight popped on and the redhead stopped in a circle of light, surrounded. Her eyes were low as they swept the darkness around her, and her body swayed like a cobra.

Behind the flashlight, a voice taunted.

"Hey sweet thing, want to party with me and my friends?"

The Harvester clenched his fists. How dare they interrupt his plans?

One moment she was surrounded. The next, she struck toward the light and the darkness was complete. Black forms moved on the road, but the shadows told him nothing.

Sounds told him everything. Thuds, grunts, and brief screams of pain filled the night air.

Then a single, slim shadow bounded away down the road.

He cautiously crept down and moved from body to body. Two of the redhead's assailants were dead; two unconscious. One writhed in pain, moaning; a switchblade was on the ground at his feet. The Harvester picked it up.

"You ruined my evening," he said calmly, without rancor, "do you know that?"

He smiled, jabbed the knife in the young Hispanic's neck and ripped. Then he moved to the closest unconscious body and slit his throat, too. Pausing at the third, he considered the possibility that these guys had saved his life. If she could handle all five of these hoodlums in such a short time, maybe he would have fared no better.

He still wanted her, but he would have to be more prepared before he tried again.

Dropping the knife, he walked away into the dark.

—⏤∪∩⏤—

Paul Demerov was trapped. Not in some shadowy dream, but in a conundrum of his own making.

In June, the Harvester Task Force had received warrants and searched the employment records of all post-secondary institutions in the Washington-Baltimore region. They assembled an initial list of three hundred seventy-seven potential suspects. During July and August, with very discreet investigations, they were able to winnow the original list down to ninety-one.

He felt certain that one of those men was the Harvester. But the others were respected, influential, intelligent professors who would raise a shit-storm of career-destroying magnitude should their hard-earned reputations be tainted in the slightest. The trap was in the fact that he could not eliminate any of the men remaining on the list without a huge risk of both igniting that storm and tipping off the Harvester. Questions of the 'Where were you on the night of...' type had to be asked. That or put round-the-clock surveillance on ninety men who were, to his knowledge, nothing more than blameless citizens whose only crime was of being in the same line of work as a character in his dream.

Having only seventy people to work with was another problem.

Once the HTF had embarked on this course, his leadership team had gotten fully behind it. They were as certain as he that they were on the right track. The last week had been full of late nights brainstorming ideas for advancing the investigation. Narrowing the search by age was the simplest and most logical step. They eliminated twenty-three potential suspects by reducing the age range to forty through sixty from the original thirty-five through sixty-five. There was a slim possibility that the Harvester was among those twenty-three, but that was a chance they were willing to take with Harvest season about to begin.

In his gut, Paul knew it wasn't enough. Using a computer modeling program, they ranked the remaining sixty-seven potential suspects. He had five teams of two agents each, whose job it would be to locate and question these men immediately after a probable Harvester abduction.

With luck, he thought that plan might get them close enough to rattle the bastard into making a mistake. His main concern was that it might not be in time to save the life of the woman in his nightmare.

As Harvest season drew closer, the nightmare had returned with a vengeance. Her face had grown so familiar that he became convinced he had seen her before. His tormenting vision had evolved. Once assembled on the table, and before being burned to bone in front of his eyes, the attractive red head spoke a foreign language while tears rolled down her cheeks and splashed on the table.

In the end, the result was the same, fiery, soul-crushing horror… with words he understood easily.

"Help me, Paul."

The pressure mounted. He had considered going to Arizona during the summer just passed. Women of the type he preferred were becoming harder and harder to find. Stalking his potential victims was becoming more difficult also. Taser and pepper spray sales had gone through the roof. People were wary, wireless security cameras had popped up everywhere, escort stations were established at major malls and shopping centers.

Like day laborers in a 7-11 parking lot, young men of a certain reliable appearance would collect at the centers. When selected by a woman, the escort's fingerprints would be scanned into a computer, ID logged, and a photograph taken with the client. All this was meant to provide a level of comfort for the women.

And the one woman that he'd thought would be an easy target had turned out to be Wonder Woman. Damn.

Oh, he would harvest her heart, no doubt; but not this year.

For the first time, he selected a victim from outside his normal sphere. She was also more 'exotic' than his usual choices, but in the end, he decided that was a good thing. His twisted imagination had developed some interesting variations to the normal pre-harvest fun.

CHAPTER 24

Sunday, October 3, 2004

L ights were out in the pedestrian underpass that carried the urban trail beneath the MetroRail tracks. When the skeletal addict shambled out of the bushes at the end of the tunnel, she didn't get the thrill that she normally felt when her hunts were fruitful.

He had greasy, long hair, a wicked blade in his shaking hand and a sneer on his pock-marked face; he would have struck fear into the heart of any other woman caught alone with him.

Leijona's reaction held no fear, only disgust and a small amount of pity.

Drugs did this to people, she understood that. Everyone in America who was old enough to purchase drugs, or alcohol and cigarettes for that matter, knew how they could destroy a person's mind, a person's body... and a person's soul. So why would even a fool come within a thousand feet of such poison?

"Gimme ya cash." Although he kept his blood-shot eyes averted, the druggy's head whipped forward, as if he had to throw the words out of his mouth.

Leijona held up her hands and stepped back. "Do you think I have any money on me?" she said. She was wearing a white compression top and black mid-thigh running tights.

For the first time, the dysphoric man looked at his supposed victim. He'd been without a fix for three days. A terrible need filled every pore of his body. He *needed... desperately needed...* something, anything.

"Ya gotta have something!" A high-pitched keening erupted from his throat and he charged.

Leijona dodged and knocked the knife from his hand as he blundered past. The sound of his head cracking against the concrete wall echoed through the tunnel. Rebounding off the wall, he fell back, and hit his head again on the tunnel floor.

Her fingers on his carotid told Leijona he was still alive. If he'd been dead, she wouldn't have felt any guilt, but she couldn't kill him now. The problem was, if she left him here, he would either die… or wake up and attack someone else.

Though he smelled like the remains of a gut-shot pronghorn left rotting on the prairie, she picked up his drug-ravaged body; he barely weighed more than a child.

———

Carlos circled the underground MetroRail lobby. The security guard was glad that service for the night would end soon. Then he could go home and soak his aching feet. Eight hours walking on concrete was brutal. Tunnels led into to the cavernous space from the east and the west. He turned into the eastern tunnel when he heard the echo of a groan.

"Damn druggies and alcoholics!" he muttered. When he got to the bench near the entrance, he jabbed the man lying there with his night stick. "Tony, wake up!" Carlos said. "How many times do I have to say it? You can't sleep in the tunnels!"

Then he noticed the blood pooling on the floor underneath Tony's head.

———

Solo mi suerte.

The bus had been empty for the last four stops. If the next stop had been the same, Hal could have ended the route, gone back to the barn, and then headed home for a well-earned night's rest. But a man was standing there, a steady rain was falling, and there was no missing the pale hand that held the umbrella.

What's a white guy doing in this neighborhood anyway? As the bus rolled to a stop, Hal noticed the dark suit and tie, the bulge under the jacket. When the door didn't open right away, the jacket flapped open just enough. The flash of the badge clipped to the man's belt helped Hal decide. The door opened and the man climbed aboard.

"I thought for a second you weren't going to let me in."

"I wasn't." Hal grinned. "I could've gone back to the yard if you hadn't been standing there. What are you doing out in this mess?"

The bus pulled away from the stop as the rider sat down.

"Chasing a perp. My car is parked up the road." He smiled into the mirror Hal was using to watch him. "You saved me a wet walk back." He glanced at the name plaque above the mirror, "Halcia... what an unusual... and very pretty name."

"Thanks, but everyone just calls me Hal."

"Well... Hal, I appreciate you stopping." he said, "And I just love your accent."

"No problem," she said. "Company policy says I don't have to pick up single males when the bus is empty. But, you know, the rain and all, I guess I have a soft heart. Is that your car up ahead?"

Hal glanced at the umbrella in the cops hand and frowned. What kind of cop would carry an umbrella on a foot chase?

"Yeah, that's mine." The dark blue Crown Victoria looked exactly like a cop car. It was so nice of Jillian to donate it to the cause. The bus pulled to the curb. "Yes, I know you didn't need to stop, Halcia... and I bet your heart is just perfect."

She set the brake and turned in her seat. "Say, why would you... "

The spray caught her in the mouth and nose as she inhaled sharply. Everything went fuzzy in an instant and black a moment later.

He shut off the wipers as he drove through the overhead door of the warehouse. At the center of the mammoth building, he backed the car to the gurney, removed Halcia from the trunk and strapped her in.

Then he pulled forward between Emily's silver Datsun and the white Sprinter. As he got out of the Crown Vic, he looked down a long line of cars, vans, and trucks; the blue and gold SuperShuttle, a yellow taxi, Gloria's vintage red Volkswagen bug and many more.

It's a good thing I have plenty of room. This has become quite a collection.

He made Halcia safe and hurried home to meet the F.B.I.

CHAPTER 25

Monday, October 4, 2004

P rofessor William Rescott, PhD moaned and threw back the covers. The clock on the nightstand read 5:04 a.m. He slipped into his robe and stumbled sleepily down the stairs. The front door of his modest home sounded like it was about to be pounded down.

"Coming! Coming!" He called, then coughed loudly. "Who's there?"

"F.B.I. Professor, this is an emergency, please open up."

Rescott undid the deadbolt and jerked open the door. "Whatever is the matter?"

"We're sorry to bother you, Professor. Do you mind if we come inside a moment?"

The two agents didn't look a bit sorry about dragging a sick man out of bed.

He wrapped the robe tighter and stepped back, pulling the door wider. He waved his arm, "Please do." Then he closed the door behind them and shivered. "I have a miserable cold or something. Don't need that damp air on me."

"We'll try not to take too much of your time. Please understand that you, individually, are under no suspicion. In connection to a lead in the Harvester investigation, we assembled a roster of potential suspects. We aren't at liberty to discuss why you are on this list, but be assured that we, at this time, have no reason to suspect you of this crime. We do not have a warrant."

"All that being said," the agent took a deep breath and got ready for a repeat of the tirade he'd endured just fifteen minutes earlier. "We have two questions to ask, and we would like you to allow us to search your house."

"Good lord!" Rescott said, "Whatever for?"

"There was a suspected Harvester kidnapping last night. We are trying to prevent another murder. You're cooperation will help us to move on to the next name on the list."

"That's awful! Of course, I'll help in whatever way I can." He coughed into his hand.

"Have you left the house since ten o'clock last night?

"Yes, I was grading papers and missed dinner, so I ran out to McDonalds. I am sure if you took a blood test, you'll find I am well over the legal limit for fat and cholesterol." His laugh turned into a hacking cough.

"Were you in the area of University Boulevard and New Hampshire Avenue last night between ten o'clock and midnight?"

"No, that's much too far. I went to the one just down the street on Route One."

The agent looked at his silent partner, who shrugged.

"I guess I'll just have a look around, then, if that is alright with you? My partner has a form for you to sign, granting us your permission to do so."

"No problem." He smiled and pointed toward the kitchen. "I'm about to fix some coffee. Would you gentlemen like some?"

A bit later, Professor Rescott closed the door behind the departing agents. He sniffed, smiled, and went to get his cell phone. He was feeling much better now, but it wouldn't hurt to take some time off. His graduate assistants could handle things for a day... or two.

Paul kept his fists clenched in his lap. He hoped that he could hold all the fury he was feeling in his hands and keep it from showing on his face. His top lieutenants were standing around the desk. The voice of the Director of the F.B.I. was coming from his speaker phone. His fury wasn't because of the call, but what the call was keeping him from; catching the Harvester.

"It was unorthodox to say the least."

The Director wasn't pleased, "A Governor, the U.S. Attorney General, and two Supreme Court Justices have called me this morning. They were asking me if the F.B.I. was out of control. They were asking for your head on a platter. How do you think I answered them?"

"Sir," Paul tried to keep anger from his voice. "I hoped you told them that you had confidence in me, and that I was doing what I thought was right, and within the law, to stop a murderer who has plagued our Nation's Capitol for twenty years." He thought, from the shocked look on his assistant's faces, that he had failed.

The long silence from the phone was another good indication. He heard whispering in the background, and then the Director spoke again.

"That is almost word for word what I did say, Demerov. But you need to know that my schedule doesn't include spending precious time on the phone explaining to powerful people why their friends are being harassed. Your reports should have included plans like this so that we could be prepared. I don't like getting caught with my drawers down, and I don't have time to waste playing catch-up."

"Every detail of the operation that was instituted early this morning is in the reports. And, sir, respectfully, I don't have time to waste explaining things either, not right now."

Paul waited for a 'you're fired' to erupt from the phone. After eleven frustrating years of chasing the Harvester, part of him would welcome the words.

After another extended silence, that part of him was disappointed.

"Point taken. It appears that someone between your level and mine should have gotten this phone call. Before the end of the day, set an appointment with my secretary, so we can resume this conversation."

Paul and his team continued the meeting that the call had interrupted, but the news he wanted to hear wasn't in their reports. They hadn't found Halcia Martinez and, so far, the Harvester had not been pressured into making a mistake. They'd been unable to locate seven of the sixty-seven professors on the high priority list. Of the sixty they had contacted, nineteen had refused to allow a search, including all five law professors. The phone calls that caused the interruption probably came from among those lawyers.

With varying degrees of indignation, forty-one had suffered the intrusion. As instructed, agents had ignored anything in a range of personal offenses. Numerous red-faced intellectuals had breathed a sigh of relief when the F.B.I. left their homes without any mention of the drugs, coeds, or pornography they'd seen.

They could not completely rule out all of the forty-one; some agents had reported that many had seemed nervous and furtive during the searches. But for now they would concentrate on the seven and the nineteen.

⸺⸺⸻⸻⸺⸺

The massive old warehouse had once been an auto manufacturing plant. A smattering of tools and equipment were left behind; he was proud of his ability to reduce, reuse, recycle and repurpose. An elaborate, electrically-powered engine hoist was being reused to support the naked form of Halcia Martinez. Chains had been recycled into satisfactory restraints that attached her to the hoist. And when he was done with his fun… and with the harvesting… her body would be reduced to ashes in the room that had once baked finishes onto cars. He'd long ago modified it to this purpose. A proud smile lit his face.

Repurpose.

Someday I'll have to turn this corded control into a user-friendly remote. The unwieldy box had four joysticks and four buttons. He pushed the second button and maneuvered the corresponding joystick, lowering Halcia until her face was even with his. *Penelope Cruz, her face reminds me of Penelope Cruz. Her nose is too broad… but the eyes and the lips, definitely the lips. I can't wait to see those lips wrapped around…*

"Halcia, dear." He slapped her face gently. "Wake up. Let's get this party started!"

He snapped a glass ampoule under her nose and dropped back as she jerked her head away and looked wildly around. After she had taken in the full extent of her position, she became hysterical, thrashing violently while screaming and cursing in Spanish. He watched in fascination as her breasts bounced like a bizarre, fleshy Newton's cradle.

The arms and legs of the hoist began moving slowly apart as he worked the third set of controls. As the chains became taut, her writhing lessened until her head was all she could move.

He stepped closer and her teeth snapped at him. Moving quickly, he grabbed a handful of silky, black hair and jerked her head up.

"My, that fiery Latin blood is certainly boiling isn't it? So sexy!"

Spit hit his face and he wiped it calmly on his shirt sleeve. Slipping between the chains that held her left arm and leg, he came up behind her. When he reached around and cupped her ample breasts, she jerked and whacked his forehead with the back of her head.

Instead of letting go, he leaned away from her, gripping her nipples and squeezing with all his strength, while her breasts supported the weight of his body. She screeched in agony until he finally stood and released her. He moved in close and grabbed her hair again, jerking her head back, so that his mouth was right by her ear.

"Keep fighting Halcia," he started out whispering in her ear as she moaned softly, "I want you to keep that fire… through everything." He continued for a long time, describing all the activities he had planned. Eventually her moaning stopped, and her teeth gnashed in anger.

"Yes! Keep that anger… All the way to the end when I put you on that table where so many others have lain." He turned her head toward the stainless steel table in the center of the room. "Please, hold on to that fire until…" His last words came out as violent shriek.

"I CUT YOUR HEART OUT!"

———

The TV blinked off, and Leijona slumped on the couch. She was tired and depressed.

Looking around the sparsely furnished apartment, she pictured a day in the future when her hair was graying, her muscles weakening. The apartment would look the same; the news on the TV would be the same. What would her life mean then?

Halcia Martinez was a stranger, but her death hurt almost as much as those of her many loved ones. Though it couldn't match the pain of the many personal losses she had suffered over the years, the Harvester had indirectly severed a piece of Elsa's heart with each victim he had claimed. The cumulative effect was devastating.

In her heart, Leijona knew that she was the one that would someday stop the Harvester.

But how many years could this go on? Tonight, even one more year of hunting the man who'd murdered her mother seemed like too much. She lay down and covered her head. Her weariness carried her off into a restless sleep.

———

Compiled from the Harvester Task Force Archives- July, 2005

The Halcia Martinez case resulted in the largest addition of material to the HTF Archives and the most lawsuits as a result of HTF activities. The lawsuits were combined by the Fifth Circuit Court of Appeals and the case found its way quickly to the Supreme Court, where, on June 23rd, it was decided in favor of the F.B.I. by a vote of 4 – 3. Two justices were forced to recuse themselves after it was revealed that they made phone calls to the Director of the F.B.I. on behalf of two of the plaintiffs.

The unusual circumstances regarding the disposition of the heart of the recent victim resulted in serious consideration being given to this being a copy cat crime.

Early on the morning of Friday, October 8, 2004, a paper bag was delivered to the gate of the Montgomery County Waste Transfer Facility with 'Halcia' written across the top in black magic marker. Inside, a food storage container held the victim's heart. Forensics determined that it had been removed with some type of chopping instrument, such as a meat cleaver or axe. The F.B.I's forensic psychiatric team concluded this was indeed the Harvester; the nature of the delivery location and the condition of the heart were signs of the Harvester's racist nature, and a worsening of the Harvester's murderous proclivities.

PART V

Avenging Angel

Everything was in place, but he checked again anyway, because he was torn between overconfidence and concern. He felt as though he was getting set for a squadron of U.S. Marines to come up the hill, not one woman.

But he had studied her for so long, he knew her to be a formidable adversary. That's why the victory to come would be sweet.

A touch of dawn was visible through the trees as she climbed the dirt trail up the hillside. Running easy, she saved her energy for the battle ahead. Her life had come down to these few moments; beyond them, there was no path for her to follow.

She wiped the sweat from her neck and brushed across the scar. Moving her finger along the three-inch ridge reminded her that the game she was playing was deadly.

CHAPTER 26

Friday, March 25, 2005

Leijona stood on the grass outside her sliding glass door and caught her breath. She'd been running twice a day for almost a year. Usually, she would go hard in the morning, and run easy at night. Once a month, she would take all the runs for an entire week as easy as possible.

She was in the best shape of her life, and some nights, dreamed of what her life would have been like if she'd taken the other path. Her husband on this path had been taken so quickly that a family had never happened. Vengeance for her mother? It was still just a dream.

It wasn't Harvest season, but she stayed alert for threats anyway. Lately, she'd taken to running away, if given the chance. Her body count wasn't as high as the Harvester's, but she was worried that someone would notice that Washington area rapists and muggers were dying at an unusually high rate.

The blackjack dazed her when she stepped into the apartment. A hand clamped over her mouth and a knife was at her throat. Dragged backward into the room, her legs caught on the coffee table and she was slammed down on top of it.

"Hold still and I won't cut your throat."

Leijona knew she was in trouble, but her first clear thought was...

Why do all bad guys have bad breath?

She held her hands up in surrender, keeping them close to her body, and near the hand that held the knife. The shot to her head had missed the sweet spot. Adrenalin drove away the daze, leaving only a lump and a headache. Against the pale light from the patio, she could see a long-haired silhouette leaning toward her. She began lifting her knees toward her chest and the knife dug into her throat.

"I said not to move." The voice was angry... but filled with a jittery excitement.

As Leijona let her legs relax, hands grabbed the hem of her running tights, working them down. She couldn't try anything with the tights around her legs.

When she didn't struggle, the blade eased away from her neck.

"That's it," the one with the knife said. "Be a good girl and this won't be so bad."

"Yeah," said the guy who'd gotten the clingy black fabric passed her knees. "We been keepin' eyes on yo' pretty ass. You is one lonely bitch in need of some lovin'." He stood and laughed, tossing away her tights.

The knife lifted a little more when its owner leaned over for a look at what his partner had uncovered.

Leijona slipped her hand under the one holding the knife. She pushed and it slid along her neck as she spun quickly off the table. When she hit the ground, she kept rolling, and hit the TV stand. She caught the small TV as it fell and threw it at Bad Breath.

Long Hair landed on her before she could get her feet fully underneath her body, she rolled with him head over heels. Pushing with her arms and legs, she sent him flying into the wall.

She jumped to her feet in time to catch the bloody knife before it could reach her stomach. With a spin and a twist, she ran it into the hip of her assailant. Releasing immediately, she stepped back to gain momentum for the violent punch she delivered to the center of his face. When he hit the ground, she leapt into the air and came down with a driving foot on his throat, ending his moans.

Strong arms wrapped around her shoulders and Leijona threw her head back, smashing teeth and loosening Long Hair's hold. Spinning in his arms, she grabbed his shirt, dropped and kicked his legs out.

As he fell on top of her, she let her weight add speed to the fall. At the moment she landed on the floor, his head hit the end of the coffee table. The splat it made was final.

Holding a dishcloth on her neck, Leijona caught her breath. She bandaged the cut and then dressed while considering how lucky she had been. Two inches to the right and the blackjack would have knocked her out. With half a brain between them, they would have had zip ties or cuffs and locked her down good. If the knife had gone one half inch deeper only a call to 911 would have kept her from bleeding to death. There were so many ways this could have been very bad.

Never again could she let her guard down; Harvest season or not.

She found the large piece of plastic in which her mattress had been wrapped and rolled Long Hair's body onto it. Then she dragged it through the woods to a culvert running under the Beltway. After repeating the exercise with Bad Breath, she put on the moccasins Bran had given her and took one more trip. She took a long time returning, covering her tracks as she went. No city detective would find his way to her back door.

—◁◁◁〇▷▷▷—

Watching from the shadows, the Harvester could only admire how cool and decisive this woman was. The noise from the apartment had been muted, but he was sure they'd had the jump on her. Ten minutes later she was carrying the bodies out the door. Amazing!

A victory over a woman such as this would be worth any risk.

—◁◁◁〇▷▷▷—

The shadowy maze of buildings was so familiar, Paul could walk it with his eyes closed; which was a good thing, since he knew he was dreaming. No desperate, manic chasing this time, though. He trudged along reluctantly, driven by routine. Clues that led to a blind alley were all he would find; and a nightmare waiting at the end.

As usual he was stalking the redheaded girl. Again he wandered along the outskirts of the plaza, beside the modern glass and steel buildings; the glancing movement in the corner of his eye that turned his head to the reflection in the mirrored glass. Once again, the image was of Paul Demerov, college professor… tweed coat, goatee, sloppy hair and jeans. He stepped closer to the glass, as did his counterpart. A hand lifted, mimicking his movement.

Paul flinched as the hand waved and his doppelganger began laughing; alternately holding his sides and then pointing his finger at Paul, who watched a wide and mocking grin spread across his reflection's face. Then the image stopped abruptly, waved as if saying 'goodbye', and stepped out of the picture to reveal the redhead standing in his place. Hands on her hips, she was breathing hard as if just completing a long run; the drops of sweat on her lovely face reflected the red of her hair. Long, tightly sculptured legs were bare up to her black compression shorts. Her muscular abdomen was revealed in a band between the shorts and a white, form-fitting compression top with red sweat soaking through between her breasts. Knowing how the dream would end, her sublime beauty was painful for Paul to behold.

With aching regret he reached for her, and his feminine reflection matched the anguished motion. Her lips began moving, but no sound emerged from the glass.

In slow motion her hands moved to the red spot between her breasts. Paul noticed that his hands had done the same, as if he were the reflection. He looked down and heart-clutching fear grabbed him; he was staring down at his rough, male hands clasped between the breasts of a naked feminine body, strapped to a metal table.

He looked back to the mirrored glass and saw the ethereal redhead as she had been, except now her white top was thoroughly stained a deep red. The image was fading, and she reached out with both hands and called mournfully. "Help me, Paul." His arms were frozen to his chest and he could only watch as she vanished.

Paul's head dropped. He saw that a scalpel was now resting between his hands, which still lay nestled between the lovely breasts. Independently, his hands rose, the right used the scalpel to draw a long, bloody line down between her breasts. His jaws were clamped shut in terror, but screams echoed through his mind.

A second scalpel appeared in his left hand. This reached across below her right breast, while the right hand crossed above the left breast. Pushing down, his hands drew the scalpels horizontally…and deeply… across her smooth, unblemished skin. Her life flowed out onto the sidewalk.

The scalpels fell to the blood-stained concrete beneath her feet; his fingers dug into the cut in the middle and began pulling the large flaps of skin back.

Unbearable pain blossomed and magnified his terror. Agony unlocked his jaws and his head jerked upright while he screamed aloud.

Through his torment, he saw the redhead return as a distant image beyond the glass, running powerfully toward him. His screams were echoed and over-laid by more and more terrified voices, until the nightmare was a clamorous, horrific chorus. In the mirrored glass the oncoming form rushed forward, and shattered the window into a rainbow of crystal shards.

The drinking glass, propelled by Paul's flailing arm, disintegrated against the concrete block. He jumped away from the table, knocking back the chair. Clutching his hands to his chest, he fought for each breath; inhaling deep, gasping lungfuls.

Minutes later, he picked up the chair and returned to the table where the Halcia Martinez file lay open. An eight by ten showed her strong, compassionate features and stirred the guilt that lay heavily on his heart. He had not been able to save her, and his dreams continued to be of the mysterious redhead.

What did it mean when the latest version of his dream showed her coming to his rescue?

CHAPTER 27

Saturday, September 17, 2005

A nother Amp Overdrive clanged into the trash can.

I wonder if I can avoid sleep for say... the next two months.

Paul turned to his computer screen and opened the calendar that contained his schedule for this Harvest season. Every slot between 5:00 a.m. and 11:00 p.m. was filled. The new Assistant Director wouldn't allow him to fill the remainder, even though the last thing Paul wanted was sleep. With sleep came dreams that always ended as nightmares.

Howard Zimmer was the type of overseer Paul wished he'd had from the start. Demanding, but realistic; paid attention to the reports he sent and asked short, incisive questions when necessary. He stayed out of the way until Paul asked for something. Mainly, he recognized that there was no one who cared more about getting the job done than Paul.

But he wouldn't let Paul work himself to death; which it certainly looked like he was trying to do.

Stalking his victims during the summer had never been a chore for him; he relished the intellectual challenge of playing cloak and dagger games with the F.B.I. But William had to admit this summer had been very enjoyable, too. Having known his harvest so far in advance had given him free time for other activities. Seattle had been invigorating. The headline 'Is there a new Green River Killer?' had been especially satisfying.

I hope Gary appreciated the renewed attention. Maybe I should visit again next year.

He'd had a year to plan this one. Her predictable Sunday morning routine had saved him much work. Logistically it was a snap.

But he would not be underestimating his prey this time. She was hunting him, and, for the first time in twenty years, he felt challenged. Surprised and out-numbered, she'd killed again, and he'd been a witness. Her instinct, strength, and reflexes were formidable.

But he had three advantages.

Knowing your enemy is the key to victory. All great strategists knew that. After a year of preparation, no one knew Leijona West like he did. Being able to choose the day and time for their meeting was also an important asset.

Best of all, he would pick the battleground. Gettysburg had shown that even a great warrior could be defeated when forced to fight on unfriendly terrain.

He would have the high ground.

———

"What you're telling me, Pablo, is that you stopped to ask some woman for directions, and she attacked you and your home boys?"

Detective Julio Alvarez was a rookie in the Major Crimes division of the Montgomery County Police. He'd been assigned to work on gang-related violence.

When Pablo Cruzon had awoken from a year-long coma, and discovered his brother and three other members of his gang were dead, it took three orderlies to get him strapped to his bed in the secure ward of the state mental hospital in Sykesville.

Once he was calm, he'd demanded the chance to make a police report.

Alvarez was here because he'd drawn the short straw.

Cruzon's jaw was clenched and his eyes tense. He nodded.

Julio checked his notes.

"You lived what, three... four miles away? And you were lost a block off Georgia Avenue?" Julio wasn't buying it. "This looks like a turf battle to me. Your brother's knife was left on your chest. Wasn't that a message?"

"I'm tellin' you, it wasn't gang shit. That redheaded bitch killed 'em!" he yelled, "Puto, Candel, Nando, mi hermano." He sobbed and Julio could see real tears tracking down the macho gang leader's face.

"This all happened a year ago and you can still describe this woman?"

"Como si fuera esta mañana." Like it was this morning.

In this, Cruzon told the truth. To him, it felt like he'd woken on the morning after.

As Cruzon gave Alvarez the description, the young detective's agile mind began to connect a series of seemingly random incidents.

A delirious junky with a cracked skull who'd claimed to have been attacked by a redheaded Amazon; two dead criminals washed out of a culvert, one with a red hair stuck under his fingernail; a higher-than-normal mortality rate among Maryland rapists; and rumors of Bruja Roja... the red witch who busted the heads of boys who didn't behave.

Maybe Cruzon and his posse had stopped on the dark shoulder of Beach Drive asking for trouble, not directions. And they'd found more than they could handle.

Was a redheaded vigilante operating in Montgomery County?

————

Professor William Rescott looked out over his Quantum Physics-401 class. There was a time when a large class would have been ten or twelve students. Thanks to the Hubble Space Telescope, Stephen Hawking, and revolutionary advances in string theory, the class had been moved to the auditorium that was usually used by lower level astronomy classes. It took a high degree of intelligence and determination to pursue a career in this field. He was continually surprised by the number of students who were convinced they had the right stuff. It was likely that only six or eight out of the eighty in the room really did.

He'd lately come to realize that he derived enormous satisfaction from teaching and research. If only the dark side of his nature wasn't so strong. Part of his mind was already focused on this weekend and eager for the class to end.

The clock above his head ticked over to 3:30, and books began to slam shut, interrupting a student. "I'll guess we'll get to that question on Monday," he chuckled, "after all it is Friday and we need to get ready for a big weekend, don't we?"

Several of the guys who would probably drop before the end of the month yelled 'hell, yeah', and started chanting 'party, party' to the amusement of the more studious in the class.

—⚞⚟—

It was a night when every caress of the sheet against her body, as she tossed on the bed, whispered 'feel me'. Air currents from the open window brought scents that wafted through her nostrils calling 'smell me'. Each exquisite note on the piano in Lorie Line's <u>Think of Me</u> that had relaxed her before bed, now echoed through her mind.

Floating, gossamer images accompanied the melody until one special moment caught and held her. Sitting on a high ledge, her body nestled against Ben's warm chest, a thick wool blanket encompassing them both, the setting sun breaking upon distant mountains and fire spreading across the western horizon. The fire burned crimson, then burgundy, growing deeper and darker. The night flowed in; she drifted on the edge of dreams for a time.

A single tear traced down her cheek before heavier sleep took her.

Leijona was struggling up a familiar, wooded hillside. Each step was harder than the one before. A sinister black cloud covered the top of the hill, but she couldn't turn back.

"Let me help." A familiar voice caused her to look up.

A blonde woman ran easily beside her. She looked like a younger version of Elsa and reached out her hand. Leijona took it and felt stronger; the black cloud ahead was less threatening.

"Today's the day," the blonde woman said. "Remember my last words."

A memory that was buried deep slipped into her dream and turned it into a nightmare.

"Don't be afraid. The fear and anger you've carried so long will give you power when you need it most."

The face and the voice joined and hovered in front of her.

Before it faded, she heard it say clearly...

"I love you, Elsa."

CHAPTER 28

Sunday morning, September 18, 2005

She awoke to the sound of her mother's voice echoing through her thoughts. As she prepared for her long run, the conviction grew that Elsa, not Leijona should be the one stepping out her door.

She checked the contents of her hip pack and adjusted her blond wig.

From the moment she stepped through the patio door, and the lamplight stitched her shadow across the grass, memories seemed to emerge from the night air and amble through her mind.

The run became an opus that encompassed her life; sun-splashed frolics on new-mown grass; cool, colorful walks in fall woods; and thrilling races across wide meadows. Mournful images of black suits and dresses, dark holes in the ground... and endless gray nights were followed by reminders of passionate evenings, adventurous days, glorious sunsets... and the love she had been given.

The modified tandem bicycle was leaning against a tree one hundred feet through thick woods from Norbeck Road. A long metal brace extended up from the second seat and would support a woman's body in a riding position. Gloves with Velcro closures, that would secure a woman's hands, were attached to the handles. The toe cages on the pedals were designed to firmly hold a woman's foot in place.

When he had put her under, he would carry her over, mount her on the bike, strap a helmet on her head, walk the bike down to the road, and casually ride away. His leg power would move both sets of pedals. It would appear they were just a loving couple out for a morning spin.

He felt over-prepared. More than a year spent studying his quarry meant that he knew this victim better than any he had taken in the previous twenty-two years. Careful planning and his special aerosol anesthetic had been enough to subdue his other victims, but he'd taken extra precautions for this one. There were surprises awaiting this quarry that he was certain would make for a quick and easy snatch, whether she was a superwoman or not.

—⸺—

At a time when other runners would be tiring, she felt at the peak of her strength. For the meeting ahead, that is where she had to be. Easing up on her pace, she drained the water bottle; warmed by the heat of her hand, it didn't cool her mouth, but relieved her thirst.

The lightly used and unnamed dirt path was just ahead. She could choose to stay on the Rock Creek Trail and skip the meeting. Searching her soul for doubt or misgivings, she found none. Turning off the asphalt bike path, she skipped lightly across the log over Rock Creek and began climbing the steep, wooded hillside from last night's dream.

By the time Elsa was winding up the slope behind Rockville High, dawn had begun filtering into the trees. She ran much slower than usual, saving her breath, and energy for the top. As she crested the hill, she saw a bike leaning against a tree, with an old-looking man bending over it. Ready for battle, she took a quick focusing breath and sprang forward.

Too late, her instinct revealed the thin wire stretched across the path. As it touched her chest, her feet slid forward and her back hit the rough trail.

She saw an orange, net-like material descending toward her and she growled, as though she were a lion about to be caught in the hunter's snare. A sweet-smelling mist fell on her face; she desperately shook her head and blew out what little breath was left in her lungs. Only seconds had passed from the moment she had first spotted him, but now she was almost helpless as he fell upon her; his weight pressed her down as her thinking became fuzzy.

Before her awareness abandoned her, she summoned all her strength in an effort to turn beneath the plastic construction mesh. If she could get on her stomach, she could push herself off the ground. Her assailant fought the attempt and she could feel her strength seeping away. She relaxed and let her head fall to the side. As she did, the locked door in her mind burst open, and a flood of anger exploded from inside; unleashing the lion.

When their brief, intense battle had begun, Rescott's dark nature had surged as always, driving him forward. In the end, it was easy, as he had expected. Each step had worked the way it was planned. Her struggles were fading and eyelids drooping as his unique halothane mixture took effect.

He began to rise, and then stiffened as her eyes snapped open. Unbalanced by sudden, snake-like twisting beneath him, he fell back awkwardly and then rolled to his feet as she turned and pushed off the ground, throwing aside the net.

Elsa took a deep breath of the humid, forest air; it helped clear the cobwebs and allowed her to focus on the man before her. The frightening surge of power that had burst from within her still coursed through her veins, she trembled under its force and her voice quavered as she spoke.

"This is the end for you," she said.

Rescott mistook her tremoring words for fear and false bravado.

"End?" His face wore a confident sneer. "After you they'll be twenty more... at least. I'll be eighty years old and still harvesting sweet fruit like you."

"However old you are today, you bastard," Elsa shifted her left foot forward into a fighting stance, "is the oldest you will ever be."

Grinning, the Harvester grabbed the Taser from his hip and fired.

Only eight feet separated them and the small darts covered the distance quickly, dragging their silky metal filaments behind. They stuck into her shirt and he triggered the voltage.

Elsa watched his grin die when she swept away the darts and stepped forward, spinning her right foot into a vicious kick below his left ear. She was surprised when the blow only staggered her assailant, but didn't knock him unconscious. But she didn't hesitate to follow up with a flurry of brutal kicks, elbow strikes, and solid punches that kept him stunned and drove him to the ground. None of them were killing blows; she didn't want him dead... yet.

The orange netting that had covered her was within reach. While he was still dazed, she pulled it over and rolled him up in it. From the backpack on the ground by the bike she pulled the restraints he had planned to use on her and cinched them around his ankles and above his knees. Twisting him onto his stomach, she secured his arms behind his back and then turned him over, pinning his arms painfully beneath him.

The shocked Professor William Rescott was trussed up in the mesh webbing like a Thanksgiving turkey.

Elsa lifted the hem of her shirt to show off the thick layer of insulating rubber that had foiled the Taser; according to internet conjecture, it was one of many methods the Harvester used to subdue his victims. The homemade rubber vest had been hot, but worth every drop of sweat.

Though well-secured, Rescott recovered his confidence, and the scornful tone of voice. "This is a long way from over," he said.

"You are right about that," Elsa replied.

Though only minutes had passed since she crested the hill, sunrise was fast approaching and light was beginning to filter into the forest. Dawn would leave her exposed and vulnerable. She had a plan that would remove the sneer from this monster's face... forever. To complete the task would take time and she had to get started.

The grunting and growling didn't affect her concentration as she began her preparations. Many nights had been spent memorizing the names of the twenty women; imagining their pain and horror as they were butchered; steeling her mind and heart for what she had planned. Her mother and all the Harvester's victims would be avenged.

On the ground beside her hip pack she laid a sturdy, cloth drawstring bag, a small plastic bottle, and a hardened case. She removed a slim, metal syringe from the case and walked to where Rescott's struggles had taken him. Flipping him on his stomach, she placed a knee just below his neck and drove his face into the dirt and leaves. His bound legs kicked ineffectually.

"I'm sure you know what this is, professor. It is amazing how forensics, technology, and a free market economy made my research so easy." Using her fingers, she found the right spot for inserting the needle. "There are internet sites devoted to the Harvester. Most of them have detailed sections on your methodology, including the drugs you use to paralyze your victims when you cut their hearts out."

Pressing down on the plunger of the syringe brought an immediate stop to his movements. Rolling him out of the net, she removed the restraints and turned him face up again. Then she gazed in his eyes as she continued.

"What I just injected into your neck is the drug you use when you want your victims to feel every agonizing moment." She was disappointed that there was alarm, but no fear. She went to her hip pack and returned with a plastic container.

"I know you," he said.

"You think you do?" Elsa moved her face closer to his.

The memory hit him with a force that caused his heart to skip a beat. For a moment, he was back in the warehouse, a long time ago. But it couldn't be. His first harvest... he had held her heart in his hands.

Now his voice was the one that trembled. "Anne Danforth?"

Elsa leaned closer still, and whispered, "I will be the death of you."

A brief flash of fear appeared in his eyes, terror even... and then the furious false bravado he'd once assumed in someone else, took its place.

"Fuc..." When his mouth opened, she squirted the bottle of mercury in it. He coughed and gagged, but no words came from his flapping mouth.

"That mercury will paralyze your vocal chords and keep you quiet. I expect that you'll be in quite a bit of pain very soon and the noise you might make would be intolerable. You'll also have trouble breathing before very long. Eventually it should kill you, but probably not for many hours, maybe even days." As Elsa spoke, she continued to work, unrolling him from the webbing and arranging his limbs until he was spread-eagle among the fallen leaves on the forest floor.

"What I am about to do, a skilled surgeon may be able to save you from. For that matter, you might even survive the mercury poisoning to live a long, miserable life in prison. And believe me, it would be miserable."

She stepped back and leaped high in the air, landing on his left knee. The sharp, cracking sound was muffled by the thick woods. His leg bent unnaturally. She leaped again and did the same to his right. Again and again she sprang high and shattered every major bone in each of his limbs. When she was done, he looked like a twisted scarecrow, his arms and legs askew.

After she had caught her breath, she noticed that he had lost consciousness.

Walking to her hip pack, she removed the final item from her "Harvester gift pack" – a baggie of glass ampoules of ammonium carbonate solution. She used the edge of her shirt to pull one out. His eyes snapped open when she broke it under his nose.

Consciousness flared and she was standing above him. A split second of anger was buried under an endless agony. Closing his eyes, he longed for oblivion, but it wouldn't come.

Elsa knelt on the ground next to him. Buttons flew when she ripped open his blue, collared shirt, revealing a mat of gray hair. She pulled an eight inch piece of metal from the cloth bag, set the point of the heavy spike against the Harvester's chest and pushed.

His eyes opened again. A drop of blood welled up and a tuft of gray hair was tinted red.

"That's right," she said, "we're not done yet. After all the misery you've caused, all the lives you've destroyed, I hope..."

Elsa felt her control slipping. She wanted to spit a lifetime's worth of anguish into his face; she longed to roar in a righteous frenzy. But that might draw unwanted attention. Her vengeance had a long time yet to run, before she would be finished with this killer. Any interruption would be unacceptable.

She clenched her teeth and allowed the fury she felt to make her tone fierce, while her words remained whispered.

"I hope you didn't think a few broken bones would be the only suffering I had for you. When I'm done, you will enter the fires of hell and consider them a welcome relief!"

A part of her mind loathed what she was about to do. That reservation was but a straw in the path of a raging fire. Elsa could feel a host of angry people urging her on. Fathers and mothers, sisters and brothers, husbands whose loved ones had been ripped from their lives by this fiend... they all screamed for revenge.

In truth, this evil creature had harvested more than the twenty hearts of his victims. Elsa's own heart was still waiting to be made whole once again. There was so much emptiness in her life that she hoped to begin to fill, once this justice was complete.

Using a heavy stone she selected from the side of the rocky trail, Elsa began to drive the metal rod into his heaving chest. She had chosen the spot carefully, to avoid any major vessels that could bleed out and kill him too quickly.

"This is for Halcia Martinez!"

Inch by inch the suffering increased. He felt each blow as the cold steel pierced his chest. The image of Halcia Martinez, rising from the flames of his crematorium, rushed to embrace him; her touch seared his heart.

Others waited in line behind her.

The rock thumped on his chest as Elsa slammed the spike home. There was little blood, since the nails remained in place and plugged the holes in his chest. The paralytic agent had rendered his face slack, but she could see the terrible agony clearly in his eyes.

"You think that hurt? Imagine watching and feeling your own heart cut from your chest. I'd do that too, you unspeakable, sick, fu…" Elsa clapped her hand over her mouth and listened as the shouted words echoed through the trees.

Her head whipped around and she peered into the woods as the dawn was breaking. She prayed that her yelling had gone unnoticed. Once her emotions were under control again, she picked up the cloth bag and upended it in front of his face. Nineteen more of the dull, gray metal spikes tumbled from the bag and bounced off his chest.

The Harvester felt the spikes hit him and watched as Elsa picked one up and held it in front of him. Though his immobilized body could not show it, and his arrested voice could not speak it, Professor William Rescott was on the edge of a wild, unrestrained madness. The agony he was experiencing did not cut him so deeply as did the crumbling of his mind. There, in the organic labyrinth of his brain, he was the one strapped to a table as Anne Danforth taunted him.

He had always been proud of his intellect. The ability to solve the most complex problem, to untangle the riddles of the cosmos, to find his way, unemotionally, through the darkest enigma; that was the foundation of his tremendous ego. Losing his mind was the ultimate humiliation. Fighting desperately, he held on to the shreds of his fragile sanity.

"Cutting your filthy, twisted heart out… that is something I could only do once." He watched her wave the cruel instrument in front of his eyes. "That wouldn't cause near enough pain to balance all the evil you've done."

She jabbed the point of the second skewer into his chest next to the first.

"I hope these will come close."

Elsa picked up the rock once more and began hammering.

"This is for Tara Whitman…"

The torment he so richly deserved continued as Elsa turned his chest into a pin cushion.

"This is for Brenda Frieson… Nina Flores… Willa Brenham."

Whenever he fainted, she broke another ampoule under his nose. Elsa was relentless and no longer regretted the lack of fear in his eyes; she knew there was only room for pain.

"This is for Andrea Hoffman." She paused and clutched the skewer to her chest.

And Alicia.

There was a dull, splintering sound when her blows drove the stake through one of Rescott's ribs. She continued to hammer fervently. Yet again, the torture went beyond what any human could handle and Rescott fainted once more. The heads of the metal rods now formed a hellish arc on his chest. Down to one ampoule, she left him unconscious as she drove the next seven stakes and completed the circle of retribution… only one to go.

Dragged from insensibility once more, he found his head being pounded on the ground as she growled angrily and slapped him. He felt like someone had used a nail gun to fasten him to the forest floor.

"Wake up you bastard!" The last dose of smelling salts hadn't fully revived him.

The Harvester found himself in the warehouse. Anne Danforth was snarling at him. The scalpel she held was thick, ugly and dull. Light from the fixture above the table was soft; at the edges of it there were hints of green and brown. A small portion of his mind recognized them as trees, and he could not understand how they came to be growing in his warehouse. His sanity was balanced precariously on the razor-sharp edge of his own harvesting scythe.

When she moved her face close to his, Anne's eyes changed from hazel to brown, the hair shortened and the face became that of his second victim. It changed again and he saw his third, and then his fourth.

"Now do you know me?" Helen said.

Her name was on the tip of his mute tongue, but then the features melted and changed again…

"You know me, don't you?" Cynthia Connolly leered at him.

And again… "Remember me? I told you I would come back to haunt you," said Andrea. Her memorable, blue-green eyes were gloating over his bewildered state.

The face altered before his eyes again… and again… and again. His failing mind knew the faces but was unable to deliver the names that went with them. Madness held him completely as he watched a fusion of faces place the final stake over the center of his heart.

The spike Elsa held was thicker than the rest. It had to be.

When she placed it on his chest, she saw in his eyes that he was in the throes of hysteria. A lunatic who could not tell mother from daughter lay beneath her hand, which held the hammering stone high.

"This one is for Anne Danforth…" Tears dripped from her face as she began driving the final nail into the middle of the gleaming circle that caged his depraved heart. "…my Mother." This one had to go through his chest plate and the first blows had little effect… except for the pain they caused. Twenty blows were needed.

There is justice in that number.

Elsa closed her eyes and remembered all the names…

Working quickly, Elsa put the syringe in the case, then put it, the empty baggie, cloth bag, and the plastic bottle in the hip pack and snapped it around her waist. Using a rag from his back pack, she wiped the blood off her hands and then wiped the top of the spikes in his chest to remove her fingerprints. Any others would be explained by the story she would tell.

She left him lying in the dirt and leaves, and continued across the top of the hill. Before she emerged from the woods into the parking lot of the Forest Apartments, she pulled the blonde wig from her head and threw it down the hillside.

Carrie and Sid were about to drive to Great Falls for a Sunday morning run and picnic lunch along the canal, when they saw the redheaded woman stumble out of the woods behind their apartment.

The horrific ordeal she'd just experienced made the look of shock and barely-contained panic on Leijona's face very real as she used the young couple's cell phone to call 911.

CHAPTER 29

Sunday afternoon, September 18, 2005

A thin slice of afternoon sun broke the forest canopy. The tiny glass tube caught and reflected the beam of light with a sparkle that brought the notice of Paul Demerov, head of a Harvester Task Force that would soon be out of commission.

The area had already been trampled by both the Rockville Police and EMT first responders before a Maryland State Police investigator realized what the strange collection of items at the scene might represent. The HTF had not been notified until two hours after the 911 call from the horrified jogger.

Paul approached the sparkle carefully out of respect for his agents. Dozens of them were scouring the woods for evidence. Others were doing their best to reconstruct the bizarre set of events involving a man the FBI had been chasing twenty years.

He knelt and flicked it out of the dirt with his pen, then lifted it to his nose with a latex-gloved hand. The whiff of ammonia was faint, but still caused him to jerk back. An agent nearby held out a plastic bag and Paul dropped it in. Another agent marked the grid location on a map. Sealed and labeled, it was added to a box that contained more of the same.

Someone had not wanted the Professor to miss any of that morning's entertainment. The rapid response team had transmitted a picture shortly after arriving on the scene, and it only took minutes to match it with William Rescott, PhD.

That identification was added to the other factors: the modified tandem bike, the unusual contents of the pack, the unique assault, and the specific count of metal spikes. The result was a feeling in Paul's gut that said the man ER doctors were trying to save was the Harvester.

Paul picked his way out of the crime scene. His next stop would be the emergency room at Washington Adventist Hospital.

The theme from "Kojak" halted Paul in his steps, and caused a rash of grins to break out among the agents nearby. He flipped open his cell phone and held it to his ear. After listening a few moments, he put it back on his hip and continued out of the woods.

Looks like I'll have to find a new obsession.

Professor William Rescott, a.k.a. The Harvester, was dead.

<hr />

Monday, September 19, 2005

H. P. Lovecraft be damned! Paul did not consider it merciful at all that his mind could not correlate its contents. If it could, maybe he would stop waking from nightmares in the middle of the night.

He zipped through the glow of the lampposts along an empty Arlington Memorial Bridge. The Lincoln Memorial and Washington Monuments glittered against the dark, heavy clouds. The classic 'movie' route into D.C. wasn't the fastest or most convenient, but the beauty was inescapable. Overnight rain gave the city a sheen that would fade as a gray dawn approached and the bridges into the city became clogged with traffic.

In the hope that another brief, mental review would clear the evolving dream from his mind before he reached HTF Headquarters, he mentally walked through the familiar shadowy maze once more.

Even in his dream, he knew the Harvester was dead, but still, some vitally important clue remained just out of reach. Again he walked through the gloom, reached the plaza and the shadows departed. Again he wandered along the outskirts, beside the modern glass and steel buildings; a glancing movement in the corner of his eye, turning to see his reflection in the mirrored glass.

This time, it was really Paul Demerov; his black shoes, dark suit and haggard look were unmistakable. He lifted his hand and his image did the same. Then his reflection dropped the hand and, with a discouraged frown, shook its head, as though disappointed by Paul's inability to unravel the clue.

When his image stepped out of view, the redhead was there once again; same black compression shorts that hugged her hips, same top that looked so white against her tan skin. She stretched her hands high in the air, her trim muscles quivering; then she spread her legs and touched the ground between them. All the time, she kept her eyes locked on Paul's. Their hazel depths hypnotized him. She stood, gestured to him, and put her hands on hips, waiting.

Stepping close to the window, he studied her captivating face from inches away.

"Paul." He looked into her eyes and felt his heart leap, touched by an unfamiliar, yet pleasant, and strong need.

"Thank you for this," she said. Then her face turned away and she began running toward a red sun that was dropping behind distant mountains.

He knew he couldn't let her go and moved to follow, only to be trapped and smothered by the glass. Although he couldn't look down, he could feel his heart being ripped from his chest as the woman disappeared into what had become a golden yellow... and rising, sun.

⬩⬩⬩

No Monday morning blues for me. Leijona rolled out of bed eager for the day to begin.

Her worries that she might feel tainted, or corrupted by what had been done on Sunday, proved unfounded. There had been no trouble sleeping, no nightmares. One brief dream had visited her sleep; she closed her eyes and tried to keep the strangely familiar images from fading, as dreams always do.

In the dream, Leijona saw her mother creep into a four-year-old Elsa's bedroom and begin to write on the easel. Elsa, too, is having this dream. She wants to wake up and surprise her mommy and jump on her back and tickle her and say "Mommy, that's my easel!" Leijona also wanted Elsa to awake, to hold her mother and keep her from going out the door, and out of her life, forever.

And she does. Tickles and laughter ensue. Mother and daughter talk about the exciting day ahead. "What do you want to wear," asked her mommy.

"The green, summery dress," Leijona heard her dream-self say, "I wanna wear the green, summery dress with the yellow flowers." Hazy sunlight was streaming into her room and everything had that blurry, soft look, even her mommy.

The hazy scene became brighter until Leijona's dream ended with a sense that something important had happened. On bare feet, she padded to the bathroom, feeling as though a dark chapter in her life was finally ended, and the page turned.

The hot water ran until it was steaming, then she soaked the cloth and draped it over her face. After rubbing her eyes, she scrubbed her face vigorously, and then used the warm cloth to massage her neck and shoulders. Out of habit, she studied her reflection and checked the roots of her red hair.

It's a good thing I've become the world's best colorist. She parted her hair and took the applicator from the medicine cabinet.

Halfway through the touch-up, Elsa froze.

Why do I need to touch up my hair? I've had my vengeance... I'm done with this.

From that dark corner of her mind where fear and anger had held sway for so long came a rough, whispered voice. There was still something more behind that door.

"No... you aren't."

The trembling started at the tip of the applicator, spread rapidly to her fingertips, and up her arm.

In the mirror, standing behind her with pale, shadowed faces, were Ben... and her father.

"Despite all the good they tried to do... maybe because of what they tried to do... they were killed... as good as murdered."

"No," Elsa's strangled words were barely audible. "That's not how it was."

"They need to be avenged," The rough voice softened, and Elsa could hear Leijona's light Finnish accent. "You loved them so much. Don't you want their lives to have meant something?"

Behind her the two ghostly images faded. Elsa's head fell and tears dropped into the sink. When it lifted, the eyes that looked in the mirror were cold and hard.

The applicator went back into action and she was pleased with the results. Elsa had avenged her mother's murder. Now Leijona had another job to do.

According to the report, Rescott's warehouse was a goldmine of forensic evidence; the missing vehicles of four victims; a fifty-five gallon drum of ashes from the jury-rigged crematorium; hair samples from a variety of equipment and devices; surgical tools; and a supply of Styrofoam containers. From the looks of it, the Harvester hadn't planned on retiring so soon.

Among the items they had found in the woods was the oddly configured tandem bike, a metal trip wire tied between two trees, a spray bottle containing a custom mix of liquid anesthetic, the orange construction webbing and a Taser that had been triggered. The investigating team marveled that anyone could have overcome such an arsenal.

In the wider area behind the high school, seven containers of mostly trash were collected: cigarette butts, beer cans, old water-logged high school text books, various articles of clothing, a pair of raggedy shoes... and even a woman's blonde wig.

Paul had spent the previous four hours going through the collection of reports and figured he still had a couple to go.

"Hey, Tom." Paul walked to his door and called to Thomas Huxley, head of the HTF communications group. When Tom's head popped out, he continued, "Our files don't have a copy of the Rockville Police report or the interview with the woman who found the body. Get them to fax all that over, OK?"

He'd only asked for the Rockville City Police report in order to make the HTF Archives as complete as possible. He was only reading the report because he had time on his hands since a scheduled meeting had been cancelled. The report held no surprises for Paul... until he got to the description of the redheaded witness.

In minutes he was on his way to Bethesda.

With every step that carried him down the hall of the Bethesda Towers, Paul became more nervous. On a professional level, nothing about this fool's errand made sense. Personally... what logic was there in chasing a character from his dreams? He could imagine the coming scene. The redhead would open the door...

"Hi, I'm Paul. I know we've never met, but I've been dreaming about you for two years. And this morning I dreamed that I love you, and can't let you go. Would you like to have dinner..."

SLAM! Goes the door in my face.

He turned the corner and saw the apartment door. It spared him worse imaginings.

Besides, she'd probably look nothing like the woman in his dreams.

Rushing to the door, he rang the bell before his courage had time to fail. Footsteps approached, and he looked at the peephole for a moment before a strange attack of shyness had him looking at his shoes.

The fish-eye lens revealed a faintly familiar, tired-looking man in a dark suit that was as good as a uniform... F.B.I. She opened the door with what she hoped was an innocent smile. The smile froze and her eyes widened in recognition as the agent lifted his eyes slowly.

She had been a blond, impressionable fourteen-year-old Elsa, and the shy, handsome F.B.I. cadet had made one. Paul Demerov. If he recognized her, she might have problems.

"Can I help you?" Leijona spoke softly and added a little more Finnish accent than usual.

Paul heard 'Please help me' in the voice from a dream. His eyes rose from the floor and, for a moment, he saw her as he had in his dream; tight black shorts, white top and smooth tan skin.

"Excuse me," Leijona repeated, "Can I help you?"

Paul blinked his eyes, and now the girl from his dreams was dressed in blue jeans and a loose green t-shirt. But the face was exactly the same. The green in the shirt drew out the emerald in her eye. He blinked again to erase the rest of his vision, but the face remained. He might have stayed a statue in her doorway, except his training took over.

"I'm sorry to bother you. I'm Paul Demerov, from the F.B.I. Harvester Task Force. If you are Leijona West, could I ask you a few questions about Sunday morning?"

"LAY... oh-na," she said, "not Lee-OH-na. I could never stand that Helmsley woman."

"Sorry... Leijona."

"If it won't take too long, I have an appointment later this afternoon." She closed the door behind him and then thought of the map on her dining room wall. "It's such a beautiful day; would it be all right if we went outside?"

"Whatever you want, I just appreciate you taking the time to talk to me."

He followed her through the living room and out the patio door. The bare apartment was more than Spartan. It had the feel of a monastic cell for a medieval anchorite.

A light breeze was blowing through the treetops, and the clouds that had lingered for most of the day were finally breaking up. He followed her to a patch of sunshine, where she plopped down in the grass.

"If it wasn't for the sound of the Beltway," he said, "this would be an idyllic spot." Feeling awkward, he pulled up his pant legs and took a seat.

"I've learned to ignore the noise," she said, "since I spend so much time out here."

"Leijona is an unusual name." He let the statement hang, as if waiting for an answer.

After a pause, she took the hint. "It is Finnish. My father was a Finnish diplomat, Aanos Westerinen. He was assigned here in Washington for a time." Leijona gave him a disarming smile. "Is this the information you are looking for?"

Paul shifted and cleared his throat. "No, sorry... I was just curious."

They spent a few minutes covering the same ground that was in the report. She apologized for falling all over the crime scene. "I hope I didn't contaminate it too badly."

Then he asked what was really on his mind. "Do you mind me asking why, with a monster like that on the loose, you would be out alone like you were?"

Leijona looked down at the grass. *Now we have come to it... how far will he push?*

"I have trained extensively in martial arts, Agent Demerov. I can take care of myself quite well."

Her eyes were telling him something important.

"Many women who became his victims thought the same," he said.

"Now we can be thankful that one of them was correct, can we not?"

Those hazel eyes said 'help me, Paul'

"I'm sure the families of all his victims are thankful." Her eyes pulled him in, pleading.

"Were you the one that was correct?" he asked bluntly.

"I could have been, given the chance," she leaned in and beckoned him closer. "Only you can say if I was. Look in my eyes, and tell me if I could have done what was done to him."

Paul gazed into swirls of brown and green that opened before him. The truth was in them, much more truth than he wanted to see. Not only could she have done it... he could have done it... would have done it to save her. The depths of those eyes held far more; flecks of gold glittered among the green swirls and made the hazel shine. He could see that layers of secrets were open to him... if only he could understand them. Bright rays of sun broke free of the clouds and blinded him; she disappeared in a golden haze.

She briefly touched his hand, and an electric charge caused his heart to leap in his chest. Then the intense connection was broken. He sat back and blinked his eyes until they cleared.

Leijona pushed off the ground, her lips in a melancholy twist. Without a word, he followed her to the door. In the hall he turned and faced her. Words careened through his mind trying to connect and find his lips.

They never had a chance. Her hand rested lightly on his shirt.

"Paul," she leaned forward and her lips touched his cheek. "Thank you for this."

Then her hand pulled away.

She stepped back and closed the door.

CHAPTER 30

Tuesday, September 20, 2005

When his alarm went off, Paul jerked and sat up. He was disoriented by the sunshine filling the room. Sitting on the edge of his bed, he tried to remember the last time he'd awoken to the sound of his alarm clock, instead of being dragged from sleep by some tormenting apparition.

He couldn't. Nightmares had become as much a part of his sleep as bed hair and morning breath. His mind was clearer and his body more rested than they had been in years.

The dark, frustrating years spent chasing the Harvester were over.

A sense of freedom crashed into him... as if the walls of the prison cell he'd constructed had crumbled. For the first time, there was the possibility of a future he could look forward to with hope.

The image of Leijona in her doorway entered his thoughts.

"Thank you for this," she'd said. Paul knew that he should be thanking her. She'd come to the rescue... in his nightmare... in his life.

Though the redhead had taken his heart in return, it was a price he was eager to pay.

Detective Alvarez examined the numbered marks on the Montgomery County map pinned to the fabric of his cubicle. The folder on his lap contained one sheet for each mark. Many of the single page reports had little detail and few hard facts. Any unbiased observer would find little concrete connection between them.

Viewed separately, they would seem only to provide evidence of the reality that Alvarez and every law enforcement officer in the region faced. Gang activity and the violence it spawned were on the rise.

On his own time, Alvarez had put them all together and started down another path. Compiling only unsolved homicides that had taken place along roadways and hiker/biker trails, or incidents in which a redheaded woman was mentioned, he'd created the file in his lap.

It held eighteen pages. A third of them were 911 calls about a woman, possibly a redhead, being chased by thugs. It was an urban myth that people ignored, or ran away, when they witnessed violence happening in their own neighborhoods. He'd found these reports in the electronic version of a 'dead-letter' file. No 911 call was ever erased. But since no evidence or report of a crime had been received subsequent to the initial calls, they'd been dumped.

Bits of gossip or rumors were on five of the pages. Some were from the squad room, some from his contacts in the community.

Five of the pages were summaries of police reports. Covering the last eighteen months, they chronicled the deaths of ten gang members in four separate incidents. The remaining two reports detailed the unsolved deaths of three others.

All thirteen dead had criminal records, many included sex offenses.

Julio was certain that not all could be attributed to one person. None of the homicide reports mentioned any witnesses or a redhead.

But Julio believed Cruzon.

And now the Harvester was dead.

There was one more incident for him to investigate. If it panned out, he would ask to see the HTF report.

—⟨⟩—

Leijona sat in the sunshine outside her apartment, and waited for a new fire to kindle inside her. Avenging her father and Ben would require a different type of vengeance, and many more years of effort. The same single-minded determination that led to the death of William Rescott, PhD was needed.

At the moment, she didn't have it. Leijona wanted to blame it on fatigue from eighteen months of intense discipline.

But the spot on the grass where she was sitting revealed the truth. Here she had sat next to Paul Demerov. He was the problem. The hunt for the Harvester had made it necessary to dam certain emotions;

Tenderness,

Compassion,

Joy,

Love.

When she'd touched his hand, a crack had developed in that dam.

The Lion of Vengeance still had a heart. It longed to feel something more than anger and hatred again. She just didn't know if it was possible.

Leijona was considering ways to repair that crack when the phone rang.

Wednesday, September 21, 2005

The restaurant was noisy, the décor bland and commercial. The food was edible, but uninspired. Taken as a whole, Paul thought the dinner was a disaster. Except for one thing; Leijona was sitting across the table. Her eyes were the most beautiful thing in the room. He'd surprised himself by having the courage to ask her out. She'd surprised him by agreeing.

The woman who'd driven twenty stakes into the chest of the Harvester was politely eating a sub-par shrimp scampi, while listening to him go on and on about his years chasing the man she'd killed.

Though she hadn't uttered a single incriminating word, Paul knew she'd killed him. She knew that he knew. Without words, each became aware that the other accepted the situation.

Contributing intelligent comments and asking insightful questions, she'd kept the conversation away from anything personal.

As he drove her home, Paul searched for a way to prolong the date. Despite the indifferent meal and one-track conversation, he was enjoying the night. It made him feel part of the human race again, after a long time away.

He didn't know that she felt the same way.

Paul remembered that the human race he'd just rejoined… loved dessert. Stopped at a light, he turned toward Leijona to suggest it, but the words didn't get past his lips.

Leijona's arms and hands were performing a complex ballet. It was strange and entrancing, and reminded him of the interpreters that the F.B.I. often used for the hearing-impaired. Her face looked subdued, and he noticed a tear as it trembled at the corner of her eye.

One of her hands wiped away the tear while the other settled to her lap.

She didn't look at him, but pointed to the Safeway in the shopping center ahead.

"Would you mind if we stopped to get ice cream and toppings?" Then she looked his way. Her smile was sad, but hopeful. "I thought we could fix sundaes at my place."

⟢⟢⟣⟣

Freddy looked like the Mummy and he knew it. TV was his only source of entertainment and that movie was showing on the screen. He didn't consider it amusing at all.

From his knees to his arm pits, he was encased in plaster. His left arm was also in a cast and was hanging from a support above his hospital bed. His jaw was wired shut and a long scar from the surgery that had repaired it stretched from ear to chin. His head was wrapped in gauze.

But the cast on his right forearm had come off yesterday, so he'd been feeling better until the man, who was obviously a cop, walked in and locked the door. Except for his skin being a shade darker, he was a good ringer for Brendan Fraser, the star of the film playing directly above the cop's head.

"How's it goin', Freddy?" the cop said, and then laughed when Freddy pointed to his jaw and grunted.

"Yeah, I know you can't talk. Tough luck, huh? I'm Detective Julio Alvarez, and I want to ask you some questions about the night you were turned into a paraplegic."

The metal braces around his head kept him from shaking his head no.

When Freddy reached for the nurse call button, the cop grabbed his arm, and held it against Freddy's body cast.

"Settle down, settle down. Let me ask my yes or no questions. You can grunt for no and blink for yes... real easy. And I know you'll tell the truth, right?" Freddy moaned when Alvarez squeezed the spot where the surgeon had put the pin in his forearm.

He blinked his eyes rapidly.

"Good boy." Alvarez took a notepad from his pocket. "On July 29th, you and your two buddies were walking along the bike path near Rockville High School when a gang of... whoa, it says here *eight*... eight guys jumped you!"

Freddy blinked.

"They busted you up real good, huh?"

Blink.

"Your buddies got off easy, but you must have fought those eight guys pretty hard."

Blink

"All three of you got broken bones, bruises... but not a single cut. Surprises me, since gangs are my business, and *all* the ones I know carry knives... at least. But not these guys?"

Freddy grunted.

"Lucky you, real lucky. It turns out... this I got from the hospital intake reports, that those eight guys didn't take a penny off any of you... or any of the drugs you were carrying either."

Alvarez leaned in and Freddy shivered in spite of the sweaty casts covering his body.

His forearm was given a warning squeeze.

"Freddy, you can keep your macho pride and it'll cause you a lot of pain." Alvarez pulled a picture from his notepad and held it up for Freddy to see. "Or you can tell me the truth."

He'd gotten the pic off security camera footage at the Grosvenor-Strathmore metro station. The tape showed a woman carrying some skinny junkie. It was grainy, but clear enough.

Freddy eyes flared as he recognized the redheaded woman who'd ripped through his crew like a chainsaw. They'd only been playin' around, and now he might spend the rest of his life in a wheelchair.

Alvarez had a firm grip on his forearm.

"This is her, right?"

Freddy blinked.

Paul blinked.

Then he blinked again.

The scene didn't change. He was sitting on a cheap metal patio chair, at a tiny round table, eating ice cream from a mixing bowl with a serving spoon.

Leijona sat next to him on her only dining room chair, eating out of her only regular bowl, with the one teaspoon she owned.

She'd gotten over being embarrassed about her lack of amenities.

She'd also gotten over being self-conscious about the large map that Paul could see hanging on her kitchen wall.

They'd hardly spoken at all, except for what was necessary to assemble their sundaes.

"Hot Fudge?"... "Yes, please." "Whip cream?"... "You bet." "Nuts?"... "Sure."

"Cherry?"... "No thanks."

From the stare she'd given him, he was sure she was about to throw him out.

"Who doesn't take a cherry on their hot fudge sundae?" she said. "It's un-American!"

"OK, ok! I'll take a cherry!"

Dessert assembled, they'd both chuckled and dug in. When they were done, she cleared away the empty bowls and fixings, rinsing them at the sink.

Meanwhile, he studied the map.

A long, green line left Bethesda, and went up and across Montgomery County, to the C&O Canal, ending in an arrow pointed north. All the rest of the loops and lines started and ended at her apartment. The black and red lines were easily understood; they represented the routes she had used to entice the Harvester. But the green line was something different.

One thing was clear - the yellowing laminate, the smudges, and number of marks...

"You've been at this a long time."

His chair scrapped on the floor and he walked up behind her.

The clanking of bowls and spoons in the sink stopped, leaving only the sound of water splashing from the tap.

Muscles on her strong shoulders tensed when he rubbed his hands across them.

He began kneading his thumbs along her spine and his fingers worked to pull the tension away. Soon her head dropped and her shoulders sagged.

Paul thought he was helping her to relax until he saw her head bobbing, and her crying was heard over the splashing water.

Pulling his hands away, he stepped back, an apology on his lips.

A wet hand reached out and grabbed his arm.

He waited, putting his free hand on her shoulder again.

After a time, her crying ended. She released him and continued cleaning.

When he resumed the massage, she turned off the water, and leaned against the sink.

"I've shut myself off for so long... I don't know if I have anything inside to give you."

Paul knew more than anyone about the damage that obsession with the Harvester did to one's soul. "I chased the Harvester my entire adult life," he said. "That monster twisted me until I wasn't sure I could be human again. When he was dead, I didn't know what to do."

"Then you touched my hand... and kissed my cheek. I woke up yesterday morning and the nightmare was gone. And I knew that my life could be my own again. That's why I needed to see you... to thank you for freeing me from the nightmares."

Her head was bowed when she turned and placed damp hands on his shirt.

He knew she would lift her head and their lips would come together.

They would embrace and his life would fill with a new purpose.

A long, happy future was, at that moment, stretched out before him.

"You're my Avenging Angel," he said.

———

Paul's words were touching her deeply. She could sense her emotional dam failing.

Leijona was close to letting all the bitterness, hatred, and vengeance leak away. Close to allowing the love and compassion that Elsa still longed for, enter their lives once more.

Then she heard... even Elsa heard, the fateful line.

"You're my Avenging Angel," he said.

Only it didn't come from the man standing in front of her. It came from men long dead. Men she'd seen in her mirror only a few days earlier. A husband and a father who'd loved her and were waiting to be avenged. Her head fell forward against his chest and she shuddered.

The pressure of her hands on his chest slowly increased... as did the pain in her heart. The crack in the dam was closed and her emotions were locked away once more.

Soon she had pushed him away.

CHAPTER 31

Friday, September 23, 2005

The amount of evidence accumulated by the Harvester Task Force in the twenty years of its existence, combined with the massive amount of material, equipment and vehicles from Rescott's warehouse, meant a lot of space was needed for the HTF Archives. An entire quadrant of the immense F.B.I. evidence storage facility in Quantico, Virginia was being devoted to the Harvester. Much of the evidence still resided in trailers and flat-bed trucks on the parking lot.

Hence the reason Detective Julio Alvarez was so far from home on a Friday morning.

The sun was still below the horizon, but Paul Demerov had been known throughout his career as an early riser, which was why Paul found the young detective sleeping by the door of the mobile trailer that served as his temporary office.

A kick brought Alvarez scrambling to his feet.

"You're Alvarez?" Paul said, "Awfully young for a detective." He opened the door and led the young man inside. The small trailer had a copier, file cabinets, a bulletin board with a floor plan of the storage facility, and two desks, one for Paul and one for an aide.

"Yes sir!" he said, "same age as you when you joined the HTF."

"Sounds like you do your homework." He pointed to a chair. "You sit and tell me what you want while I get settled." The first thing Paul did was head for the coffee maker.

"Part of my job with the major crimes unit has me tracking gang violence. As a result of that and other factors, I became aware of a vigilante that I believe was attempting to lure the Harvester into an attack."

Young Alvarez had Paul's full attention, although he tried not to show it as he got the coffee started.

"I've accumulated a lot of evidence. As many as thirteen people may have been killed by this suspect."

"Thirteen people! You can't be serious!" Paul was shaken. It couldn't be true.

"Thirteen, yes sir... not including Rescott. Here's the summary."

Paul took the folder from Alvarez and sat down. He scanned the information quickly, soaking up the important facts. The bodies of two victims were found just across the Beltway from where Leijona lived. Those two had a rap sheet so long it could serve as a case study of what was wrong with the criminal justice system.

"Looks like she... I mean your suspect picked the right people."

"They all had records, yes sir. But I don't believe she picked them. My theory is that she was making herself a target for the Harvester. These guys were drawn in unintentionally, and paid the price."

"You're saying they were all self-defense?"

"No, not really. Two of the victims had their throats cut while they were injured or unconscious...."

The shocked agent inhaled sharply and choked on his coffee. "Sorry," he said, "went down the wrong pipe. You were saying?"

Alvarez continued. "Based on the evidence, I don't think self-defense would fly. This woman is a lethal weapon."

Paul held up the folder. "You think a woman did all this?"

"Yes sir. I'm sure of it." Alvarez pulled a photo from his jacket. "I even have a picture."

He flicked it across the desk like a playing card.

The photo spun and floated until Leijona's face landed in front of Paul.

For a moment he was back in his nightmare, with the face he'd assembled on his desk. "Help me Paul," it said. His hands gripped the arms of his desk chair as he fought to keep an interested, but neutral look on his face.

"OK, I'm convinced." Paul stood and pulled a ring of keys from his desk. "I can't stay, but my aide will be in soon." He handed the keys to Alvarez and pointed out the window.

"That first trailer should have the files you're looking for. Obviously, you can't leave with anything, but feel free to make copies of anything you think you might need."

Once Alvarez went out the door, Paul sat back down at his desk. He opened the bottom drawer and pulled out an item he'd removed from an evidence container earlier in the week. Even now he wasn't sure why.

———

The Brazilian Samba ringtone triggered a brief, horrifying nightmare of falling planes and fiery buildings. Then it pulled Leijona from her sleep.

"Hello?"

Paul's impassioned voice helped sweep the cobwebs from her head.

"Did you cut the throats of those two guys on Beach Drive?" He sounded torn and tired.

"What? No!" The abrupt question confused and frightened her. "I did what I needed to defend myself, but I've never used a weapon."

"I saw your map; I know those guys attacked you. How did their throats get cut?"

"I don't know…"

Paul heard doubt and concern in those few words.

When she'd been surrounded by those men in the darkness, the violent, angry beast within her had broken free of its cage. The mental images of what happened in the shadows on Beach Drive were indistinct and blurred. Leijona felt like crystals of ice were flowing through her veins, as the thought that she may have become a cold-blooded killer ran through her mind.

Have I turned into a monster no different than the Harvester?

"No! I couldn't have done something like that." She had to believe this was true. Then a faint memory became clearer and she latched onto it.

"When I hit the last guy, I knew he was going down and my next thought was that I needed to run. The first clear memory I have is of running along the road as if I was running away from a nightmare. Guilt was chasing me because I was sure that I'd killed at least one more person."

That thought triggered a need inside of her... a need to acknowledge the guilt that had grown into a terrible burden. "All I ever wanted to do was find and kill the Harvester. After the first time, I never went out with the idea in mind that I was going to kill another person. Once I knew it wasn't the Harvester that was attacking, I would run away if I could."

"The first time?" Paul had to know her story; he was desperate for something that would convince him that she wasn't a calculated killing machine.

Leijona sighed. The guilt was buried deeper than she'd realized.

"It was a long time ago... Tolin and Peters"

"My God! Have you been doing this for five years?" Paul was almost overwhelmed by the memories from that year. If it hadn't been for the death of Tolin and Peters, he might not have become the SAC.

"Not consistently. Something..." The silence on the line was drawn out as Leijona struggled with her own memories of a time when Ben... and Alicia were still alive.

"...stopped me... kept me away... for a long time."

"When did you start again?"

"May, 2004"

Paul knew he didn't have much time before Alvarez would be back. He had to make a decision... and for that he had to know.

"How many have you killed?"

Leijona's eyes squeezed shut as the question hit her. Her hand rapped the phone painfully against her head while she considered the awful number. Whispered and unsteady was her reply.

"I'm not sure... six... maybe seven. I never set out to kill anyone... anyone but the Harvester." She fought with her emotions as ugly images flickered through her head.

"Two attacked me in my apartment... I had to drag them through the woods to a culvert under the Beltway. Others... I usually didn't know they were dead unless I saw it in the paper the next day."

A part of her refused to let the guilt consume her. She felt compelled to defend herself.

"I'm not a monster! I've never killed anyone who wasn't planning to rape or kill me."

"What about the two guys with their throats cut? I have to know what happened."

The answer tripped into Leijona's mind… and it felt right.

"Rescott must have been tracking me for a long time. As I started to run away, I felt that someone else might have been there, but I didn't want to hurt anyone else… I just wanted to get free. Maybe he killed them for getting in the way."

Leijona sensed that trouble was coming. She could tell that Paul was on the other end, thinking.

"Where is all this coming from?"

Paul took a deep breath and crossed over the line.

"There's a Montgomery County detective here at my office in Quantico. He has evidence connecting you to some of the criminals you killed. He's going over our files, and he'll find your address from the police report."

He never knew why she'd pushed him out that night. Part of him had hoped that they still had a chance. Now it was gone.

"He'll find what he's looking for soon…

"Run, Leijona"

⟨⟩

The preparations she had made against this day proved their value. Leijona made her way around the penthouse without thought, blindly following her pre-arranged plan. In minutes, her hydration backpack and hip pack were loaded and at the door.

Closing her eyes, she tried to focus. The map from her wall was already destroyed. Nothing left in the apartment could identify her. His face kept interrupting her thoughts.

Paul was risking his career to save her even though she'd pushed him out.

Confused by her conflicting emotions, she shut them down, went to the bedroom, and changed into her running clothes. After tying her shoes, she slipped into the backpack and buckled the hip belt.

Then she took a deep breath. The longest run she had ever attempted was about to start. She would be trying to run from this life to the one she had left behind.

⟨⟩

Paul pictured the green line on the map in her kitchen. It was Leijona's path to freedom. He believed this with all the blind faith he could muster.

That's why he was thirty miles northwest of the Beltway heading for a nineteenth century ferry that still operated across the Potomac River. The incoming barge was named after a confederate general, Jubal Early. After it unloaded cars traveling from the Maryland side, Paul's flashing lights and badge got him front and center for the return trip.

On the other side was the C&O Canal… part of the green line.

Though sunlight was flooding over the trees, the opposite shore remained shadowed and indistinct. The placid but powerful river flowing between Paul and that distant goal was transformed into a shimmering stream of sparkles as it passed before him.

While waiting for the remaining cars to load, he leaned against the front hood. Shading his eyes, he gazed into the river and tried to fathom the decisions that had brought him to this riverside. They were as impenetrable as the murky depths he was about to cross.

All the years he'd dedicated to the F.B.I. were put at risk by what he had done.

He could recoup it all by bringing her in.

For two years, she had been in his dreams. In less than a week, she'd captured his heart.

Now, no matter what he did, she would be out of his life.

—◦◦◦—

Towering high above her, the transmission lines hummed as Leijona sped below. This right-of-way provided a hidden path through the dense suburbs. A left at the gas pipeline and she was headed straight for the C&O Canal. The miles flew by and soon she was cruising north on the towpath along the Potomac River.

So many memories had been created here with her father… and with Ben; but all were from another life that was gone forever. Now, her existence as Leijona had imploded and would soon be discarded. She felt like a person with no identity, nothing to connect her to a real life.

Torn by decisions she'd made, she felt nothing but regret for the path she had chosen.

But the choices *were* already made, and the course set.

Leijona ran on and kept her eye on the horizon...

But the path ahead was blurred by the tears in her eyes.

After forty miles on the towpath, she would hit the Appalachian Trail and head south. For the next week, she expected to be all but invisible to those who searched for her. After that, Leijona would disappear.

—◦◦◦—

General Early arrived at White's Ferry on the Maryland shore. The attendant unlatched the chain, and then jumped back as the impatient Fed gunned his engine and the car leapt off the barge.

Paul sped out of the ferry staging area and rapidly approached the crossing at the C&O canal. Then the car skidded to stop in a cloud of dust. A bright spot of red moving among muted greens and browns had caught his eye. He jumped from the car and ran up to the towpath.

The dusty haze drifted away on a breeze from the river, and the Leijona of his dreams charged up the short hill toward him.

In one coat pocket were his handcuffs; in the other, the item from his desk drawer.

—◦◦◦—

Her eyes were finally dry, but the path ahead was far from clear; it held nothing but loneliness. When Paul appeared like a wizard from a cloud of smoke, Leijona was stunned. Then the dam inside broke and she was overwhelmed.

She raced up the hill and into his arms.

Hugging him, for a moment she dreamed that he might run away with her. But she had pushed him away.

Now he did the same.

"I'm sorry... I couldn't let you go." His face was etched with agony. The choice he had to make was ripping him apart.

"I would have kissed you... that night in the kitchen," Leijona said. "I wanted to... with all my heart. But you said it. It may sound naïve or corny, but I am the Avenging Angel. My father taught me to make what's wrong, right. And I'm not done yet."

She looked in his eyes and saw the conflict in them.

"When I'm done, I'll come back to you."

Their eyes were locked together and she saw sorrow replacing the conflict. He reached into his pocket.

Then he pulled his hand out and pressed something soft and silky into her hand.

Leijona looked down and saw that she was holding her blonde wig.

"They have your picture, Leijona. Hikers will notice a redhead as beautiful as you."

Her lips reached his. Their kiss conveyed longing and regret. It was a kiss that told of the deep gratitude that each felt.

But, in the end, it was a kiss goodbye.

Stepping away, Leijona fit the wig over her short red hair.

When she looked up, Paul felt himself pulled back twelve years in time. He was in the Hoffman's doorway, and couldn't keep his eyes off the young blonde girl in the living room.

Why didn't I see it from the first moment? She was there in my memory all along.

Leijona saw the glimmer of recognition and her words were an echo from the past.

"Yes, I am Elsa, Anne Danforth's daughter."

She gave him a final kiss. He closed his eyes and imagined the kiss gave him hope for the future. Then she slipped by him and away.

When he turned around, Elsa was moving swiftly down the sun-dappled trail. From out of the shade of a majestic oak, she appeared in a shining patch of sunlight; a fantasy image that was escaping with his heart. Then the vision vanished into distant shadows.

THE END

Acknowledgements

Throughout my life I have been a writer who wore a variety of disguises: UPS driver, woodturner, cabinetmaker, electrician, business owner, and many more. The writer chafed, but waited for the responsibilities of life to ease.

The first lines of what became Harvest of the Heart were written in 1999, an early indication that the writer would one day lose his patience. Since that time, many people have supported and encouraged me during what must have seemed like an extended mid-life crisis. Foremost among them has been my wife, Kathleen, who refused to allow me to become the starving artist that it appeared I wanted to be. My children: Chris, Brian, Philip and Carrie showed remarkable patience as I foisted various versions of this story, and others, upon them. Their keen eyes and loving criticism helped to improve the final version of HotH. Special thanks to Carrie for helping with the online web development that I dreaded; and to Phil for catching the errors so many others missed. And finally, to Chris, who keeps pushing me in the right direction.

Bill Thompson (yes, that Bill Thompson) was the first real editor to see Harvest of the Heart. His compliments lifted me and his critique was invaluable. Sorry Bill... in the end, the title meant too much to me. Angie Schneider, along with her copy editing, provided a push in the right direction for the crucial part of the story.

RUNNING
SCARED

MICHAEL
SELMER

GRIPPING STORIES FOR THE RUNNER IN ALL OF US

RUNNER'S HIGH
One recovering addict discovers what running high is all about when he is caught in a blizzard.

PROGRAMMED
A distraught husband searches for his wife, who is trapped in a body that refuses to stop running.

DRIVEN
In a town full of runners, a detective fights to keep pace as he chases a murderer.

THE MONEY CLIP
An average man picks up a lost money clip while out for a run and his life is turned upside down.

COWBOY JOE
To unravel the mystery behind an ultrarunning legend, a New York writer travels to the high plains of Wyoming.

THE GHOST RUNNERS
A winner with an oversize ego learns that it is sometimes better to finish second.

SHEILA'S MARATHON YEAR
An abused woman's mental breakdown leaves her unable to record memories of her life except while she is running.

AVAILABLE IN MARCH 2012

www.ingramcontent.com/pod-product-compliance
Lightning Source LLC
Chambersburg PA
CBHW071323250626
47159CB00004B/1438